INTO THE CATACOMBS

Into the Catacombs

By Paul McCusker

AUGUSTINE INSTITUTE
Greenwood Village, CO

IGNATIUS PRESS
San Francisco

Author's Note: *Catacombs* was originally written as a three-act play premiering in 1982 and published by Lillenas Publishing Company in 1985. The play was novelized by the author and published by Tyndale House in 1996. *Into the Catacombs* is an extensive revision of those earlier works.

Uncertain Light and *Assurance* by Joseph Christian Freiherr von Zedlitz (1790–1862); public domain translation.

Jesus Loves Me was composed by Anna Bartlett Warner (1827–1915); public domain.

Cover Design: Zander Renault

28 27 26 25 24 23 22   1 2 3 4 5 6 7

Paperback ISBN: 978-1-955305-14-3
Ebook ISBN: 978-1-955305-17-4

Library of Congress Control Number: 2022934822

Printed in Canada

To John Gunnoe

CONTENTS

Father Bannon had hoped to be more comforting with his final homily. From the expressions of worry and fear on the faces of his congregation, he knew he was failing.

"Many of you are grieved by suffering and trials," he said, "but Our Lord Jesus calls us to embrace them as He embraced the Cross, knowing that suffering unites us with Him. As impossible as it seems, God wants us to rejoice as we share in Christ's sufferings because, after a little while, God, who has called us to eternal glory in Christ, will restore, confirm, strengthen, and establish us."

He had served the people of this parish as their priest for the past seven years. His words shouldn't have been a surprise. He had tried to warn them. But he now thought of all the things he wished he'd said in his homilies, in the pastor's column he'd been given in the parish newsletter, in the many conversations he'd had in the confessional, over tea in their rustic living rooms, at the local shops, in the hospital.

"Meanwhile, we need to stand firm and open ourselves to the comfort He gives to us now. It is there. He *knows* our suffering, having suffered worse than us. And, in that knowledge, He knows best how to comfort us. We, in turn, must give the same comfort to one another."

His gaze landed on Jason Fitzgibbons, who was glaring at him. This was just the kind of homily the man *hated*. Jason often told the priest to back off—allow that the authorities knew what was best; embrace the many executive orders, emergency acts, laws of protection, and committee decisions. The authorities were trying to set things right, Jason had said repeatedly. We should yield to them.

"If we have any hope," Father Bannon continued, "it is not in anything of this world, but in the world to come. God the eternal Father, the burning passion of Our Lord Jesus Christ, the ever-wise Holy Spirit, the aching heart of Our Lady—hope must come from them."

He leaned forward on the lectern. "But make no mistake. The wolves are coming—even now they are at the door."

He saw dear old Christie Mills turn to look at the door behind them, as if she expected the wolves to burst through at that instant.

"Now we must prepare. We must begin with the Precious Body and Blood of our Savior," Father Bannon declared. "So, let us stand and profess our faith."

The congregation—there weren't many of them left—stood, shuffling uneasily. The Creed had been removed by the auxiliary bishops. To say it now was an act of defiance.

The priest began. "I believe in one God, the Father Almighty . . ."

In the distance, he heard helicopters approaching.

PART I

THE ESCAPE

The gray dusk bled through the bars on the high, narrow windows. The light spread like ash over the prison cafeteria, filtering out any semblance of color on the cold stone walls, the prison overalls, the trays, the metal tables, even the faces of the men. It could have been a scene from one of the black-and-white movies Murphy loved so much. Back when they gave him the first round of shock treatments, those old films seemed like the only reality he could wrap his mind around. He lost track of the line between his life and those movies. Maybe the line never existed.

Who am I? Murphy asked himself as he stepped beyond the double doors into the cafeteria. He hitched up his trousers until the waistband hit his belly and fell again, barely hanging onto the curve in his back. No matter. *Am I George Raft or Jimmy Cagney?* He glanced to his right to make sure Fennis was keeping the guard occupied. Then he gave a glance left and upward to the surveillance camera. It hung limp in the corner—the victim of a wayward basketball earlier that morning. *I am Humphrey Bogart*, he decided.

He strode across the cafeteria, weaving his way through the tables like Rick in *Casablanca*. He had his eye on Mr. Smith, a man hunched like a question mark over his tin plate of food. Smith was new. But everyone knew who he was.

Murphy cleared his throat and sat next to Smith. Smith's fork scraped the bottom of his plate like a metal claw across a car hood. Glancing again at Fennis and the guard, Murphy leaned back, his elbows on the table, facing away from Smith. He didn't want the scene to look obvious—not as if he was there to *talk* to Smith. As he looked around, he had the uncomfortable feeling that he looked exactly like a man who was trying not to look the way he was looking.

Smith slowly lifted his head. He turned to look at Murphy.

"Don't—" Murphy started to say but realized it was ridiculous to act as if they weren't talking. He adjusted himself to face Smith and flinched. The pale skin and the gaunt cheeks were familiar. But those eyes. Dark, almost black. It was as if somebody had soaked up every ounce of despair ever felt by the inmates of the rehab facility and squeezed it like a sponge into Smith's eyes. Murphy tilted his head as if Smith had said something to him.

Smith simply stared at him.

Murphy cleared his throat again. But there was no clearing the raw rasp of nicotine. "Glenda, in the office—"

Smith turned his plate and jabbed at the leather-like meatloaf and the congealing gravy. "Glenda," he repeated mechanically.

"She overheard a call between the warden—Chapman— and that captain. You know who I mean."

"Slater."

"He knows you're here," Murphy said, sure it was dramatic news.

Smith didn't seem surprised. He only shrugged, as if to say that, somehow, *they* knew everything. Sometimes they knew sooner and sometimes later, but they always knew eventually.

Murphy coughed, thick and congested. "Slater will come for you tomorrow. But he doesn't want anyone to know he's coming. Not even the guards. He's afraid they'll talk." A sardonic smile. "He wants it to be a surprise."

Smith nodded as he gently put down his fork and pushed the tray away. He tipped his head. "Who is that?" he asked quietly.

Murphy stole a glance over his shoulder to look. A wizened old man sat at the far end of the table watching them. "We call him Preacher—because he used to be one," Murphy explained. "Don't worry about him. He's had too many shock treatments. They're letting him out tomorrow."

Smith scratched at his short brown hair, then rubbed the day's growth of stubble on his chin. He kept his eyes on the old man.

"We have a plan to get you out," Murphy whispered.

"Just me?" Smith asked.

Murphy smiled like Bogie to Ingrid Bergman. "Passage for one."

Smith pressed his palms against the top of the scarred table as if it might blow upward. His voice was low. "Do you have any idea what they'll do to anyone who helps me escape?"

Murphy nodded. "No one cares anymore."

Smith didn't say anything.

"You have to get out of here," Murphy said. "You're too important—"

Smith's eyes—those wounded eyes—interrupted Murphy. "Are you a transient?"

Murphy frowned. "Transient" was slang for people who followed Christ; the old-fashioned terms like "Christian" and "believer" were long gone. He shook his head.

"Then why should you care what happens to me?"

"Because you're a rebel," Murphy replied. "I don't care what you believe; I just want you to bring them down."

"I don't want the responsibility."

"You've got it whether you want it or not." Murphy was now being Bogie in *The Maltese Falcon*.

Smith studied his hands, still pressed against the table. That was all.

Murphy was disappointed. This wasn't how he expected Smith to act. Smith was supposed to be upbeat and brave. He was supposed to be Errol Flynn in *The Adventures of Robin Hood*. What was he up to? Was he simply putting on an act to keep the guards from getting suspicious? *That had to be it.* Smith was being noble, chivalrous. A man like Smith would hate for others to have to sacrifice for him. He wanted to carry the burden himself.

"This is something me and the boys are proud to do. What else is there in this place? They might knock us around for it, but that's a morale builder. It sure beats the boredom."

"You don't get it ..." Smith said, then his voice faded away.

When Murphy was sure that Smith had nothing else to say, he leaned closer and whispered, "Be ready at lights out ..."

Smith didn't look at Murphy. His whole demeanor, the way he stared straight ahead with those eyes, gave the impression he didn't want to know about the plan. Murphy felt annoyed. It was a clever plan. Far cleverer than the time Murphy smuggled out a prisoner in a refrigerator truck. He got a beating and thirty days in solitary confinement for that. It would have been worse if the prisoner hadn't suffocated en route. But today he was Bogie, and Bogie didn't care about those kinds of things. Murphy laid out the plan for Smith.

Afterward, Smith shook his head as if a curse had just been placed on him. "I'll do what has to be done," Smith finally said.

It was a simple proclamation that Murphy didn't know how to interpret. What role was the man playing in this movie? Was he affirming his duty with grim determination like a Jimmy Stewart? Or playing it like Gary Cooper in *High Noon*? Murphy couldn't sort it out. Did Bogie make any movies with Jimmy Stewart or Gary Cooper? He didn't think so.

Fennis coughed, the signal that the guard was watching them. Murphy stood up. He wished he could get a better sense of what Smith was thinking at that moment. The slender, pleasant face with the martyr's eyes didn't give him a clue.

As he worked his way through the cafeteria tables again— *oh, if only he had a white tuxedo!*—he couldn't shake the feeling that Smith's words weren't really a proclamation of duty, but an announcement of resignation. Murphy caught a quick glimpse of the scene one last time before he rounded the corner out of the cafeteria. Smith's eyes were on the old man at the end of the table. The old man stood up. Their mouths didn't move, but Murphy got the feeling that something was said between them.

CHAPTER 2

Captain Robert Slater, field director of the government's Special Forces division, rode the last five miles to the State Rehabilitation Center with an impatient glee. He watched the speedometer inch past ninety miles per hour, then turned to Agent Williams, his assistant. "Is that the best you can do?"

Williams glanced at him out of the corner of his eye. "I assumed you wanted to get there alive. These back roads are treacherous."

"You've driven on worse," he said.

"Our industrials will burn away." Williams was referring to the government-issue tires they were forced to use. Everything made by the government—which was most things now—got the catchall name of "industrials." He spoke with derision.

They raced past the dead corn fields and skeletal trees that jabbed at the morning sky. It had been a cold autumn for this part of the country. Barbed wire, normally hidden by vegetation, sat thorny and exposed. On the horizon, some unidentified camp barracks stretched out like round gray ships on a brown ocean.

Slater fidgeted in his seat. He clenched and unclenched his fists. He ran his fingers through his wavy red hair.

"Relax," Williams said.

Slater pushed himself against the cheap vinyl seat of the black sedan, knowing he couldn't relax. Every second counted. If those morons at the Rehabilitation Center had processed his fingerprints right away, he'd have the fugitive bagged by now. "*Two* days, right under their noses."

"The system keeps malfunctioning," Williams reminded him.

Slater couldn't deny it. The government's infrastructure—especially the technology—worked intermittently at best. Even now his phone, which should always have a steady and secure signal, wasn't connecting to anything.

"Maybe you should have had the guards put him in solitary," Williams offered. "Just to be on the safe side. They have solitary in the rehab facilities, don't they?"

"Solitary there is getting sent to bed without cookies and milk. It's not like the maximum-security centers." Slater shook his head. "And to give him special attention would've told him I'm coming. The roaches would've come out of the woodwork to steal him away."

"Roaches?" Williams asked.

"The transients. They're roaches ... vermin," Slater explained. "They sneak around in the night, behind the walls, skitter across your face while you sleep. And just when you think you've exterminated them all, another batch shows up. They are tenacious."

"Roaches," Williams repeated, as if he wasn't sure what he thought of the description.

Slater dug a hand into his pocket. "You want a breath mint?"

"How long has it been in your pocket?"

"I don't know."

"Then no thanks."

Slater popped the mint into his mouth. He remembered how, early on, the Christians were pitied for being so completely outside modern thinking. They were quaintly old-fashioned, pathetic remnants of another age, treated like a senile relative who should be sat in the corner of the room and ignored. Public opinion slowly turned as people became impatient with the Christians' defiance of the new norms, for their not having the intelligence to embrace the flow of humankind. Then the Christians were marked as hateful and bigoted for maintaining an archaic moral code of conduct that made others feel guilty or inferior. They were narrow-minded. They were propagandists for daring to argue their point of view in a way that influenced others. They were self-delusional, cultish, and, finally, insurrectionists.

"If I had my way, they wouldn't be put in Rehabilitation Centers. They're traitors."

"The government doesn't want to look intolerant or oppressive," Williams said with a cynical tone. "Better to treat them as mentally disturbed. Arrest them quietly; hospitalize them."

"Is that what you think?"

"It doesn't matter what I think. It's the law." Williams glanced at his boss.

Slater turned away, his jaws working, cracking the mint between his teeth. He didn't believe the transients could be rehabilitated. Destroying them was the most effective way to purge society of their poison.

He checked his phone again. He had a signal—weak, but enough to let the center know he was almost there. He punched a button to speed-dial the number for the warden.

The internal car speakers clicked, then connected.

Bernard Chapman, the warden, picked up. His face appeared on the dashboard monitor, but the signal couldn't sustain the image. It pixelated, froze, came back, then pixelated again. Chapman was a round-faced man with unfashionably long sideburns. "Hello—"

"Slater here. We'll be there in ten minutes."

Chapman was in an instant flap. "You said this afternoon—" he sputtered. He wiped a collection of crumbs from the corner of his mouth. Had they interrupted his breakfast?

"And that would give your prisoner more time to escape."

"I assure you he does not know anything."

Slater grunted. "Prepare the prisoner for transfer."

"But transition staff doesn't come on duty until nine," Chapman stammered.

Slater leaned toward the in-dash camera and spoke in low, measured tones. "Chapman, I'm going to be there in nine minutes. Do you really want to be reported for obstructing the transfer of a prisoner who is considered a threat to national security?"

Chapman's jowls flapped as he shook his head briskly, "No, sir, I'll see what—"

Suddenly the speaker was filled with a shrill scream. Williams instinctively hit the volume button. "What in the world?"

Chapman looked confused as he turned from the screen. He spoke to someone out of view. "Why's the alarm going?"

The line crackled and the picture pixelated, then went dead.

Williams looked at Slater, puzzled.

Slater scowled. "*Go!*" he shouted.

━━━ •••• ◆ •••• ━━━

Slater and Williams arrived at the Rehabilitation Center amidst screaming sirens and the general chaos of something gone terribly wrong. A guard at the front gate looked panicked and threatened to keep Slater from entering because of the lockdown. Slater showed him his government credentials and pushed past to go inside the main entrance.

As the guard hit the appropriate buttons to open the gate, Slater asked, "What happened?"

"That's the riot alarm." The guard touched a finger to his crackling earpiece. "I have to go," he said and waved them through. Other guards raced across a courtyard wearing riot gear and carrying AK-47s.

Slater and Williams found Chapman in his office barking orders alternately into a phone and then a walkie-talkie. A bay of television monitors showed uniformed guards battling the prisoners.

Chapman stiffened when he saw Slater. "The perimeter has been sealed; the guards have everything under control," he reported.

Slater glanced at the monitors again. Whatever had happened was concentrated in the exercise yard and the cafeteria. "Where is my prisoner?" he asked.

"In his cell."

"Are you sure?"

The blood drained from Chapman's face. "The guards reported that all the inmates in that block are accounted for."

"Show me," Slater said.

Chapman turned to the security guard seated at the bay of monitors. "Sector C."

"Yes, sir." The guard swung around to the archaic control panel and fiddled with the switches. He pointed at one of the monitors. "Sector C."

Compared to the rioting in the other areas, it looked serene.

"Cell 47," Chapman said.

The guard toggled the camera down a track that ran in front of the cells, their numbers clicking away in blue on the bottom left-hand corner of the screen: 52 ... 51 ... 50 ... but at 48, the camera suddenly stopped. The guard navigated the toggles and knobs, but the camera wouldn't move any further.

"It won't budge," the guard said nervously. "Something must be blocking the track."

"Call the sergeant in that sector," Chapman commanded. The guard reached for the device.

Slater snapped, "Forget it. Take me there."

"It may not be safe," Chapman said.

Slater glared at him.

Chapman yielded. "This way."

"Tell me what happened," Slater said to Chapman as they descended a stairwell and walked at a brisk pace down various corridors. At checkpoints, buzzers sounded and doors were opened.

"Some of the prisoners were out for their morning exercise and started fighting. It got out of hand."

Slater asked, "Do your prisoners often fight?"

"No," Chapman replied. "Most of the inmates are—er, *were*—transients. They've all had shock treatments. They're generally compliant."

Slater glanced at Williams, then asked Chapman, "Was my prisoner in the exercise yard? Was he part of the fight?"

"No. He's been in his cell, as per your orders." Chapman brushed the back of his hand across his glistening forehead. His walkie-talkie crackled.

"Yard and cafeteria are secured," a voice said.

Snatching the device from his belt, he asked, "*Everything is secured?*"

"Yes, sir," came the voice.

"Good." Chapman gave Slater a satisfied look.

At the next checkpoint, a guard behind a large metal desk asked Chapman, "Are we still in lockdown?"

"What?" Chapman asked, annoyed.

"They're asking at the front gate," the guard said. "The next shift needs to get in."

Chapman waved a hand at him. "Yes, yes, everything is secured. Cancel the lockdown."

Slater was about to challenge the decision, but his eyes landed on the door ahead. It was marked with a large "C".

<hr />

Patowski, one of the new recruits, led the old man down the passageway to the main exit. The inmate had wild white hair and beard and clutched his gym bag with a trembling hand. This was the first time Patowski had been so close to the Preacher, who'd become something of a legend for his stream-of-conscience ramblings and apocalyptic visions.

The old man faltered and switched the bag to his other hand as if it was too heavy for him to carry.

"Why so slow, Preacher?" Patowski asked him. "I'd have thought you'd be rushing to get out of here."

The Preacher didn't reply. He lifted the gym bag and clutched it close to his chest.

Patowski looked at the man's rubbery wrinkles and vacant eyes. This one could have been let out a long time ago. He'd had enough shock treatments to ensure that any semblance of belief was deep-fried away like yesterday's onion rings.

The old man shuffled along.

Patowski wanted to ask him how he felt about being released and what his plans were. Did he have any family left? But the old man would have quoted a Bible verse in response. Even new recruits like Patowski knew not to get in a conversation with the Preacher.

A flickering fluorescent light above seemed to catch the old man's attention. "Am I working in the laundry room today?" he asked.

Patowski shook his head. "It's your big day. Your release. No more laundry room."

The Preacher said nothing. They reached the final processing counter.

Frank O'Connor, the bushy-haired man behind the desk, had the paperwork ready to go. "Anybody know what started that ruckus this morning?" O'Connor asked.

"No idea," Patowski answered.

O'Connor brought out a large yellow folder. "Grady said a couple of big shots came in."

"Big shots?" Patowski asked.

"Two guys in government suits," O'Connor said. "They've got Chapman in a sweat."

"Bad timing for the inmates to act up." Patowski's thoughts were already on ditching the Preacher and getting back inside. The right word, the right action, and Patowski could get the big shots' attention. He knew he was capable of better work than this. Thankfully, his wife had cleaned and pressed his shirt.

The old man hardly seemed to recognize the old watch, key ring, and worn wallet handed to him from the large personal possessions envelope. O'Connor checked them off. "You want them in that gym bag?"

"Just do it," Patowski said, his impatience showing.

O'Connor unzipped the bag and put the meager inventory inside next to a spare pair of trousers, a shirt, and a shaving kit. There were books, too, but Patowski couldn't see the titles.

"I can't imagine what got into them," O'Connor said, still talking about the riot. He counted out the State-sanctioned release money—enough to get the Preacher started in proper conditions of poverty—and handed it over. The Preacher took it but didn't seem to know what to do with it.

"Put it in your pocket," Patowski told him.

The Preacher obeyed and tucked it in his shirt pocket.

"Take care, Preacher," O'Connor said. "Do you know where you're going? To the end of the courtyard and through the gate. Got it? If you don't have anyone meeting you, then turn left and walk for about a quarter of a mile. That'll take you to Beeson's Grocery and Gas. A bus will come by there within the hour. Do you understand?"

The Preacher nodded and, clinging to his gym bag like it contained precious jewels, stepped up to the large iron door. O'Connor hit the buzzer and the latch clicked free.

Patowski opened the door for the old man. "See ya, Preacher."

The Preacher stepped into the light, shielded his eyes, then hobbled through the courtyard to the larger gate beyond. The wind caught his hair and beard and blew it around like a white wildfire.

"I don't know why they bother," Patowski said.

O'Connor shrugged. "Makes them feel *just*, I guess."

A black sedan pulled up at the gate and an old woman got out. She gingerly went to the Preacher and hugged him. Patowski thought she was weeping as she held him at arm's length, then pulled him close for another hug.

"His wife, do you think?" O'Connor asked.

Patowski didn't answer. What little training he'd had in observational work told him that something wasn't quite right. The old woman guided the Preacher to the passenger side of the car, then lightly stepped back around to the driver's side. She crawled in.

Something didn't ring true. What was it?

The sedan pulled away and out of view.

Patowski frowned. "His daughter?"

"Too old for his daughter," O'Connor said.

"But ... the way she walked around the car," Patowski began, but he didn't know where he was going with the thought. "Didn't you see it?"

"No."

Then it occurred to him. "She looked like an old woman but walked like a *young* woman."

O'Connor looked out as if the scene would replay for him. "I didn't notice."

Patowski thought nothing more of it, keen to get back inside the prison.

By the time Slater and Williams entered the "C" block, curious guards had appeared. The prisoners in the cells came forward, pressing against their bars to see what the stir was about.

"Stand clear!" a guard shouted. The inquisitive inmates stepped back.

Chapman reached number 47 first. He put a hand up to the wall as if to steady himself. Slater and Williams stepped next to him.

"Open it up," Chapman shouted. "*Open it up!*"

There was a distant buzz and the door to cell 47 slid open.

Slater took a step inside and swore under his breath. Williams remained behind him. Chapman let out a small choking sound.

An old man with wild white hair and beard sat on the edge of the bed, his hands folded politely in his lap. He looked up at Slater and smiled like a child greeting a trusted adult.

Slater choked down lukewarm coffee at Chapman's desk. Ostensibly, he was calm and cool. In reality, he was in a red-raged fury. Williams alone knew it.

Searches for the escaped prisoner had turned up nothing. An all-points bulletin was issued for the black sedan and its occupants, but Slater made it clear he didn't believe they'd be found. "The car will turn up," he said. "And it'll have the wigs and makeup in it. Nothing of any use."

Frank O'Connor, the guard in charge of the front desk, stood by the wall with the new recruit named Jeff Patowski. Chapman stood off to the side, wringing his hands.

"Explain it to me," Slater said. "You simply *look* at a released prisoner and let him go? Don't you have a scanning system?"

O'Connor and Patowski glanced at Chapman.

"We did but it stopped working," Chapman said. "I put in the requisition forms months ago."

"Fingerprints? Identification tags?" Slater continued, this time to O'Connor.

O'Connor shook his head. "No, sir. That isn't part of the protocol for low-security Rehabilitation Centers like ours."

Slater shot a look at Williams, who nodded and made a note to address protocol issues with the central office when they got back.

Chapman looked helpless. "We're not a big-city operation like you're used to, Captain. The inmates we have here—they're mostly harmless. We don't have to go through a lot of bells and whistles. It's not like they're hardened criminals."

Slater stared at Chapman with a cold expression. "What do you consider a hardened criminal, Chapman? A murderer? A thief? A child-enslaver?"

"Well ... yes."

"And what do you think *makes* a criminal hardened? I'll tell you what it is: the *idea* that killing people or stealing others' belongings or enslaving children is a good idea. Criminals are criminals first in their ideas. Do you understand? It's what they have *up here*"—he pointed to his temple—"that makes them hardened criminals. These Christians have an *idea* that leads to action against our state—against *us*. It's the *ideas* of men that bring down a world, not guns or revolution."

Chapman should have let it go but didn't. "But these ideas are just the superstitions of the weak-minded. You don't seriously believe they're a genuine threat."

"I believe it," Slater said through clenched teeth. "Now, I want to talk to the accomplices."

Chapman rapped on the door and a guard brought two men into the office. They were manacled from head to foot.

Roaches, Slater thought. He could tell by the obsequious posture and lamb-like eyes.

"These are the two," the guard announced.

"Thank you," Slater said. He leaned against the desk and eyed the two men with a long and purposeful look. One was a medium-sized creature with a face and beard that looked like a purple leather couch with cat hair all over it. The name Fennis was stitched to the breast of his overalls. The other was sandy-haired, larger, and more substantial in build. "Murphy," the stitching said.

"So, you don't have anything to tell me about the escape, Mr. Fennis?" Slater asked.

Fennis shook his head. "No, sir. I don't have anything to say about it."

"It's not Christian to lie," Slater smiled.

"It's not a lie to say that I don't have anything to tell you," Fennis countered.

Slater conceded the point with a nod. "Fennis, I saw in your file that you're up for parole in three months. Only three months after—how long has it been? Four years? Four years in here for what? Teaching the Bible to a bunch of bikers. Was that your crime? Turning Hell's Angels into Heaven's Angels?"

Fennis looked impassively at Slater.

"You're so close, Fennis. Why would you blow it by helping someone to escape? I don't understand. Help me, will you?"

Fennis kept his eyes locked on Slater's. "You wouldn't understand no matter what I say."

"I could release you in *one* month if you choose to cooperate," Slater offered.

Fennis' face tightened as if the offer caused an internal tremor somewhere deep inside of him. He pressed his lips together, then relaxed. "I still wouldn't have anything to say."

"Patowski." Slater waved his hand.

Patowski nearly leapt across the room. "Yes, sir?"

"I want you to take your nightstick and hit it as hard as you can across the bridge of Mr. Fennis' nose."

Fennis took a step back. Williams stood up straight as if to brace himself.

Patowski went pale. "What?" The question came out as a strangled sound.

Slater spoke slowly. "I want you to take your nightstick and—"

"I heard you, sir, but I ..." Patowski didn't have the words.

"You don't want to do it, I know," Slater said sympathetically. "And I don't want you to do it either. But Mr. Fennis refuses to help and, frankly, I can't imagine that talking will persuade him."

"But ... why me?" Patowski asked.

Slater addressed Patowski as if talking to a small child. "Because you let our prisoner escape, and this will go a long way to making amends. You want to make amends, don't you? You don't want words like 'incompetency' and 'recommended for immediate dismissal' to show up on your record, right?"

"No, sir ..."

"I'll be asking Mr. O'Connor for a similar favor," Slater said casually.

Chapman stepped forward, still wringing his hands, "Captain, I don't think—"

Slater held up his hand. His tone was as hard as a block of cement. "Warden, I don't care what you think. Patowski, go on. You can do it."

Patowski slowly pulled out his nightstick. He was turning green, working his mouth as if he might vomit. Fennis was wild-eyed as he backed away. There was nowhere to go.

Slater made eye contact with Williams, tipping his head to watch Murphy. He was bigger and stronger and might be the one to take action.

"Well?" Slater asked impatiently.

Patowski held up his baton like a baseball bat.

Chapman was red-faced. "I'll file a report."

"Do it, Patowski," Slater commanded.

The recruit with the clean and pressed shirt positioned himself in front of Fennis, who was still trying to look tough, but squirmed against the guard.

"I don't have anything to tell you because I don't know anything," Fennis said, his legs trembling, his knees beginning to buckle.

"No good," Slater said and signaled Patowski.

With shaking hands, Patowski brought the baton back.

"Go," Slater prompted him. Williams touched his fingertips to the butt of the pistol in his shoulder holster.

Patowski closed his eyes, his entire body went taut.

"No!" Murphy shouted. "Stop! He's telling you the truth. I'm the one you want. I concocted the whole scheme. He was just a bit player."

Slater moved next to Murphy and looked into his grizzled, pock-marked face. "You're another biker who saw the light, huh? I'll bet you miss those roaring engines and the feel of leather against your enormous backside."

Murphy straightened up and lifted his chin in a weak show of defiance. It reminded Slater of James Cagney in a movie he'd once seen.

"Tell me what you know about the escaped prisoner."

"You may as well kill me," Murphy told him. "I'm not afraid of death."

Slater smiled. "Death is going to be the least of your worries, Mr. Murphy." He nodded at Williams. "Let me tell you something about my associate here. He doesn't like inflicting pain on people, or animals, or even insects like roaches. But it is never a matter of liking or disliking it. He's been trained thoroughly to use the art of physical violence to extract whatever information is needed from anyone at any time with any tools available. I've seen him do things with a toothpick that would make you cry like a little girl. Now,

I know what you're thinking. He looks like a charming and friendly fellow, but he's actually a cold clinician. You will be a dissected frog under his scalpel."

With surprising speed, Slater grabbed the baton from Patowski and swung it hard against Fennis' nose. Fennis screamed and brought his hands up, dropping to his knees. In a return swing, Slater caught him hard on the back of the head. Fennis fell hard. Blood poured from both wounds.

"That's what happens to bit players. Imagine what happens to the star of the show." Slater handed the baton back to a stunned Patowski.

Williams carefully took off his jacket as if he didn't want to wrinkle it. He removed his shoulder holster and gun and handed them to Chapman. Politely, he said, "I'm sorry, Mr. Murphy; it's nothing personal."

Murphy didn't die that day, though he wished many times that he had.

Chapter 3

For Sam Johnson, the journey began with two events that happened on the same day: he was fired, and someone slipped a mysterious note under his apartment door.

He guessed that the note had been delivered even while he was across the college campus at the chancellor's office being dismissed.

Burdened with a box of books and sundry belongings from his small office, Sam had trampled the note as he entered his apartment. If his paperback copy of *Candide* hadn't slipped from the top of the box, he might not have seen the plain white envelope until much later—perhaps when it was too late.

He put the boxes down and shoved the note absentmindedly into his jacket pocket.

It was hard for him to believe that he'd been fired. Sixteen years of classes, seven years of tenure were quickly dismissed by a nervous administrator who wouldn't look him in the eyes.

It was an odd scene for two old friends to share. But Sam shouldn't have been surprised. Wasn't he the one who often told his students: "Your enemies can't betray you; only your friends can do that"?

Just three days before, he had gone fishing with Bill. Then they weren't chancellor and professor, but two pals standing hip deep in the cool river, smoking their pipes, and talking about nothing in particular. But it wasn't *nothing* talk, was it? Bill must've been making mental notes.

What had happened? That night, as the fire filled the air around the tent with the smell of smoke, bad coffee, and pine, Sam felt at ease, comfortable in their friendship. He said something he shouldn't have said. He admitted that his studies of history and literature had led him to a belief in the impossible, a search for God that had taken him into a great mystery called Jesus Christ. He hadn't meant for it to sound so serious or profound, not even a declaration of faith. It was merely something he'd been thinking about.

Now, standing in his apartment, Sam remembered the uneasy expression on Bill's face as he had stoked the fire. It was an expression that asked, "Why did you have to tell me? Why couldn't you keep your mouth shut?"

In Bill's office, after his-friend-now-chancellor delivered the blow, Sam was too shocked to say anything. He imagined his expression at that moment was pure comedy.

The chancellor muttered something about the college's economic woes and "signs of the times."

They both knew the real cause. "The fishing trip," Sam said.

"It has nothing to do with that," the chancellor snapped. He spoke without conviction. "But Sam ... you were supposed to research that nonsense to refute it. You weren't supposed to *believe* it."

Do I believe it? Sam thought as he walked out of the chancellor's office. *Wasn't it foolishness to pay this kind of price for something he didn't believe?*

Sitting on his apartment sofa, surrounded by his boxes, he felt like a lover spurned. It was an appropriate analogy. The college had been Sam's girlfriend, his wife and mistress. The joy of standing in front of a class filled with open minds ready to receive the world's great literature and history was like some kind of conjugal rite. It gave him a sense of fulfillment no human could have provided. Gradebooks, exams, and class itineraries were the duties of a loving husband.

Even after college regulations limited what books they could read ... and debates were reduced to repeating and reiterating the latest platitudes from the cultural gurus ... and scientific theories were held as indisputable facts ... and students' once-eager expressions turned to contorted looks of anger and indignation ... he still taught with every ounce of passion he had. He remained faithful to a lover he suspected would one day spurn him.

The surprise, he had to admit, was how he'd been spurned. It wasn't the college's administration and faculty, or even government regulations, that cut him off. A disgruntled student wrote about him on one of the social networks, quoting something he'd said in a class that contradicted an established point of view. Then someone else searched the internet for past writings and unearthed an essay he had written in graduate school. The essay put forward the unintended consequences when freedom of speech is slowly strangled. "As with any strangulation, oxygen to the brain is cut off, and we know what happens then."

The social networks set themselves alight. The usual voices, and a few new ones, argued that freedom of speech didn't mean that every stupid opinion should be tolerated. Even a few of his fellow professors declared in a joint statement that the "weeds of bad thinking needed to be pulled and thrown out." They stated that what he'd called strangulation was actually *pruning*, "which is a necessity if one is to maintain a thriving garden."

Sam was forced to defend a twenty-year-old essay. But when he tried, using the same networks through which he'd been attacked, his responses were blocked as a violation of the networks' policies of "advocating points of view that were liable to incite violence or to offend users through unscientific or bigoted methods of expression." He couldn't imagine what they were referring to until someone pointed out that his use of words like "strangulation" and "cutting oxygen to the brain" suggested violence. He was told that such expressions might upset those who had once suffered from strangulation.

"Do we have a lot of students who've had that experience?" Sam had asked a co-worker.

His wording might also offend those persons in the medical community, he was told, or distress families who were even now serving as caregivers for victims whose brains had been denied oxygen.

The whole incident happened without any sense of irony. According to his co-workers, stopping his freedom of speech seemed to be the only way to maintain freedom of speech.

Sam braced himself for an official reprimand. When it didn't come, he thought he'd escaped a dangerous close call.

Then came the fishing trip. Likely his admission there was the last straw, giving the chancellor an excuse to do what he might have been planning to do anyway.

Sam's mind now went to all the things you say you'll do after a breakup. He'd have more time for those writing projects. He could go out more often. He might finally get to clean out the closet in the spare room.

He leaned back and put his hands over his face. His head ached and his eyes burned. What was he going to do now?

The mysterious envelope rustled in his pocket. He pulled it out, looked at the unmarked front, then tore open the back. He expected it to be a cheesy announcement for an event in the student lounge. Instead, he saw a note with only three typed lines on it.

"They won't leave you alone," the note warned. "Be at 11 Camden Court at ten o'clock tonight. Bring your essentials and warmest clothing. *No cell phones.* Destroy this letter."

The print near the end of the message was faded, a telltale characteristic of the printer in his department. Was he being warned by one of his co-workers? An intern or student? Or maybe it was the ever-faithful, ever-diligent Dolores, who had been the department secretary for as long as anyone could remember. He never spoke of Christianity with her, but always suspected she was a believer.

He slumped against the sofa and felt like someone had pulled the plug on his body and let the air out. He had to concentrate. Someone was trying to help him. Or it might be some kind of trap.

But who would go to the trouble of trapping him? The authorities? Why would they bother? It was easy enough for them to simply arrest him on some pretext. They had done it enough with others. Everyone had become quite familiar with the sound of heavy footsteps in the halls at odd hours, fists pounding against the doors, the muted voices from the other side of the wall, a quick peek through the curtains to see men in suits ushering the accused away, ostensibly to answer only a few questions at headquarters. But somehow the accused never came back. And which friend or neighbor would dare to inquire into their whereabouts?

Signs of the times, all right. Sam had a student in a class only two semesters ago who unwisely defended Christianity during a discussion about Constantine and the Roman Empire. It was hardly a defense. Just a couple of comments that seemed to favor a few of the basic tenets espoused by

Christ. He remembered how she had stood. Her lithe body straight and determined; her long sandy hair cascading halo-like around her fresh face. She spoke in a matter-of-fact tone about Christ, as if she hadn't grown up in a state where matter-of-fact tones invited betrayal. Doubt and fear were what the State liked. Trembling lips and shaking voices.

Class monitors were secretly posted in each class by then. One must have reported her. Two days later, while Sam was teaching about the merits of State-sanctioned censorship, the girl burst into the class. She was frantic, wild-eyed. She begged for help. Two police officers raced in, catching her in the gallery. "Won't anyone help me? Won't anyone stop this?" she had screamed as they dragged her out. Sam felt a pang of conscience then. Not because she had been arrested, but because he and the class had watched the scene with all the concern of a flock of grazing sheep. Once the doors had slammed shut, they simply went back to what they were doing as if nothing had happened. He never saw the girl again.

Signs of the times, indeed.

He remembered the night he was abruptly awakened by a commotion one floor up. At first he thought it was the recently arrived newlyweds having a fight. But then he heard a third voice talking in that dull procedural monotone the security forces often used to convey their emotional detachment. The girl cried out, the boy shouted, a scuffle followed with the sound of furniture being knocked over and glass breaking. Sam lay there listening, sweating. He felt conflicted. His freedom-loving instincts said that they had no right to barge in on people in the middle of the night like that. He should do something about it. Step into the hall. Say a few words of protest.

He didn't move. He dug his claws into the blanket and waited. The silence would come. He knew it would eventually. And when it did, he felt the relief of his safe anonymity.

Leon and Margaret Maxwell, the couple living with their three kids in the efficiency next door, predicted the same end for Sam if he didn't keep his mouth closed.

"You professors are all alike," Leon said, waving a spoon at Sam during dinner the night after the newlyweds had disappeared. "You can't keep your thoughts to yourself. Gotta act like the whole world is your classroom. What happened to those kids will happen to you one day if you don't watch it."

Embarrassed, Sam laughed—but not too loudly—and that night they drank wine together until Margaret urged Sam to go home so she could put the children to bed.

When Sam began to entertain an appreciation for Christianity, he used Leon as a sounding board.

Leon—liberal-minded as he was—stated clearly, "I don't like it and don't approve."

"Why?" Sam asked. "How can we look at history and literature—its beauty and continuity—and not be affected? It's like they're all pointing to something or someone, as if God buried clues inside of our artistry, inside of our stories, for us to find. I'm only now seeing them."

Leon furrowed his brow and lectured Sam for an hour about the dangers of such thinking.

They saw little of each other after that. Just an occasional hello in the hallway. It was safer that way.

Sam wondered what Leon would think if Sam disappeared in the night. Just another missing person. Another enemy of the State. Maybe Leon wouldn't think anything at all. It was safer that way, too.

He tucked the note back into the torn envelope. *Who sent it?*

Maybe someone in the Resistance. Not that he knew much about it except from the inflammatory reports in the newspapers. "Revolutionaries," they were called. And they were mocked for their biblical code names. Moses and Elijah were the leaders. They used a network of followers to help the offenders escape. *It was their own version of the Underground Railroad,* Sam thought wryly.

How did they know to contact him?

He thought of Angus McLeod, another professor at the college who'd been Sam's nemesis for years. They rarely agreed on anything. Angus was rumored to be a Catholic and, ironically, became a catalyst for Sam's growing faith. They were having one of their typical lunchtime debates, this time about the nature of Christ as expressed in medieval literature. The debate shifted to the Reformation and its merits—or lack thereof. Angus then took the position that the Reformation did not reform anything but simply wrecked what had been core Christian belief for 1,500 years. He quoted pieces of Scripture that sent Sam home to find a Bible—his mother's old leather-backed version—buried in a box with other family heirlooms.

Sam read the New Testament. He couldn't put it down. The Gospel of John was as beautiful a work of poetry as he'd ever read. Over the course of two months, he read the entire Bible, viewing it in the context of history and as a great work of literature. He yielded to the mystery of Jesus Christ coming as the Son of God, dying for him, and rising from the grave. He accepted that this Jesus demanded to have a place in his heart and life.

The Protestants might have called the moment "asking Jesus into his heart." He thought of it more as a decisive pivot point in what had become a series of pivot points. But what was he to do next?

He mentioned to Angus that he was curious about the historical nature of discipleship. What did Christians do once they actually became Christians?

"Protestant Christians don't have to do much of anything," Angus admitted. "Accept Jesus, claim salvation as something God-given through grace, and they're good for heaven."

Sam nodded. His mother, a staunch Protestant, expressed something very similar. She had taken the family to church services, Sunday School, and Vacation Bible School. Saved by grace and not works. That was the position. Which meant she didn't have to do much apart from bake casseroles for church functions.

"The Catholic route would have new believers go through some form of catechesis and sacramental training," Angus continued. "Baptism, confession, confirmation ... that sort of thing."

Sam asked more questions about the Catholic route.

Angus looked at him with narrow eyes. "Be careful, Sammy. One might suspect you're asking for yourself."

Sam had laughed at the suggestion.

Thinking about the letter, Sam wondered if it was Angus trying to save him. *Maybe, maybe not.*

Did it really matter who'd sent the note? The question now was whether to go. Looking around his apartment, Sam realized that all his worldly goods were not enough to hold him back. Was there anything worth staying for? He went through a mental checklist and found himself even more depressed. Any reason to stay? No. Family? No. Friends? No. A place to call home, any attachments at all? No and No. What had he done with his life?

He had spent it with an inanimate lover who'd rejected him. Even now she kept her distance, across a bed of fallen leaves, remote and indifferent to whether he stayed or left.

He thought of the girl who'd been arrested—*was Leanne her name?*—and tried to imagine the indignity of being dragged from his apartment in the middle of the night, or chased across campus, or led in handcuffs from the cafeteria in front of the students and faculty.

He began to pack.

CHAPTER 4

Number 11 Camden Court was a row house that sat behind a low brick wall with a mangled iron gate. The house had chipped and faded paint, the shutters hanging on for dear life from their hinges.

It's a mistake, Sam thought. He considered strolling on past. But the dark road ahead gave him no other options.

He walked cautiously up to the door. Clouds filtered the light of the full moon. Stark shadows drifted like ghosts across the cracked gray sidewalk. A blast of cool air started a small whirlwind within the confines of the bricked garden. Trash ran like rats around his feet. Despite the breeze, he sweated. The stuffed overnight bag tried to slip from his damp fingers. His knuckles ached as he clenched his fist around the handle.

Swallowing hard, Sam gently knocked on the scarred oak door. Everything seemed to go quiet. Even the breeze had stopped. Then he heard a soft scraping noise from inside. A pinpoint of light betrayed the peephole in the middle of a panel on the door. He was being checked out.

Sam waited for an uncomfortable amount of time. Just as he started to think that he'd made a big mistake and should leave, he heard the slide of the bolt. The door opened slowly.

A middle-aged woman with sharp eyes and wiry hair tied in a tight bun peeked out at him. "Yes?" she asked. Her gaze took him in from head to toe. She had the look of someone who could make you feel at home or like an unwanted stranger. Right now, he felt like an unwanted stranger.

"My name is Sam Johnson."

"So?" she asked.

Sam was bewildered. "I got a note saying to come here tonight."

"Did you?" she asked, then gave him a mischievous smile. "Then I suppose you should come in."

She stepped aside so he could enter. By the time he closed the door behind him, she was walking briskly down a thin, stale-smelling hallway. "Come along," she said over her shoulder.

He followed her to the end of the hall and through a small room that might have been a kitchen once. They went through to a rear room, its peeling wallpaper smelling of damp and mold. A bare bulb hung above a wooden table in the middle of an uneven dirt floor. Around the table sat a young woman—she might've been nineteen or twenty years old—and an old man with an explosion of white hair and beard. The girl had a wide-eyed look, as if she expected something to suddenly jump out at her. The old man looked oblivious to his surroundings.

Sam sympathized with the girl's expression. He wanted to tell her that he felt frightened, too. Maybe they could share the emotion and somehow draw up courage between them. But embarrassment constrained him. They managed only to mutter their first names to each other. The young woman was Amy. The old man was Luke.

Sam heard footsteps and realized that the woman who'd brought him down was leaving.

"Welcome." A stocky man stepped out of a shadowed doorway. He was bald and sported a large walrus mustache. In a smock, he would have looked like an old-fashioned town butcher or baker. A plain white shirt with gray pants held up by black suspenders added to the effect. "I'm Ben."

When Sam started to introduce himself, Ben held up a thick hand with sausage-like fingers. "We don't have much time. Follow me." He shuffled into the shadows of a side room. A loud click and a dull yellow light buzzed over his head.

The young woman and old man looked confused but followed slowly. Sam hesitated. *This could be a lure into a house of horrors.* Nonetheless, with little option he passed through the door into the room. It was filled with broken wooden shelving.

Ben opened another door and the smell of gasoline, old grass, and garbage wafted in. The four of them entered a narrow garage. A large windowless van sat with its doors open.

"I hope you brought warm clothes," Ben said. "Throw your bags in the back."

Sam obeyed, dropping his bag onto an oil-stained carpet just inside the rear door. Other bags and boxes were piled behind the driver and passenger seats.

"You three will hide under the false floor of the van until you're safely out of town," Ben continued. "It won't be comfortable, but you'll survive. I'll be taking you to the next rendezvous point, where you will meet the rest of your group."

"Group? What group?" Sam asked.

"Please," Ben said patiently. "I can't tell you anything more. The less you know, the better." He pulled up the carpet and rolled it to one side. Then he used a crowbar to dislodge the panels that made up the false floor.

The three travelers moved to get in, but Ben stopped them. "Any cell phones?"

"What's wrong with cell phones?" Sam asked.

"They're used as tracking devices," Ben replied.

"Even if they're switched off and the battery pulled out?" asked Amy.

"They broadcast your whereabouts no matter what you do to them," Ben stated. "I took a sledgehammer to one and it still—well, never mind. The only safe bet is to leave them behind." He eyed them. "Please don't make me have to frisk you."

The three looked at each other, then shook their heads wearily, handing him their phones.

Placing each of the surrendered devices in a box a few feet from the van, Ben smiled. "Okay. Get in."

Sam, Amy, and Luke lay down side by side in the shallow bed, Amy between the two men. *This is what a pauper's grave looks like*, Sam thought.

"How will we breathe?" Amy asked.

"Ventilation," Ben explained.

"And if we need to get out?" Sam asked.

"Push and kick as hard as you can," Ben said. He lowered the panels back in place. Then came the thud of the carpet on top. The darkness was offset by small holes drilled into both sides of the bed.

Soon, the van was backing out of the garage and onto the road. Heavy exhaust fumes wafted in. Sam felt sick. Then, as they moved, fresh air eased the feeling. They hit a few hard bumps and Amy grabbed his hand. Startled, he jerked away.

"I'm sorry," she whispered.

He felt his cheeks burn. "It's all right," he replied.

Time blurred. Sam may have fallen asleep. He hoped they weren't being asphyxiated. Then the van came to a stop, and, through the side of the coffin, Sam could hear the barking voices of authority. They must have reached a checkpoint.

Sam easily imagined what it looked like: the pristine, blue-uniformed guards, a cold-white fluorescent-lit box with papers and stamps and metal desks and roller chairs. It was potent in a sterile way; inhuman. He wondered if this one was equipped with the new scanners: large machines that used thermal imaging and X-ray technology to scan every vehicle, identifying everything on board. The scanners had become standard equipment for the checkpoints in the big cities. He hoped that this one was remote enough not to be equipped with the latest technology.

The guards yapped at Ben for his papers and sniffed around the van like bloodhounds. Ben told them something about being on his way to pick up goods for a delivery.

No scanners, but Sam still held his breath, expecting the false floor to be yanked up at any moment. He heard a low growl and was alarmed to realize that the old man was snoring. Amy must have nudged him because he suddenly stopped. Long minutes went by. Some final shouts and Ben wrenched the truck into gear. A few jerks and they were on their way again. But only for a few minutes. Ben pulled off the road, bumping on an uneven pavement. The van stopped. A few moments later, the panels were pulled up.

"Stretch your legs," Ben said. As the passengers crawled out, he explained that it would be two hours to the next rendezvous point. He had pulled into a rest stop near a patch of woods. A single streetlight stood above them, its light fading in and out.

"Was everything all right with the guards?" Sam asked.

"No problem." Ben patted the side of the van with affection, smiling. "I'm surprised they haven't figured it out by now."

Sam's arms and legs ached. He rubbed at them and looked around. Luke strode into the trees, disappearing into the blackness. Amy seemed unsure of what to do.

Pacing along the edge of the road, Sam wondered where they were going—and where they would ultimately call home. He noticed that Amy hadn't moved from her spot. She looked ready to make a run for it at the slightest hint of trouble. He drifted in her direction, surreptitiously looking at her without intending to be creepy about it. Her brown hair was tied back into a bun, giving a clear view of her face. He thought she was pretty in a wholesome, sweet way—likely the kind of girl who did well at school, knew her Bible, and dated only virtuous young men. She wore a thick ski jacket, a plaid flannel shirt, jeans, and hiking boots. He imagined that she once had a nice figure, but now she looked thin, maybe even undernourished. Though she wore a constant expression of anxiety, he suspected she'd be particularly radiant when she smiled. *If* she ever smiled again.

Her eyes darted to the woods at a loud rustling. Luke stepped out again. Sam guessed Luke was in his sixties, maybe seventy. His hair was white and uncombed. A Moses-like beard hung from his face. Now, he had the look of a young child who was thrilled to be having a nighttime adventure.

Ben passed around bottles of water and protein bars. "There won't be another checkpoint," he said. "Make yourselves as comfortable as possible in the back. Just be ready to slip under the panels if I say so."

They picked their spots around the floor of the van. Sam leaned against his bag of belongings and tried to relax. He couldn't. Amy and Luke both seemed to stare into the spotted blackness of the van, avoiding Sam's and each other's gazes.

In the scattered light that sprayed them through the windshield, Sam saw Amy's lips moving as if in prayer. He glanced down and saw a rosary threaded through her fingers.

Luke stared straight ahead. His eyes were wide. *Maybe too wide*, Sam thought, remembering eyes like that from a picture in a psychology textbook he had once read. They were the eyes of someone who had suffered a serious mental or emotional trauma.

Sam eventually dozed, cast adrift in a small boat on a rolling sea. Not only was he a lover scorned by his academic mistress, but he had now banished himself from her presence by taking a voyage to parts unknown. Would she miss him? No, probably not. Apart from being unloving, she had always been demanding and jealous. And he had been unfaithful—giving his mind and heart to another. Her lack of forgiveness would display itself as a willful indifference. He never existed for her. He was like the dead unremembered.

Now he was alone. In his half-sleep he prayed for a grace he hadn't yet felt.

The lulling vibration and bounce of the van suddenly stopped. Sam jerked up his head.

"Our next pickup point," Ben announced. He climbed out of the van, leaving the door open. The burst of air was crisp and carried the distinct smell of hay and animals. Sam scooted forward to look. A farmhouse and barn stood off like giant specters.

Urgent whispers outside of the van. Sam cocked his ear to listen more closely but couldn't make out any of the words. Amy had tilted her head slightly as if she too was trying to hear. Her brow was knitted with worry.

"Sounds like a couple of parents trying to figure out what to do with the kids," Sam said.

Amy gave him a disapproving look, as if he was the man on the elevator who'd broken the rule of silence.

The rear doors made a loud metallic click and swung open.

"Make room," Ben said. "We have five more people. But, please, *no talking*."

Sam shuffled to the side, pressing behind the driver's seat. Then the newcomers appeared, their names quietly offered by Ben as they climbed in. First, a pale woman with Madonna-like eyes, red and bloodshot from shedding endless tears for the troubled world. She held onto—dragged, actually—a young boy of six. He had dark wavy hair, an oval face with a pale complexion, and eyes that looked around with all the wonder and excitement of a child on his first school field trip. They were mother and son, Mary and Timothy.

"Can I ride up front with the man?" Timothy asked.

"No," his mother replied sharply, her tone enough to make him sit down as if she'd yanked his arm.

Ruth came next. She was a stout woman of "pioneer stock," as Sam's mother might have said, with a square build and a face deeply etched by laugh lines and too many days working in the sun. She glanced at Sam and smiled. It surprised him. He smiled back.

A distinguished-looking gentleman poked his head in and looked the van over. "This?" the well-bred voice asked, offended. "You expect me to ride in this?"

"Please, Mr. Beck," Ben sighed. "We don't have time."

The head peeked back in, and Sam caught the quick, darting eyes, the natural frown that pulled down heavy jowls, and the thinning hair gone gray at the temples. Howard Beck sighed, sniffed, and pulled himself in.

Ruth chuckled and shook her head.

Peter climbed in last. He was a handsome young man in his early twenties, muscular and lithe. He moved with self-confidence and, as he made his way through the van to sit down, patted shoulders and grinned reassuringly at everyone. He had the look of a high schooler running for student council president.

Peter winked at Sam, then reached for his hand and shook it vigorously. "Peter," he said simply.

"Sam."

"Quiet *please*!" Ben snapped.

"Okay, okay," Peter mumbled and slid down next to Ruth.

"He's my nephew," Ruth whispered to Sam.

Sam nodded.

Ben passed in some additional boxes of provisions, to be placed wherever they could make room.

"What if we're stopped?" Beck asked. "How are we supposed to hide?"

"No one will stop us," replied Ben. "Not where we're going."

Ben slammed the doors closed. A moment later he was in the driver's seat again. The starter churned, then the engine roared. More exhaust fumes. With a grunting protest, the van took them away.

They drove up winding roads. Sam thought he could smell snow. He burrowed deeper into his coat. He began to second-guess his decision to join them. It was possible he wouldn't have been arrested. He was a new believer, certainly no threat to anyone. Just the opposite, in fact: his faith was academic, not passionate. For all he knew, it was nothing more than a romantic interlude that would have quickly ended if it came to the choice between it and time in a Rehabilitation Center. *But,* he reasoned, *if that's true, then I am an even greater fool for making this journey. To do this without a heartfelt motivation is ridiculous. What am I doing here?*

Sam looked into the shadows, catching the outlines and silhouettes of his fellow passengers. He wondered about their stories, their reasons for escaping. He sighed. They probably felt something deep and stirring, a furnace of faith that burned within their very souls.

He wished he felt that kind of passion—felt something other than an intellectual predestination about his choices. Those initial talks with Angus, reading his mother's Bible, pretending he wanted to study it just to disprove Christianity more effectively ... when did he ever feel like he had the choice to stop? But it was the intellectual stimulation that pushed him along: How could he be truly open-minded and not consider the mystery of Christ from an academic point of view? Or maybe it was simply an adolescent desire for the forbidden. In this government-induced paradise of emotional jackboots and unified thinking, the State had said not to touch the fruit of that particular tree. "Touch it and you shall surely die." But another voice tempted him, and, for intellectual reasons, he couldn't resist.

He eventually accepted what Christ offered, but without tears. He gave a thoughtful assent. *There should have been tears. I should have red eyes like Mary the Madonna.* He had once read that the first-century Christians had bloodshot eyes from so much crying and knees like a camel's from so much praying. Sam had neither.

He shivered. Even though the van was now quite toasty, something cold touched him.

It was autumn in the towns and cities below, but snow had fallen in the mountains. He'd seen the peaks of the

Rocky Mountains from the campus. Then he had his doubts. Which direction had they gone? North? Or were they headed south?

He tried to create a mental picture of a map and find the "You Are Here" point on it. Had it been two hours or four since they left the farm? Where were they when they stopped to get gas? He'd lost track of direction and time.

The van hit a hard curve and Sam slipped against Timothy. "My turn," Timothy said. They went into another hard curve in the opposite direction and Timothy slid into Sam. "Your turn," Timothy giggled.

"Quiet," his mother whispered.

Another sharp turn and the van slipped in and out of the ruts of what must have been a dirt road. Rocks and gravel machine-gunned the chassis as they bounced along the pitted path. "This is ridiculous!" Beck said after they hit a pothole and he bumped his head. Tim seemed to think it was a game to bounce the highest.

Ben swung the van in a semicircle, then brought it to a hard stop.

"You can get out," he announced just as he climbed out of the front cab, "but stay close. It's dark. You don't want to get hurt."

A moment later the back doors swung open.

They crawled out, their feet making loud crunching sounds on the gravel. They stretched and groaned intermittently. The smell of pine filled the air. Somewhere a creek gurgled and splashed. The moon had slid behind some clouds, leaving only a gray veil.

Sam made out that they were in a clearing of some sort. A forest edged around them, broken by a patch of open ground that rose onto a slight hill away from them. The hill was covered with something that Sam couldn't quite see.

Then the moonlight returned and cast everything in an ice blue. Sam now saw stones of various shapes and sizes poking out of the ground on the hill. He recognized the shapes. A chill went up and down his spine. He was standing at the edge of a graveyard.

The rest of the group gathered around him. They saw what he saw.

Ben called them from the van. "Give me a hand. The boxes go inside."

The group turned to him, speechless.

He looked at them, puzzled. "This will be your home for the next couple of weeks until your contact comes. You have a little over a three weeks' supply of food and, praise God, a furnace that works well despite its age. There are cots in the rooms to sleep on, a kitchen, and a freshwater creek over on the other side. It has everything you'll need. You should be safe," he chuckled. "It's such an obvious hiding place that no one thinks to look here."

Sam glanced around, "*Where? What's* such an obvious hiding place?"

"This must be some kind of a joke," Beck scowled. "We're staying in a cemetery?"

"Of course not," Ben said. "You'll be staying over *there*." He pulled a flashlight from his belt, turned it on, and pointed the beam at a path that stretched between the graveyard and the forest. At the end of the path was a small building, half-hidden by the spruces and firs.

"What is it?" asked Ruth.

"You'll see. Grab your things. Help me with these boxes."

They each grabbed some of the supplies and followed Ben down the path. As they got closer, the beam of Ben's flashlight showed them what they couldn't see before: a building with boarded windows, decaying wood that splintered through broken paint, the roof and walls covered with leaves and sticky pine needles. A "condemned" sign was nailed on the wall next to a set of double doors. Yellow crime-scene tape hung from the doorway itself and ribboned across the grass like decorations for a party gone wrong.

"A *church*," said Luke.

"You see?" Ben smiled. "Who would think to look for Christians in a church?"

"Anyone with half a brain," Beck muttered.

"It'll work," Peter said as they paraded up the rickety wooden steps into what was once the vestibule.

"Wow!" Timothy cried, looking as if he might run off to explore. Mary jerked him back by his shirt collar. He yelped like a puppy.

Ben produced a box of matches and lit a few lanterns sitting on an old table by the door. The vestibule was paneled, with doors to the left and right and a hallway straight ahead. Sam saw remnants of a life that has passed: a long pew against an open wall, a bulletin board with ripped papers, an empty book rack, a half-shell basin attached to the wall.

Peter touched the basin. "This is a Catholic church?"

"*Was*," said Ben.

"What happened here?" Ruth asked.

Ben shook his head.

Beck dropped his case. "This is where we're staying? Really?" He spun on Ben. "*Really?*"

"You were expecting five-star accommodations?"

"I won't do it. I won't stay."

"That's up to you," Ben countered. "But you're not going back with me. I risked getting you up here. I'm not taking another risk to get you back."

Beck glared at him. "I'll go somewhere else."

Ben's tone was calm and reasonable. "You don't know where you are. You haven't a clue where the nearest town might be. You'd get lost in these woods and never be found. And if I were them," he hooked a thumb at the fugitives, "I wouldn't want you wandering off and *maybe* getting caught and *probably* confessing about this hideout."

Beck glanced at the others, as if assessing whether they might physically stop him. He lowered his head.

"Any other complaints?" Ben asked. "Good."

Later, Ben led Sam and Peter down to the cellar. They passed rows of metal shelves with the remnants of church-type supplies. Sam saw boxes of church decorations, a busted-up Nativity set, a large cross with a discolored shadow that had once been a figure of Jesus, pages torn from liturgical books, candle stubs, and only God knew what else.

A large gray beast of a furnace sat in the corner.

"Coal?" Sam asked.

Ben nodded, but then pointed to a smaller furnace nearby. "Gas," he said. "We have a local source that's kept us hooked up."

"A local source?" Peter asked.

"Not everyone around here joined the mob that wrecked the church." Ben gestured to the older furnace. "You can use that one for wood-burning, if it comes to that." Skirting around to the side, he went to a fuse box fastened to the wall and opened the panel. He flipped the master switch.

A bare bulb above their heads turned on.

Sam looked up at the light. "Isn't it dangerous being on an official grid?"

"I wouldn't call the grid up here 'official.' If you're worried, there's a generator you can use. But it won't last for two weeks—not without a delivery of fuel."

"It's not solar?" asked Peter.

Ben gave him a *you must be kidding* look. "No budget," he said.

After a bit of cajoling, Ben got the furnace started. "You're already doing better than some of the folks who've come through here. But you want to be careful. A local might see the lights on, or smoke coming from the chimney. But I doubt it. This place is fairly remote."

"Why did they build a church in the middle of nowhere?" Peter asked.

Ben wiped his hand on a handkerchief he'd pulled from his back pocket. "There was a gold-mining town not a stone's throw from here. It lasted about twenty years. But the gold ran out and the town was left to ruin. The church stayed, serving the ranchers that had made this mountain their home. Eventually a real estate developer leveled the old town with big plans to build expensive vacation homes. But the crisis came and put an end to that."

Big plans, Sam thought, remembering a time when people had such things.

Back on the main floor, everyone was busy choosing their rooms and settling in. Ben called out a goodbye as he left. "God be with you all," he said.

Sam walked Ben back to the van. They shook hands in silence. Then Sam watched helplessly as Ben drove away. A sick feeling of finality turned in the pit of Sam's stomach. He had cast his lot with this group, for better or worse. Their lives were in each other's hands—the hands of strangers who may or may not be trusted. Theoretically, the only thing that held them together was a shared faith. Was it enough? Did the question even matter?

There was no turning back now.

CHAPTER 5

Williams was glad that he and Slater hadn't gone back to Central as planned. Unlike his boss, he enjoyed the small rural communities, the open land, the array of forests. It was a vast difference from the steel-and-cement-encased claustrophobia he had to endure back home. Apart from following Slater from town to town, looking for leads and filing reports, it was like taking a vacation.

Slater, on the other hand, was restless and annoyed. He saw the small towns as havens of stupidity and the thick woods at nothing more than hiding places for the enemy. Even now he hadn't rushed back to the city because he was convinced that their escaped prisoner was still in the area somewhere. He counted on the slim chance that one of their informants might come up with a location. Williams wasn't convinced.

"Nobody here likes us," Williams reminded Slater over breakfast. It was their fifth day in Tannerville and their fifth cold breakfast in the diner. "Everyone else is enjoying hot food. Ours is always cold."

"Tell the waitress."

"I'm sure she already knows."

Slater was vindicated a few mornings later when an informant—a grizzled old wretch called Stumps—gave them a tip-off. The escaped prisoner had been seen in an abandoned building next to Tannerville's long-forgotten train depot.

Slater and Williams had pulled together a strike force made up of local police from the surrounding towns. They were a hodgepodge of old and overweight men who couldn't stand straight, picked their noses, and kept hitching up their trousers. A dozen of them.

Slater grumbled to Williams, "This isn't a strike force. It's a baby-slap force."

Slater briefed the men, then warned them that any slip-ups would be construed by him as subversive action to aid the insurrectionists. "I want this man alive. Kill him and you'll wish the same would happen to you."

Williams watched the men glance nervously at each other. That was the kind of inspiration his boss instilled in those around him.

"Now, let's go roach-hunting!" Slater shouted.

The men looked confused.

"The *traitors*," Slater added, to mumbles of "oh" and "ah" and even a "never heard them called 'roaches' before."

Shortly before noon, the so-called *force* descended upon the abandoned building, coming from all directions in police cars and on motorcycles. Slater would've brought in tanks if he thought he could get them there in time. The 327 citizens of Tannerville came out in their rusted cars and pickup trucks to watch, their mouths agape and their eyes like saucer plates. It would keep them talking for weeks, Williams figured.

Williams hit the brakes, bringing the car to a sliding stop in front of the derelict building. A faded Victorian-style sign announced that it had once been the Imperial Hotel. Slater jumped out and made his way through the positioned officers to the boarded-up double doors. Officers with axes and picks broke through and pushed inside. They attacked every door and wall that got in their way.

"Nowhere to run, nowhere to hide!" Slater shouted over the racket of crashes and shouts. The place smelled of dead animals, excrement, and mold.

Styrofoam cups of coffee were handed to them by a young-looking officer who smiled with all the optimism of a new recruit. The two men leaned against what must've been the front desk of the hotel. "I hope your informant knew what he was talking about," said Williams, sipping the drink.

"Stumps wouldn't let me down," Slater said. "He wouldn't dare."

Within minutes the report came from the captain of the wrecking crew. "Unless he turned into a termite, we can't find him."

Slater tossed his coffee aside. "You can't find *anything*?"

"There's a room—it looks like someone *was* here, but—"

Suddenly a walkie-talkie crackled and a voice from the helicopter shouted, "There's a woman running across the roof! On the south side! She's headed south for the fire escape!"

"Get her!" Slater barked into the device. "*Alive!*"

Slater and Williams rushed out to the open lot, navigating to the south side of the building. The woman had just hoisted a leg over the rail when the officers grabbed her. She shrieked and clawed at them.

Slater and Williams sauntered back to the car and waited.

The woman was feisty and still fighting with the three officers who half-dragged, half-carried her across the lot to Slater. One of the officers had a large gash across his forehead. Williams had to admire her tenacity but knew that his boss wouldn't. Who admired tenacious roaches?

The girl was young and wiry, a twig between two large trees. She stopped fighting and looked at Slater with a child-like defiance. Williams now recognized her from a security video at the Rehabilitation Center.

Slater did the same. "A little makeup and a wig ... you're the old woman in front of the rehab center. Far more attractive, though. That was a very clever stunt you pulled."

"I didn't do anything," she scowled, struggling again. "Tell these baboons to let go of me."

Slater leaned close to her slender face, now smudged with dirt. Her black hair was disheveled, her dress clung damply to her body. "I'll tell them to let go. But you should know that there are *crack* marksmen prepared to shoot you if you so much as blink the wrong way."

Williams suppressed a smile. The only cracks on the cops around them was what he saw when they bent over.

The woman glanced around quickly and seemed to relax. Slater nodded. The officers let go of her arms.

"Good," Slater said. "I'm looking for an escaped prisoner and you know where he is. Tell me, please."

She shook her head. "I don't know."

Slater rolled his eyes. "Really? That's how you want to play it?"

"I'm telling you the truth. I don't know where he is." She gave him a *really, I'm telling you the truth* look.

"You're also going to tell me that you're not a member of the Resistance?" Slater asked.

"I am," she admitted, "but we only know enough to help with one part of the operation. Because of *you*. I can tell you where he was, but not where he is."

"Clever." Slater held his eyes on her. "Where was he?"

"In there." She pointed at the old hotel.

Slater looked disappointed. "I know that much."

The girl fell silent. Williams watched her eyes. She was looking at Slater but, for a fraction of a second, she looked at something past him.

Slater frowned at Williams. "She's stalling."

"Definitely." Williams was about to turn when Slater struck the girl hard—an open palm across the side of her face. The sound echoed like a gunshot.

"Where is he?" Slater asked.

Tears came to her eyes.

Just then a motorcycle roared to life. A uniformed police officer revved the engine, then pulled away with a spray of gravel. Williams recognized him as the cop who'd given them coffee.

"*Him!*" Slater shouted at the officers standing around. "Stop him!"

There was a massive scramble of cops and cars. The motorcyclist zoomed out of the lot and sped to a dirt path along the railway tracks, plumes of brown dust billowing behind him.

Williams dreaded how his boss would react to this *second* near miss with his prey.

Slater grabbed the girl's face in his hand, squeezing her jaw tight. "You can't imagine all the things we'll do to find out how much you say you don't know."

He pushed her back toward the three officers who'd been holding her. With a signal to Williams, they leapt into the car and joined the chase.

◆

Slater took to calling the woman Gypsy, even after he'd learned that her real name was Jennifer Walters. As usual, Williams did the actual interrogation. He was surprised by her performance. Someone had trained her well. She knew how to answer just enough questions to give the impression that she was cooperating. Of course, the information she told them was useless. Slater was no closer now to catching his man than he was after the entire convoy of police had lost the fugitive outside of Tannerville.

Gypsy sat slumped in a metal chair. Other than what she'd received back at the old hotel, she had no new bruises or scars. Williams proudly subscribed to a "pain without blemishes" technique. And she had indeed suffered a lot of pain.

Williams turned to his boss. "I think she's finally ready to talk."

Gypsy looked up helplessly at him. Her eyes told him everything. They were empty. The defiance was gone.

Slater leaned on the edge of the table next to her. "I want to believe you, Gypsy. I really do. When you say you only know part of the plan, I think you're telling the truth."

"I am," she whispered. "Please ... I'm so tired. If I knew more, I'd tell you. But I can't tell you what I don't know. Please. Can't you leave me alone? For just a minute."

Slater wagged a finger at her. "Here's the problem. You helped him escape from me—not once, but twice. I'm sorry, but I can never forgive you for that. But let's forget about locations," Slater said. "Let's talk about the man himself."

"I don't know anything about him."

Slater feigned disappointment. "How can you tell me you don't know anything when I haven't asked my question yet? You were with him. You must know a lot of things. Unless he had a hood over your head. Did he?"

"No," she answered.

"So, you *can* tell me what color his hair really is, right?"

"Brown."

"Good for you." Slater gave a stiff smile. "Tell me about his frame of mind."

"His frame of—?"

"Mind, yes. Did he seem happy? Sad? Determined? Playful? Confident? Tired? Energetic? Just jump in here and grab a word. Depressed? Wild? Adventurous? Melan—"

"He was sick. A fever, I think. Kinda depressed," she said. Her eyelids were half-closed. She looked drugged, though she wasn't.

"What makes you think he was depressed?"

She smacked her dry lips, then licked them slowly. "He didn't go when he was supposed to."

"Didn't go?" Slater repeated.

"He was supposed to leave a day after he escaped from the center. The next rendezvous. He didn't go. He kept hanging around, as if ..." She faded for a moment. Her head slumped.

"*Gypsy.*"

She lifted her head again. "I was confused." Her words slurred now. She stared, her lips moving but without a sound.

"Gypsy. What else?" Slater tucked a hand under her chin and lifted her face.

"For misfortunes beyond counting press on me from all sides—"

"What did you say?"

She mumbled, "I cannot see. They are more in number than the hairs on my head. My courage fails. Show me favor, Lord, and save me. Lord, come quickly to my help."

"What is she saying?"

"Sounds to me like a psalm," Williams said.

The girl was quiet.

Slater hit the table with his open hand. The sharp report didn't get a reaction from her.

"We've taken her as far as we can." Williams unrolled his shirt sleeves.

Slater looked annoyed.

Williams stepped forward to check her condition. Her breathing was shallow.

"She needs to go to the hospital now." Williams picked up his jacket.

Slater waved his hand in an *I don't care what you do with her* gesture.

Williams signaled the two officers by the door. They picked the girl up and carried her out.

"Sick and depressed," Slater said thoughtfully. "Do you think she was telling the truth?"

"It might explain why he was still in the area," Williams observed.

The phone buzzed on the table. Williams snatched it up and glanced at the screen. "The police captain at Tannerville."

Slater cocked his eyebrow. "Put him on the speakerphone."

Williams obligingly pushed the button.

"York here," the voice crackled. "We found the motorcycle."

"Where?"

"Outside of Henley. Under a railway bridge."

"And?"

"There's a path that leads deep into the woods. It's at the base of Providential Mountain."

Slater snorted. "You're kidding."

"The bike was a mess," the captain said. "I think he crashed. We found some blood on the uniform."

Slater looked hopeful. "He left the uniform? Then get some dogs to pick up the scent. I want every nook and cranny searched within a five-mile radius. Send me your coordinates. I'll get there as soon as I can." He disconnected the call, then eyed Williams. "Are you up for the drive? You want a nap or anything? I know how tiring interrogations can be." A glib tone.

"Only for the ones being interrogated," Williams said.

Slater smiled. "You're my hero."

PART II

THE CHURCH

CHAPTER 6

Death. I can't pinpoint what I think about it. Which is funny since we seem surrounded by it lately. When I think of death, I think in terms of literature. Death comes to me in words. Poetry, mostly. It is noble, lofty, multi-syllabic.

And it has a British accent.

I like to think I'm prepared for death now. I'm not. I don't think anyone really can be. How can one fully prepare oneself for something one experiences only one time?

Yet, it's a paradox because Death is such an important part of living.

Don't ask me to explain that because I can't.

—from *The Posthumous Papers of Samuel T. Johnson*

Sam sat with a pen in his hand poised above a piece of paper. He was at an old wooden table in the corner of what had once been the sanctuary of the Catholic church. A baptismal font was upended only a few feet away.

The look and feel of the church—especially in this decayed state—was unfamiliar to him. He knew the functional hotel conference-room style of the various Protestant churches he'd attended. But this was something different, something he'd glimpsed only when forced to attend a Catholic wedding a long time ago—the architecture and adornments pointing to something more than mere functionality.

What was left of the altar—now hacked to bits—suggested a beautiful gold-framed, marble-topped table. The lector's stand had been a carved mahogany but was now suitable only for a fire pit. The pews were upended and torn apart. Stone bases testified to the existence of statues that were now stolen or possibly pulverized into what was now little more than dust on the floor. A box that Ruth had identified as a "tabernacle" looked as if it had been battered with an iron bar. The stained-glass windows were now broken shards and mangled leading.

Cobwebs haunted every corner, shivering like timid spirits. The place reeked of animal excrement and urine. The day after they'd arrived, they had wrenched a few of the boards away to let some light in. It didn't help much. They replaced the shutters at night to keep their light from being seen by strangers. "The opposite of Jesus' command," Ruth had said.

Sam could guess when the desecration had happened: four years ago, on the Night of the Purge, when citizens all over the country rallied to ransack the churches as a show of protest against the Christians.

It had been coming for years, of course, but that night was the culmination of the defiance everyone felt against organized religion and its advocates. Few doubted that the Committee had quietly stoked the rage, pointing persistently at the Christians' ongoing and, most said ignorant, resistance to the Committee's very reasonable and necessary mandates.

Sam remembered that night on the campus, watching from his apartment window as the flames reached for the sky. The chapel was vandalized, then razed. He was angry at the time, but only because he thought the building could have been used as a study center.

Glancing around the sanctuary now, he could imagine the frenzy of the local townspeople marching toward this little church, torches held high, ready to destroy Frankenstein's monster. No doubt they started here in the sanctuary, then made their way through to the rest of the building.

That was one reason Sam used a table in the corner here, rather than the desk in his assigned room. His excuse was that it gave him more surface space on which to work. That was a half-truth. The full truth was that Sam's room had once been the priest's office and the desk there had blood stains on the top. Not just one or two drops as if the priest had accidentally cut his finger one day, but a stain that looked as if an impressionistic artist had taken a large brush of dark red paint, flicked it suddenly and violently at the desk, then changed his mind and smeared it all around instead.

Sam shuddered every time he thought of it.

He had covered up the stain with a large piece of cardboard from a box in the cellar. That helped for appearance's sake, but Sam could never use the desk for reading or writing. How could he? Not while that stain made him wonder what had become of the priest.

It took him back to the nagging questions that had plagued him since he'd become a Christian: How in the world did they get into this mess? What forces were at work to strip all elements of faith from their society? How was it possible that a modest priest's office could become a chamber of unthinkable violence—that simple room where church bulletins were created, words of counsel offered to a husband who wanted to leave his wife, consolations given to the mother of a wayward child. Here baptismal and marriage certificates were created, funeral papers signed, obituaries finalized, all the key moments of life passed through, oblivious to the ticking bomb that would explode and ... and ... splash blood across a desk.

Sam adopted the old wooden table in the corner of the sanctuary. Everyone took to calling it "Sam's desk." Peter had carved Sam's name in the upper right-hand corner just to make it official.

They had been at the church for over three weeks. In that time, they'd grown from being frightened strangers to uneasy friends. Sam equated it to co-workers stuck on a broken elevator, or castaways marooned on a desert island, or inmates in a concentration camp.

They had initially established a practical routine: a rotation of chores and responsibilities that gave them the comfort of order. Normality, even in the most abnormal circumstances, was a salve. They established a daily get-together for worship that usually ended with a "business meeting." They attempted a "let's get to know each other" time, but that got a mixed response. They were each aware of how their knowledge of one another could be used as a weapon against them if they were captured.

For the first couple of weeks, they seemed close-knit, polite, compassionate, and generous. But a change had crept in over the last week and a half as they began to get on each other's nerves. Personalities clashed on a regular basis, patience was as rationed as their food, and panic disguised itself as claustrophobia.

Where was their contact? Surely, he should be here by now? The questions were on everyone's minds, if not their lips, and they preoccupied Sam as he sat at the desk.

His thoughts were interrupted by Mary scolding Timothy somewhere in the hall. "Look at you! You're a mess! I thought I told you not to play in the cellar. It's dirty down there and dangerous. Something could happen to you and we'd never know until it was too late!"

"But I found cans of food down there," Tim said as if his find justified his disobedience.

Sam's ears pricked up. He remembered the cans. Peter had found them hidden behind a shelving unit the day after they'd arrived. The cans were old and dented and, as Peter put it, probably filled with as-yet-to-be-discovered cultures of bacteria.

"Just leave them alone," Mary said firmly.

"But it's *food*. We need food, don't we?" the boy asked.

"It's *bad* food," Mary replied. "Don't touch those cans! Why were you in the cellar anyway?"

"I was looking for Joshua," Tim told her. Joshua was a chipmunk he had befriended.

"That's even worse! I want you to stay away from him. He probably has rabies. He could bite you."

Sam could hear the pout in Tim's voice. "But he's the only friend I have."

Mary wasn't moved. "I'm your friend. Now let's get you cleaned up."

"When are we going to eat? My stomach hurts."

The voices became footsteps retreating down the hall.

Sam shook his head sympathetically. Poor Tim. Six years old and forced to confine all his youthful energy in a boring old building and very limited time to play outside.

Poor Mary. Her nerves were so tightly bundled up that her fears dictated everything she said and did. Every minute that Tim was out of her sight, she wrung her hands and lamented his absence. She was the kind of woman who lived for that inevitable calamity.

After their second "let's get to know each other" meeting, Ruth observed that Mary could find a dark cloud behind every silver lining. Sam wondered if she had always been that way or if it was the result of losing her husband to a Rehabilitation Center.

Behind the walls a rat scratched at the plaster.

Tapping his pen against the paper, Sam realized he had written the word "Desk" across the top of the table. He didn't remember doing it. What had become of his mental discipline? There was a time when he had only to line up his thoughts like books on a shelf and pluck off the one that suited him. Not now. He intended to write about Ben and their escape in the van but found himself encountering feelings and memories he had thought were sufficiently buried. Mostly feelings about death. That's why he called his journal *The Posthumous Papers of Samuel T. Johnson*, which Ruth thought was a terrible title. He couldn't deny it. But that didn't make it any less appropriate. Death was all around them. He could sense its presence—a whisper on the other side of a heartbeat, an inevitability that took away their illusions of dignity and pride. Death was the great equalizer, leaving nothing behind but vague memories and fading shadows. Ashes to ashes, dust to dust. *In the scheme of eternity, what we do and say here doesn't amount to much without us around to say it does*, he thought, and remembered a verse from a psalm about the curse of being "the dead unremembered."

"Sam?" a voice whispered.

He looked up to see Ruth peeking in at him from the doorway.

"Hi," Sam whispered back and then wondered why they were whispering.

"Lunch is almost ready."

"Thanks. I'll be there in just a minute."

She hesitated, then walked up to him. "I hate to bother you, but we've got to talk about our food situation." She spoke quietly, seriously, but without panic. Sam had learned that much about Ruth. She wasn't the type to panic in a crisis.

"I know what you're going to say." He stood up and stretched.

"We had enough food for three weeks. That was all. We're running out."

Sam nodded. "We should have rationed it better."

"True," she said. "But we assumed … I suppose we were naïve to think things would go smoothly."

"I guess so."

"I wish we knew what was going on down there—in the world, I mean."

Blind again, Sam thought. *Just like they were in the back of the van. All darkness, no sense of time or direction, no answers, just riding blind. But wasn't that what constituted faith? Give God the steering wheel and wait for the arrival, right?*

Ruth gazed at him patiently.

"We have to wait. Have faith and wait." He spoke sincerely but knew he didn't sound convincing or convinced. "Peter went to check his traps. Maybe he caught something."

Ruth fiddled with the makeshift apron tied around her waist. "Well, I've already cut our portions for lunch. Then we'll have to ration more. Maybe to a fraction of what we've been consuming."

Sam winced. Rationing would not be accepted happily. He thought of the cans in the cellar. Dare they open them up? Boil the contents and hope for the best?

"Maybe we can put our heads together and come up with some alternatives," Ruth suggested.

Sam wasn't sure what the alternatives might be, though. "I have some experience with fishing," he said. "But real wilderness survival isn't my forte. I read *Walden* once, but that only inspired me to speak profoundly."

"Profound speech isn't edible," Ruth quipped, turning for the door.

"I don't know about that," Sam replied, smiling as he followed her. "I've had to eat my words on many occasions."

CHAPTER 7

He made it to the woods just as the daylight began to fail. Running as hard as his weary legs would allow, he pushed forward, ignoring the branches that lashed out at his face, the nagging stitch in his side, the chafing breath that only added to his pain. It didn't matter that he had lost track of who he was running from or where he was running to. He had to keep moving. The mountain stood before him, and his instincts told him he must reach it. He hoped to find safety there.

Every muscle ached, every sinew begged his fevered brain to stop and rest. But his instinct for survival was a slave driver who cracked a whip across the back of his need to live.

So he rushed onward, though the forest conspired against him. Obstacles rose and fell in the shapes of decaying logs, thick bushes, and sharp briars. Finally, a large root grabbed his ankle, causing him to stumble, spin, whirl drunkenly like a puppet, then collapse as if his strings had suddenly been cut. He landed facedown in a pile of leaves. The smell of old earth filled his nostrils. The sound of his own breathing whistled in his ear like a hot tea kettle.

The slave driver screamed for him to get up and run. He clawed at the brittle leaves and rolled onto his back. With his eyes closed, he listened to the sounds of the forest. A faint mountain breeze rode through the naked treetops. A maverick leaf slid across his cheek. The birds called out to one another and, for a moment, he heard them. But it lasted for a mere second before the slave driver twisted the sound into a scream. It began as the scream of one person, then became the chorus of a thousand. He heard the boots of uniformed men rushing, crushing twigs like brittle bones, their guns cocked, dogs barking and chains rattling. He could smell their leather and sweat. He could taste blood filling his mouth.

His own blood.

He opened his eyes, hoping reality would take away his nightmare. The branches above him reached out like jagged fingers and pointed accusingly at him. The darkening sky frowned in agreement with their condemnation.

You don't belong here.

Get up, you fool. The mountain waits for you. You will find safety and peace there. No one can touch you or harm you. It will be like returning to the warmth of the womb, like being swallowed up into . . . into what? A positive image failed him. He could think only of being swallowed up in the belly of a whale.

Don't just lie there. There's no point in giving up now after you've come so far.

So far . . .

Run before it's too late. Run and soon you won't have to run anymore. It will be very comfortable for you there . . . in the belly of the whale.

Just a few more miles . . . a few more miles . . . a few more . . .

Slowly, he got to his feet.

CHAPTER 8

"It's pointless. Do you think the animals up here are morons? They'd never fall for your stupid traps." Howard Beck was sitting beneath a tree.

"Look, Beck, I never said I knew how to do this."

"Good thing, because you obviously don't."

Peter bit his tongue. *Count to ten slowly*, he thought. He'd inherited his father's propensity for anger and, through the hard lessons of experience, clung to this one proverb from his mother. Count to ten. That would help to clear his mind and strengthen his resolve to keep from doing or saying something he would regret later. In this instance, it was his desire to punch Howard Beck in the mouth. That was number one on his Top Ten. Number two—and rising fast—was to nail Beck's tongue to the side of a tree. Both appealed to him more and more as their time together dragged by. Both appealed to him now as he knelt next to the small crate he'd set up as a trap to catch some food.

"We've been duped," Beck said. He dug at something under one of his fingernails. "No one's coming for us."

Four ... five ... Peter continued to count. Yes, he could be hot-headed, but what he felt toward Beck was new and foreign. It was a feeling dark red in emotion. At first, he figured it was simply a personality clash. After that, he blamed a touch of cabin fever. Maybe it was anxiety from the fear that no contact from the Resistance would come, that they'd been left on the mountain with nobody to lead them on. Those would be enough reasons to make anyone edgy. And he accepted them as valid excuses for his impatience with Beck—the first week, even the second. By the third week, they'd dispensed with their strained mutual toleration to a more active dislike for each other. Beck called him cocky, egotistical, rude, brash, and a delinquent. He called Beck an over-stuffed, whining lazy snob.

Today, as he hopelessly checked his traps and had to listen to Beck's color commentary about all that was wrong with their situation, Peter had to admit what that dark red feeling really was. *Hatred.* Hatred like a cold, throbbing black heart. It stung Peter's conscience like one of the nettles that threatened him in the forest. It made him feel deeply ashamed of himself.

Before he became a Christian, he honestly believed that he'd never hated anyone. Conflicts were merely problems to be tactfully worked out. Then, as a Christian, he knew he *shouldn't* hate anyone: not his persecutors, not the agents who took his parents away, not Eddie Richie for that low, dirty hit during football practice, and especially not a fellow Christian. *Love one another as I have loved you,* Jesus had said. If that didn't quite work, then *love your neighbor as yourself.* And if Howard Beck didn't fit those two categories, Jesus had also said to *love your enemies.*

If the church had a priest, Peter would have had to go to confession several times a day.

Beck continued, as if he didn't care whether anyone was listening. "If you think I'm going to sit around while we starve to death, well you have another think coming ..."

"Is that 'thing'?" Peter asked, trying to derail Beck's grumbling. "'If you think ... then you have another *thing* coming."

"The expression is *think*—which is something you can't seem to do," Beck complained.

Peter hated Beck for making him hate. It was a nice cycle of resentment. Beck brought out the worst in him. Beck exposed his hypocritical view of forgiveness. Beck showed him that his understanding of love was childish.

"Sometimes the substance of love can't be known until it's pressed into service by hate," a priest once said to him. He thought of that now and prayed for God to forgive him, and to give him strength to love Beck with the heart of Jesus. Then he despaired that, within the next few minutes, he'd hate Beck all over again.

"We should send Luke down to the town," Beck was saying.

"Why?"

"To find out what's happening down there," Beck said. "And if he's caught, we won't be missing anything."

"Howard!" Peter snapped. He'd lost count somewhere between six and eight, between the prayer to be forgiven and his appeal for strength.

"I don't know why we brought him along. The odds are against us to begin with, and we're lessening them by dragging around excess baggage—*crazy* baggage, at that!"

"Do you ever listen to what you're saying?" Peter marched into the woods to check the next trap.

"I'm just trying to be practical," Beck said as he followed. "It's absurd for us to continue a charade of compassion when our lives are hanging by a thread. You know his story. They've put enough volts through him to light the capital. He's a burnout. He's useless."

Peter considered the pleasure he'd get from stuffing Beck into the next trap. He pushed the thought away. *Be calm, be reasonable: count to ten.* "He'd be more helpful to me right now than you're being."

"I'm asking a simple question. Why did they put him in with us? What were they thinking?"

"Maybe they were thinking about the years he spent as a pastor. Maybe they remembered how he stood up for the Gospel when nobody else would. Maybe they felt loyalty to him because he'd suffered so much. What do you think?"

"I think our contact—if we ever hear from a contact—should take him back to the town. He's oblivious anyway. What does he care whether he's with us or in a rehab center somewhere? Escaping doesn't mean a thing to him."

"And if they kill him?"

Beck snorted. "Then he goes to heaven. It's his gain, right?"

They'd reached the edge of the woods where Peter had set up another trap. He'd precariously balanced a crate on a thin stick, with a piece of carrot tied to the stick by a small string. The carrot was untouched.

"You might want to take that carrot back with us. We'll be needing it before long," Beck said.

The woods opened to a sprawling meadow. The sun, a stranger to them for the past few days, shone brightly. The chill of the mountain air was ever-present. It was November, after all. Peter paused and looked up, wanting to bask in the golden warmth for a minute.

"Well? What are we standing around here for?" Beck asked.

Peter gritted his teeth and hooked a thumb back into the woods. "That way."

"Why that way? What about putting a trap in the field? Rabbits are known to run in fields."

"There's a farmhouse just beyond those woods. We can't take a chance of them seeing the trap—or us. Sam said it's best to stay clear."

"A farmhouse?" Beck was surprised. "What's a farmhouse doing way up here?"

"I don't know. Next time I stop by to visit, I'll ask." Peter pushed back into the forest. He picked up his pace. He figured they were about two miles from the church.

Beck groaned behind him. "Where are we going *now*? Haven't you seen enough empty traps?"

"No," Peter said. "I have three more up ahead." He shoved through some branches to a thicker, darker collection of pines and sycamores. "Why? Do you have a pressing engagement somewhere?"

Beck puffed, "I have more important things to do than wander around in the woods with a smart-mouthed kid."

"Then go back to the church," Peter grunted as he stamped through the underbrush.

"And get lost on the way? You'd like that, I suppose."

"You should've left a trail of breadcrumbs."

Beck mumbled under his breath as the branches poked, prickers jabbed, and leaf-covered roots caused him to stumble. Peter knew an easier way to go, but he was enjoying Beck's discomfort. Revenge tasted only slightly sweeter than anger, but the aftertaste was like poison.

Suddenly, Beck stumbled, crashing down on his knees. He let loose a string of expletives. "That's it. I can't go any further."

Peter gave him an impatient frown. "The trap is just on the other side of that ridge. I'll check it and come back."

"You'd *better* come back," Beck snarled.

"I'll send Luke to find you." Peter walked away.

Brat, Beck thought as he watched Peter work his way through the vegetation. Few things irritated him more than a know-it-all kid whose arrogance was unsupported by experience. Youthful, cocky, mindlessly energetic, ready to face any danger ... all the things Beck himself was like when he was a young man. For that fact alone, Beck knew that he and Peter had a lot in common. But he would never have said so aloud. It was something he acknowledged in that secret, rational place in the back of his mind, but nowhere else. He might even concede that their similarities were the cause of their conflict. But the thought bored him and the acknowledgment that Peter was like his younger self generated no appreciation or respect. Peter was a nuisance, no more and no less.

He looked up at what he could see of the sky through the tangled web of branches. It was time for lunch. He should be on the corner of First and Centennial trying to hail a taxi to Tony's Italian Restaurant. There the large dining room hummed with the latest deals, investments, and mergers. He'd slide through, a quick nod or handshake to go with *Hello, Frank ... Hi, Bill; did you hear the latest?* Then he'd sit down with the world's best meatball sandwich and a glass of red wine while watching the stocks rise or fall on the TV monitor. Closing his eyes now, he savored the memory like a tender piece of filet mignon. It melted in his mouth and dissolved into dry mountain air.

What am I doing here?

He asked himself that question often: *more* often as the days carried them along.

Did I have a choice?

It was the most practical and expedient thing to do, surely. It was one thing to take risks with other people's money, another to take risks with his own life.

A ray of sunlight hit the tops of the trees and fanned out like a garden sprayer. Beck caught part of it with his upturned face. A breeze rustled through the forest with a sound that reminded him of waves on a beach. He thought of Louise and their last vacation together. He could hear the water hitting the shore, the gulls crying overhead, a radio playing somewhere, a blonde in a rather optimistic bathing suit looking for shells, and children kicking sand on them as they ran past.

Brats.

He could see Louise turn to him from her blanket with that grief-stricken, cow-eyed expression that made him feel both small and angry at the same time. He disliked children for their assumption that all people should like them. They were intrusive. Yet, Louise felt it was her duty to bring children into the world. She couldn't be fulfilled as a woman otherwise. Dear Louise. Sweet, sensitive, self-righteous Louise. He bought her a poodle instead and it seemed to placate her for a while. Chi-Chi became her baby. She pampered and coddled and spoiled it. Beck hated the animal as much as if it had been a child.

When Louise became ill, he locked the dog in the cellar except when she asked to see it. When Louise died, he had the dog put down. It wasn't a malicious act—he felt nothing; rather, it was the practical and expedient thing to do. Much like authorizing the removal of Louise's life-support equipment. It was perfectly legal. He had spent three years dutifully caring for her while she died. He had made his sacrifice; he had given her life as much as he planned to give it.

His wife's death had been his resurrection. His plan was to structure his life to receive maximum pleasure with minimum pain. That was his deal with God. And since God was made in his image, agreeing was the least God could do.

Except. Hiding in a run-down church on the top of a mountain certainly wasn't part of the idea. God wasn't keeping His part of the deal.

Oh well. Beck considered it a momentary inconvenience— a small price to pay for being foolish enough to get caught with his hand in the wrong cookie jar. He would get out of this one way or another, with or without God's help.

Beck looked in the direction of the farm. The seed of an idea dropped into the fertile ground of his mind. The seed, carefully nurtured, might grow into a plan. He had to be practical—and this was one possible way to do it.

"Beck!" Peter called out. "Help me!"

"What now?" Beck mumbled. He considered pretending like he didn't hear Peter so he wouldn't have to respond. And if it was trouble—if the police were wrestling Peter to the ground—he didn't want to be anywhere close by.

"Beck!"

He caught sight of Peter now, stumbling toward him through the dense forest, waving frantically. Maybe he caught a deer, Beck thought hopefully.

He slowly got to his feet and headed in Peter's direction. "What? What's wrong?"

Peter's arms were flailing. "This way!" he cried out breathlessly.

Beck eyed him with suspicion.

"Come on." Peter was close enough to catch hold of Beck's arm.

Beck jerked his arm away. "This better not be a trick."

They didn't go very far before Peter stopped and pointed. "There."

Beck's first thought was that Peter had indeed caught a deer somehow. It lay half-covered in leaves. He ventured closer and realized it was too small to be a deer. He focused his eyes, squinting in a way he knew made him look foolish. He took a few more steps, then froze in his tracks. It was the body of a man.

Chapter 9

Sam finished helping Ruth and Amy clear up lunch. Even after a month, the scene was awkwardly played out, as if behaving like a family and washing dishes in that mildewed and rotting kitchen had become part of some ancient liturgy they'd newly discovered. Luke stared silently at a cross he'd made of his fork and knife. Timothy fidgeted in his chair while Mary gently explained why he shouldn't allow his chipmunk inside the church.

Sam nodded. "We might have him for lunch."

Mary shot him a sharp look.

"I'm teasing," Sam said to Timothy. Timothy already knew it and was giggling.

The whole scene was so domestic, so mundane, that Sam felt comforted by it. These little things were the true stuff of life. He imagined it was a form of church that he'd never been allowed to enjoy in his adulthood.

"I'm going to wash clothes this afternoon," Amy stated.

"Oh good. You got your rock fixed." Sam smiled.

Amy looked at him as if she wasn't sure whether he was joking or not. He appreciated the expression, and the fresh-faced innocence that came with it. His students often gave him the same look when he made jokes in class.

"I'll help you, Amy," Ruth offered.

"No, thank you," Amy said. "I'd rather do it myself. I like doing it. It's therapeutic."

"Laundry is therapeutic?" Sam asked.

Amy nodded soberly. "Being alone in the woods—it gives me a chance to think and pray."

Luke held up his hands. "Mark, chapter 1, verse 35: 'And in the morning, while it was still dark, Jesus got up and went out to a secluded place where he prayed ...'"

"Thank you, Luke," Ruth smiled as she grabbed up his cutlery cross and took it to the sink.

What a collection of misfits we are, Sam thought. *Of all the runaways that could have been assembled, why these? Is it God's peculiar sense of humor ... the same sense of humor that had assembled the mismatched disciples, so different in personalities, so unlikely as saints?*

A loud bang at the main door startled them all. Then Peter yelled for help.

"Good heavens!" Mary cried out. She put a protective arm in front of Tim.

Sam was on his feet, heading into the hall to investigate.

Peter shouted again, and Beck made sounds as if he was in pain.

Sam raced in the direction of the noise. Ruth and Amy were hot on his heels. Sam's first thought was that the two men had encountered the police and now the church would be surrounded. His second thought was that Peter or Beck had been hurt. His mind shot immediately to the simple phrase: "Lord, have mercy on us." In the past three weeks it had become his default prayer when his mind didn't know what else to think. He wasn't even sure where the phrase came from. His mother said it perhaps as he was growing up and he'd hidden it away in the unattended rooms of his memory until he'd arrived at the church. Then it suddenly appeared like a jack-in-the-box from a lost toy chest.

Rounding the doorway into the sanctuary, Sam saw Peter and Beck laboring to put something onto the floor. His eyes played tricks. He thought they were carrying a large, rolled-up carpet. Then he saw that it was a man.

"Get blankets!" Peter shouted.

Amy spun on her heels and raced back into the corridor.

Beck wheezed and puffed, "He's heavy ..."

Sam came alongside them. "You were supposed to catch rabbits and deer, Peter, not human beings."

"Is he alive?" Ruth asked.

"We wouldn't have bothered to bring him back if he wasn't," Beck growled.

"You didn't want to bring him back at all," Peter said.

Amy returned with the blankets and spread them out on the floor next to a radiator on the side wall. "Here; this will be warmer."

Sam helped Peter carry the man to the blankets. They carefully put him down, then stepped back.

Ruth knelt next to the stranger, putting a hand on his forehead. "He's burning up. Get the first aid kit."

Amy dashed away.

"We found him in the woods," Peter gasped, catching his breath.

"Who is he? Do you know who he is?" Mary asked from the doorway. Tim was straining to come in, but she held him back.

"No identification, no marks ..." Peter replied.

Beads of perspiration dotted Beck's face. He pushed his disheveled silver hair away from his forehead. "We should have left him where he was. He may be one of *them*—sent to catch us."

"Or he might be one of us." Amy handed the first aid kit to Ruth. Sam noticed that her eyes were fixed on the stranger's face. "Maybe he's our contact. Maybe Moses and Elijah sent him."

Beck shook his head. "Moses and Elijah? You may as well wish for the Easter Bunny and Santa Claus to help us. It's a big mistake bringing him here. Like I told *whiz kid* here—"

"He would have died out there," Peter said defensively.

Sam put a hand on Peter's shoulder. "You did the right thing. Don't worry."

"We still have a responsibility to help others, don't we?" Amy asked.

"See if you feel that way when he turns us in," Beck snarled.

"I checked him out for broken bones and wounds," Peter explained to Ruth. "A few scratches and bruises. But, besides, that . . ."

Ruth looked up. "It looks like he hasn't eaten in days."

"I wonder how he got so far up here?" Amy asked.

"Help me get his coat off," Ruth said to Sam. They sat him up and wrestled his arms through the sleeves. "Get a damp rag, will you, Mary?"

Mary looked unsure about having anything to do with the stranger, but then nodded and moved off, dragging a whining Tim with her.

Ruth pulled a second blanket over the man and tucked it around him.

Sam noticed Luke lingering in the doorway, stretching out his hands and moving toward the stranger.

Peter intercepted the old man. "Hold on, Luke; stay back. We don't know what's wrong with him."

Luke smiled. "The Lord can heal him. Let me lay my hands on him."

"Crazy old fool," Beck muttered.

"Let's try some conventional approaches first," Sam suggested.

"You should trust more," Luke said.

"I'm sure you're right," Sam said.

Beck gave a loud snort.

Mary returned with the damp cloth and handed it to Amy.

The girl knelt and gently touched it to the stranger's slender face. Then she guided it over his patchy beard and matted brown hair. "I wonder if he's our guide."

"Just our luck," Beck said. "A sick guide. Big help."

The stranger suddenly groaned and tossed his head from side to side.

"Take it easy." Amy pressed the cloth to his forehead.

The man's arms pushed at the blanket. Deliriously, he mumbled something that sounded like "Moses."

"Did you hear that?" Peter exclaimed. "He said 'Moses'!"

Beck sneered at Peter. "You'll grab at any straw, won't you?"

"Moses." The stranger spoke louder and sat straight up, nearly knocking Amy over. He looked at her, then his eyes rolled upward, and he slumped. Sam caught him by the shoulders and eased him back.

"You have to check him more thoroughly than I can," Ruth said to Sam.

"His mind is in turmoil." Luke came close again. "I can give him peace and rest."

"Sit down before you hurt someone," Beck shouted.

"Not hurt, *heal*," Luke corrected him. "You have no faith."

Beck scowled. "Lunatic."

Peter grabbed Beck's arm. "Look, Beck. I told you—"

Sam moved between them, his eyes on Peter. "Get a jug of water."

Peter glared at Beck as he backed away to the door.

Sam turned to Beck. "A little compassion, please."

"We're trying to survive here," Beck asserted. "What chance do we have if we take on every nutcase and runaway we come across?"

"Be glad they didn't ask that question before allowing you to come," Sam said.

"Meaning *what*?" Beck demanded.

"Think about what the Bible tells us," Ruth said, tipping her head to the stranger. "We could be entertaining angels unaware."

"Angel's underwear?" Tim called from the door.

His mother shushed him.

"Am I the only one who understands our situation?" Beck fumed. "We're fugitives trapped in an abandoned church on some desolate mountain. We've got the police looking for us, we're running out of food, winter's coming, and that furnace we've been using is more likely to blow us to smithereens than keep us warm. All while we wait for some mysterious contact from the Resistance to come and lead us to the promised land! *Now* we've taken in a sick stranger and—" He seemed to lose the words in his red-face apoplexy. "Why don't we just send up flares to say, 'Here we are! Come and capture us!'?"

"God has taken care of us so far," Amy said. "Why should we believe that He'll stop now?"

Beck was scornful. "Taken care of us? You call *this* being taken care of? Didn't you hear anything I just said? Look around you! If this is being taken care of, then I've got some ski trips in the Sahara I want to sell you."

Amy looked at him, undaunted. "The Bible said it would be like this for believers. History proves it." She glared at him. Then her cheeks flushed. "His will be done."

Peter approached, carrying a large jug of water. "You were probably asleep when they taught it, Beck, but the Bible talks about the joy of being persecuted for Christ and the crown that awaits us if we die for our faith."

"If you're so hot to die and get a crown, why don't you turn yourself in?" Beck challenged him. "Then you can have all the joy of persecution you want."

Peter jabbed a finger at him. "If you spent as much time praying as you did complaining, you wouldn't be worried about a thing."

Sam held up his hands like Moses parting the Red Sea. "Stop it. We need to be calm and sensible about this new development. Everyone to the kitchen while I examine him."

The fugitives paraded out of the sanctuary.

Sam knelt next to the newcomer. "I sure hope you don't die."

Everyone was seated around the large dining table when Sam walked in. There was a tense silence and a lot of looking at the tabletop. Sam went to the sink and washed his hands.

"Is he one of the police?" Tim asked.

No one answered, so Sam said, "No, I don't think so."

Tim dug in his pocket and pulled out a Swiss knife. "I can protect us."

"Take it easy, Daniel Boone." Peter smiled at the boy.

"I'm not Daniel Boone," he protested, "I'm Moses. And Joshua is my assistant. Just like in the Bible story."

"Joshua? Your chipmunk?" Amy asked.

He nodded earnestly. "He went away, but he came back this morning. I worried he would starve without me."

Beck grunted. "You've been feeding chipmunks? Terrific. Now we've taken in animals."

"It's just a few crumbs." The boy gave him a guilty look.

Sam grabbed a chair and sat down. "Let's talk about his condition. I saw only what Ruth saw—bruises and scratches. He might have a head injury, but there's no knowing without X-rays."

Ruth shrugged. "It looks to me like he's sick from exposure. He probably hasn't had anything to eat or drink in days."

"What should we do?" Amy asked.

Ruth sighed. "We *should* take him to a hospital."

"What?" Beck cried out.

"I know, I know." Ruth held up her hands. "But if he dies because we can't treat him properly—"

Peter stood up. "I'll take him."

Beck waved his hands at the young man. "Sit down, hot shot. We have to talk about this."

"I'm not asking you to go."

"Wait a minute," Sam said. "Nobody's taking him anywhere. For one thing, we don't know the way to the nearest town, but we know it's miles from here. For another thing, carrying him all that way to the town might do him more harm than good. We should do our best to take care of him for a day or so and, if he gets worse, then decide on a plan."

"A plan?" Beck demanded. "What kind of plan?"

"We could take him to the farmhouse," Peter suggested.

A derisive snort from Beck. "And what? Leave him on the doorstep in a basket with a note pinned to his diaper?"

"Do you have any other suggestions?" Peter countered.

"I made my suggestion earlier," Beck said. "We should've left him where he was."

"How could you even think of that?" Amy glared at him.

"Please calm down," Sam said, then turned to Ruth. "What can we do to help him?"

"I'm no nurse, but I suggest we take shifts. Stay nearby, keep him hydrated, maybe give him some broth later. We need to keep applying cold cloths to try to break that fever."

"Do we have ibuprofen in the first aid kit?" Mary asked.

"Yes," Ruth replied, "but it expired three years ago."

"Let's try it anyway," Sam said. He pushed back from the table. "I'll watch him this afternoon. We can take shifts through the night if anyone wants to volunteer." He glanced at Peter.

The young man nodded.

Amy raised her hand. Then Ruth. Finally, Mary also said she'd help if she could.

Beck sat sullenly. Luke had been gazing at the ceiling, in a world of his own.

The gathering broke up with everyone going their separate ways. Sam returned to the stranger. Ruth followed him in. She lingered as Sam applied a fresh rag to the man's forehead.

"Well?" he asked.

"I want to know what you *really* think," she insisted.

He shook his head. "I don't think anything right now. We could nurse this man back to good health, only to have him turn us in. That's the gamble, isn't it?"

Ruth nodded. "It's certainly a risk."

"I don't see us following Beck's suggestion," Sam said. "So, all we can do is wait to see what happens."

There was nothing else to be said. Ruth walked away. The soft heels of her shoes brushed against the floor, echoing throughout the sanctuary like a servant's broom. Sam then noticed Amy standing in the doorway. As Ruth passed by, the girl turned and followed as if she'd been pulled into a slipstream.

Sam looked at the sleeping stranger. He had a growing suspicion that this man was going to determine their future, whether he knew it or not.

CHAPTER 10

From Williams' vantage point on the sixteenth floor of Central, the people on the plaza below looked like punctuation marks. The rain had been falling nonstop since yesterday morning, and the standard black umbrellas, open against the depressing drizzle, turned the entire scene into a massive ellipsis moving across a gray page—with the occasional exclamation mark supplied by the stiff soldiers who appeared from or disappeared into doorways. They were everywhere, those soldiers, those exclamation marks, nestled conspicuously among the more functional dots and dashes. From his position, Williams detected no rhyme or reason for all the activity. How easy it was to forget that those were people. This was the point of view the Committee wanted all good citizens to have: no individuals, just a collective mass of disposable punctuation marks.

He wondered if that's how everything looked to God: small dots moving helter-skelter for no obvious reason. A sentence run amok. An explosion in a typesetter's shop. Did God see only a collective mass, disposable marks on a page?

Williams didn't believe in God as an ongoing concern but found the concept of some entity over and above them intriguing. It could be the Force or a Being or Zeus or Mother Goose for all he cared. It didn't matter. He liked to think that there was something or someone up there, if only to give the Committee a bit of competition. Competition was healthy for everyone.

Fingers of lightning fractured what piece of sky Williams could see between the two high-rises across the street. Perhaps *that* was God. A sky that might be blue or sometimes black, sometimes pleasant or sometimes stormy. Anything but the boring gray of the Committee. At least God had a name—or many names. The members of the Committee were unnamed and faceless. No icons or statues or photos on the office walls, just slogans and catchphrases to inspire all good citizens everywhere. Williams was amused to realize that, for him, it took as much faith to believe in the Committee as it took to believe in God. And, if you put him down on the street with everyone else, he would be just another punctuation mark to someone above him.

He suddenly felt self-conscious and looked up, half-expecting to see someone watching him from a higher window across the street. He wasn't wrong. The giant face of a generic-looking man on a billboard glowered at him. In bold, authoritative neon, the words "Do Your Duty!" matched the man's stern expression. Otherwise, the buildings—non-descript offices for the government's countless clerks—merely winked at him with dull fluorescent eyes through the gray rain.

He looked at his watch. Already 4:50 p.m. In a moment, lights would be turned off and ID cards scanned as bureaucrats joined the ellipses going home.

Home wasn't on the agenda for Williams tonight. It rarely was. Home for him was an efficiency apartment two blocks away with an unmade bed and a pile of dirty laundry in the corner. There was little point to it being otherwise. He knew when Slater hired him that he was taken on for one reason alone: he was unattached to hearth and kin, completely dedicated to his work at all hours of the day or night. Just like Slater. That's what made their relationship work. They were kindred spirits haunting the same graveyard—or two parts of a semicolon.

He turned away from another flash of lightning, the dying day, and the mixed metaphors, and looked across the mess they'd made of the conference room. The long table was littered with reports, files, communiqués, and the Thai food they'd had for lunch. Three weeks had gone by since they had heard anything at all about their escaped convict. Arrests had been made, suspects questioned, and informants paid off, all without satisfaction. No one knew what had become of him. The tracks were getting cold, and Williams knew that Slater was worried about losing the scent completely. The fiascoes at the State Rehabilitation Facility and in Tannerville didn't put Slater in good graces with his supervisors either. They expected results and if he couldn't deliver, then he'd be moved to other, more mundane, assignments. A punishment. And that was the rub: Slater didn't do other assignments well. He wanted to catch the roaches.

Why Slater was so determined to eliminate the Christians was something Williams hadn't sorted out yet. He had theories, but nothing he could prove.

"Are you listening to me?" Slater asked. Williams hadn't noticed that his boss was standing in the doorway. "I asked if you want some coffee."

"Sorry," Williams replied. "I was just thinking."

"About what?"

"You," Williams said as he sat down at the long table. He began to organize the papers into relevant stacks.

Slater moved to the table without sitting down. "What about me? Is someone asking questions?"

"Not at all. I was just wondering why, of all the things you could be doing with your career, you're so determined to arrest the Christians."

Slater looked at him, surprised. "Why shouldn't I? I'm a law enforcer. They're breaking the law."

The fluorescent light above their heads crackled and flickered. Slater went to the coffeemaker on the side counter and poured himself a cup. Williams flipped through a binder of police reports that had been passed on to them from other offices. He wished he hadn't said anything. It was dangerous to be too inquisitive about one's superior—or his private motivations.

"It's simple." Slater leaned against the counter. "I want to round up these roaches for the sake of our children."

"You don't have any children."

"For the sake of the next generation then," Slater said impatiently. "Don't be so pedantic. I want them to have something we didn't have: the chance to grow up in a world without the kind of neurotic fears and crass manipulation the Christians have used to get their way. They're roaches who breed and pass on their sick thinking like a disease. Have you ever read a Bible?"

"Not really, no."

"You should get one from the Evidence Room. Then you'll see." Slater sipped his coffee, winced at it, then continued. "It's a collection of myths that, as ancient writings go, are curious when they aren't downright grotesque. I can hardly imagine how those books could be twisted around into an actual system of belief—and an oppressive one at that. Think about it. Their God offers a terrible punishment in the afterlife if you don't fulfill His unrealistic expectations in *this* life. He forces children—*children*—to worship Him without question. It's beyond reason. Young, innocent minds are filled with nightmares and rotten images: eating flesh, drinking blood, burning in eternal fire, denying their natural impulses, crushing their pride underfoot, praying and praying and praying to a great void and ..." He paused, swallowing as if the memories had become a collection of phlegm to be spat out. "You get the idea."

Williams got the idea, all right. In some ways, it was more than he wanted to know.

"Open rebellion is easy to deal with. But the insidious nature of their teaching—that's a greater challenge."

Williams' eye caught a report from College Park, a university town in the north. A van driver had been questioned on suspicion of bootlegging, then released for lack of evidence. Bootleggers were a dime a dozen these days.

"My father was one of them, you know. A Christian, I mean," Slater said. "Don't deny that you've heard the rumors. Or the theory that my resolve is based on daddy-complex."

Williams had heard that—and nodded.

"I'm not exaggerating when I tell you that my father's beliefs literally killed my mother and very nearly ruined my life. If it hadn't been for the Committee ..."

Williams tried to downplay the moment. "Most of us were rescued by the Committee in one way or another."

"*All* of us were. Make no mistake about that. The hope it gave, the clear thinking, the chance to break free from the chains of our backgrounds ... it made all the difference in the world."

Williams glanced at his boss and wondered if he was being sincere. It wasn't like Slater to be emphatic about the State. In fact, Slater often came off as one who had no particular ideology and only the most practical allegiance to those in power.

"I've surprised you." Slater smiled. "Maintaining an air of detached objectivity keeps *certain people*"—he pointed to the ceiling—"from taking you for granted. Give your heart to anyone or anything and let them *know* they have it, and they'll use you up. That's something they don't teach you in the schools, but take it from someone who knows. Now, aren't you glad you asked?"

"Asked what?" Williams spoke innocently.

Slater laughed. "Smart boy. Now tell me what's in those police reports. Time is wasting away."

The two men got back to work.

———————————◆———————————

"Did you see this?" Slater asked, holding up a report.

"Probably," Williams said, stifling a yawn. It was past one in the morning. "What is it?"

"A report from College Park."

"The van driver who was questioned about bootlegging. Yeah, I saw that one."

Slater stood up, "But did you *read* it? This driver—Ben Greene—gets pulled over on a routine offense. One of his headlights is out. The officer decides to do a check of the van. Greene says it's empty. He says he made his delivery of dry goods earlier, which makes perfect sense. But the officer goes ahead with the check, probably to fulfill his quota for the day. Rather than flash his light around, this bright boy climbs *inside*. That's when he notices that the flooring has a peculiar sound. 'Hollow,' he noted. He looks down and sees a bit of cloth sticking out from under the carpet. He pulls the carpet up. That's when he discovers the panels."

"The van had a false floor," Williams said. "That's why they questioned him about bootlegging."

Slater nodded. "Why else would a van have a false floor? But Greene explains that it's not intended as a false floor.

It's simply another storage area that helps maximize space in the van. But the officer is still curious. He lies down in the bed under the panel. He fits. But he doesn't have any proof of bootlegging—Greene's papers and identification are in order—so he lets Greene go."

Williams yawned again. "Sorry, Captain, but I don't get the significance of this."

"A bed in the van to store *people*." Slater was pacing now. "It's such an old trick. Illegal aliens used it. So did the sex-slavers. Why wouldn't the Christians use it?" A frown. "I thought we sent out a directive about vans with enough spaces for humans to hide?"

"We did. But I assume it was treated the same way as all our directives are treated. They're ignored."

"Let's talk to the driver of that van."

Williams glanced at his watch. "Right now?"

"Right now."

CHAPTER 11

Peter was sitting at Sam's table. It was the middle of the night—his shift to watch the stranger. He must have fallen asleep because the church sanctuary had returned to its former glory. The stained-glass windows were intact once again, the pews polished, and the parishioners now stood with hymn books in hand, singing a song that Peter recognized as old and traditional: the kind of song his mother sang around the house when she was clearing the dishes or folding the laundry. The congregation was radiant with joy, unafraid, lifting their voices until the harmonies echoed up to the rafters, high above the glittering chandeliers. The whole scene was bathed in a golden light.

It was a loud *click* that yanked Peter from the dream. He lifted his head. Yes, he had fallen asleep. The sanctuary was as dark and gloomy as ever. The stranger was still asleep on the table.

So ... what was the *click*?

He stood up, rubbing his eyes. Was someone in the hall? He'd learned the normal sounds of the group: Sam's light-footed step, Beck's heavy shuffle (as if he was too bored to pick up his feet properly), Amy's ballet-like steps, Mary's walking-on-eggshells footfall, Timothy's boyish thumps, Luke's steady march, Aunt Ruth's quick and purposeful stride. This was something different. This was the sound of someone heavy *trying* to walk softly.

He suddenly imagined soldiers burdened with heavy tactical equipment, creeping down the hall, guns ready.

Peter's eyes darted to the doorway just as they burst in. They were crouching, all in green fatigues, helmets with night vision goggles, and the red lasers on their weapons scanning in all directions.

The crashes, shouts, and screams started.

"No, wait!" Peter cried out, putting up his hands as if he could deflect the barrage of bullets.

He jolted awake.

The sanctuary was just as he had always known it: dark, battered, and desolate. No soldiers, no gunfire, no shouts, not even the echo of his own scream. Just silence.

The stranger had not moved. He remained perfectly still under the blankets by the radiator. Peter went to him to make sure he was still breathing. He was. Slow and deep. Peter dabbed the man's brow with a cool, wet cloth.

The violence of the dream was shocking. Peter shook his head, as if that might loosen the memory. He stood up, stretching long and hard, thinking about the various stories he'd heard of mob violence against churches and Christians. *Mobs*, the news media had assured everyone. The attacks were random, uncoordinated, and unsanctioned. Soldiers were never involved. The Committee would never lower itself to the use of excessive force.

When the persecution came, it was calm and reasonable and, at the worst, coercive. The best minds in the schools and colleges supported and justified the anti-Christian laws. Only idiots would disagree with the assumptions and policies of the Committee that were driven, of course, by fact, data, science, and philosophy. Even when the Committee's logic was completely illogical and its statements defied common sense or rational thought, the people still felt the pressure to be agreeable, even grateful.

Then it came to a point when those who disagreed were maligned socially and tagged officially. They needed to be corrected. If correction was refused, then they must be ostracized, outcast, and then, ultimately, taken to Rehabilitation Centers for a complete overhaul, like computers being rewired and reprogrammed. The average citizens didn't flinch. Especially when it came to the Christians. After all, the Christians had had their chance—*hundreds* of years to fix the world. They had failed completely. The Church became a scandal, entangled in all the wrong things. It treated temporal issues like dogma and dogma like temporal issues—and attacked its own for not agreeing. It was as if the Church became a martyr to itself. The Committee didn't need to use violence. Insistence was enough to knock over a cathedral of straw.

One of the double doors to the hall creaked open. Peter fixed on it with a feeling of dread, a residue of fear from the dream, like Scrooge waiting for the appearance of a ghost. Amy stepped in. She was carrying a tray with a mug and a thermos. She showed no signs of anything being wrong. He took a deep breath and relaxed.

The dim light of the lantern gave her the look of a specter—just like one of Scrooge's ghosts. "Tired?" she asked softly as she approached the table.

"Just a little, I guess," he answered. She was dressed in her usual attire of jeans and hiking boots, but tonight she wore a turtleneck and cardigan sweater. It was his favorite of the three outfits she wore. "Why are you awake?"

She gave a slight shrug and sat the tray down on Sam's table. She filled a cup from the thermos. The smell of coffee was strong. "This should help keep you awake."

"Thank you." He sipped the drink. It tasted stale and burnt. "It's perfect."

She gestured to the stranger. "It's good of you to stay up with him tonight."

"Nice has nothing to do with it," Peter said, appreciating her attention. "I don't want to let him out of my sight."

She gazed at the stranger, a long and intense look. The expression on her face—there was something about it. What was it? It was normally radiant, so fresh and pure. He often thought he could sit and look at her face for hours. Her eyes, too, haunted him. He knew them well. So, what was it that he saw now? Definitely more than mere curiosity. Sympathy? Intrigue? A girlish crush over a man of mystery? Love? She was looking at the stranger the way he wanted her to look at him, with a desire to know him more.

He took another sip of coffee, hoping the action might mask the twinge of jealousy he felt. "I think his fever is going down."

"Thank God," said Amy, her gaze still fixed on the sleeping stranger. "Who do you think he is?"

"I wish I knew." Peter looked away, scanning the gloom of the sanctuary. The memory of the dream came back to him. What would the soldiers do to her if they burst in upon them?

"I keep praying that he's our contact," Amy added.

"So do I."

She pulled the sweater tightly around her. Whatever her expression was before, it gave way to one of distinct sadness. She finally turned from the stranger. "I thought hiding in a church would give me a sense of peace. It hasn't."

Her tone—with that expression—squeezed his heart. He wanted to say something hopeful and encouraging but the words wouldn't come. "Sure beats jail" was the best he could come up with, and he loathed himself for it.

"Sometimes I don't see much of a difference." She hesitated as if she immediately regretted her honesty. "No, I'm sorry. I'm being childish. I didn't mean that."

"It's okay." He put down his mug of coffee and took a few steps closer to her. "We all feel that way."

"I don't ever want to be ungrateful to God for what He's done," she said. "This is better than any of the alternatives. I have to remember that. It's just that I've been feeling so homesick lately, remembering how it used to be, when my parents were alive ..."

"Don't go there, Amy. It doesn't help. Dwelling on memories, on the losses ... it's a particular kind of torture." He knew it well and had blocked out as much as he could. To do otherwise was to invite a mental breakdown.

A thin smile worked across her lips. "I know. It's not something I do often. I think it's the weather. It must be. Certain times of year always trigger memories for me. I've been tough until now. But today turned overcast—did you notice?—sunshine, then those big gray clouds came in. They smell of snow. And I thought of walking home from school, stepping in the back door of my house, smelling my mom's chocolate chip cookies baking in the oven." She choked back a sob.

"You see? That stuff will drive you crazy." He wanted to take her in his arms.

She suddenly straightened. "I don't care. I'd rather have the memories with the pain than no memories at all." She looked at him with defiance and he felt the rebuke. "If it weren't for the pain, I wouldn't feel anything at all. I'd be a ... a walking corpse."

"I've seen those movies. You don't look anything like that." He hoped she might smile.

Instead, she shook her head. "But I *am* a corpse. We all are if we bury the memories and the pain. Do you know what I mean? I can tell by your expression that you don't."

Whatever his expression was, he tried to change it. "Hey, I grew up Catholic. I know all about memories and pain." Another unsuccessful smile. But he knew she was right. He *didn't* understand. It hadn't occurred to him that all his attempts to bury his feelings, his memories, would make him a walking corpse. "We do what we have to do to keep alive."

"There's a difference between keeping alive and living," she said. "That's the contradiction, isn't it? I came here to stay alive, but I don't feel alive. Maybe that's why I hate it here. This church is—oh, what was the word in the Bible? *Ichabod.*"

"Like the story? Ichabod Crane?" Peter asked, feeling stupid.

"Ichabod was a word from the Old Testament, I think. It means something like *the glory has departed.* The glory has departed from this church, maybe from everyone. And I hate it. But hatred is the only emotion I've felt since we got here."

Peter's heart sank. "You haven't felt anything else?"

"No." A sigh. "I suppose being here is like spending a night in a tomb. We hope morning will come and we'll come out alive."

He struggled valiantly to connect with what she was saying. "Look, Amy, all I know is that being alive ... well, that's part of being a Christian, right? We were dead, but Jesus brought us to life. The dead ones are *them.*" He gestured to the darkness as if it contained the very people he was referring to. "The ones who want to lock us up. They're dead. And they're jealous because we're not. They want us to be like them and that's why they want to lock us up, kill our very souls if they can." He stopped, suddenly aware that she was looking at him with an expression of pity. He felt exposed and embarrassed. He'd overplayed his hand, tried too hard, and she noticed it the way girls do when guys are trying to impress them. "I'm sorry. I'm talking too much."

"You are very sweet, Peter," she said gently. "Under normal circumstances, a girl would be very lucky to have you."

His heart skipped a beat. His mouth went dry. "How about *you*?" he asked.

There. It was out.

She smiled indulgently at him. "These aren't normal circumstances." With that, she walked to the doorway and disappeared into the shadowed corridor.

He wanted to kick himself around the room. Turning to the sleeping stranger, he said, "Don't say a word. Not a single word."

———◆———

Like Peter, Sam was visited by dreams. And now he lay awake on his cot, trying to piece together the various subconscious fragments. First, he'd dreamt he was a young boy again, playing hide and seek in the woods with some friends. He was *it* and, after counting to ten, began to search diligently, checking the usual places and the not-so-usual places. He couldn't even find Fast Freddie, who was named not for speed but, ironically, for the obesity that made him so slow. You knew you were in trouble when you couldn't find Fast

Freddie. He continued looking until boredom overtook his determination and he decided it was time to quit.

"Olly Olly in-come-free!" he shouted. No one responded. He shouted again. An upset bird caring for her young screamed back at him. Finally, he heard rustling in a thick overgrowth of bushes. Certain that he'd found at least one person, he raced into the bushes, scrambling furiously to catch whoever it was before they could get away. Pushing through, he stumbled into a small clearing. He was startled to see under a netting of camouflage a large military tank waiting like a sleeping giant. The turret suddenly turned to him.

This was part memory, Sam knew as he stared at the ceiling of the pastor's office. As a boy he had stumbled onto an arsenal of tanks: a base for the militants who would later lead the country to a failed revolution. It was what happened afterwards—in the dream—that had him perplexed.

Afraid of the tank, Sam turned and ran back through the bushes. But as happens in dreams, he was no longer a young boy but his adult self, clawing frantically through the underbrush. He was lost and panicked, driven by an anonymous fear. The woods gave way to a large, sunny field. As he stumbled forward, tombstones sprang up in front of him, then open graves and upended coffins, scattered and disheveled. He ran, tripped, gashed his forehead against a marble cross, and fell in a heap onto the soft earth.

He heard gunshots and looked up toward the church. It was still and silent. Suddenly the ground beneath him shook, then cracked and split. A hand broke upward through the dark soil only inches from Sam's face. The patchy flesh barely held onto the bone as it reached for him from the green moss. He saw maggots squirming between each finger and smelled the stench of death.

Screaming, he jumped up, the hand clawing for his ankle. He ran for the church, dodging the constantly moving headstones. Hands pushed up out of the ground all around him. They strained for him as he ran past. One grabbed his pant leg; another caught his shoe and pulled it off. He ran ahead without it. He made it to the gravel parking lot as the sun vanished behind swirling black clouds. Lightning flashed. Some part of Sam's mind told him not to worry—it was only a dream; he would wake up and all would be well. But he couldn't wake up. The rain fell in fat black drops, drenching him. He turned to the church door and was surprised to see that it was five times its normal size. It swung open, looking like a mouth ready to devour him. He drew back, but something pulled him toward the door, toward an inevitable end. A machine-gun turret poked out of the shadows in the doorway—and unleashed a fury of bullets. Then he woke up.

He sat up, throwing his legs over the edge of the cot. He rubbed his hands through his hair. Then he heard someone walking down the hallway. He could tell by the footfall that it was Amy. She had probably taken a snack or some coffee to Peter.

Sam wondered about nightmares like the one he'd just had. Without the benefit of a proper clergyman or a theologian, he didn't know the Christian stance on the subject. There were dreams in the Bible, he remembered. Two Josephs had dreams, among many others. They were interpreted for spiritual insight or prophetic messages. In the age of Freud, they were interpreted for other insights and messages. But what now? What about tanks and convulsing graveyards and a church that seemed to symbolize death?

He stood up and turned on the desk lamp. Where was his Bible? He'd lent it to Ruth. He wished he had it now to read a psalm for comfort. He knew he wouldn't get any sleep until he could erase the images from his mind. Reprimanding himself for not memorizing verses for just such an occasion, he paced the room.

He tried to create his own words for an elaborate prayer, but they didn't come. So, he simply asked God to show him the meaning of the dream or take it away. It didn't seem too much to ask. Though he hated to bother God with a silly request. Or maybe it wasn't so silly.

After all, this was the sixth time he'd had this particular dream.

Peter felt the stranger's forehead. It was still warm. He stood up and nearly jumped out of his skin when someone tapped him on the back.

"What're you doing, frisking him?" Tim asked.

"No," Peter replied, relaxing. "What are you doing up?"

"I can't sleep."

"Why not?"

"Mom's snoring."

Peter placed his hands on Tim's shoulders and gently pushed him toward the door. "Women don't snore; they just breathe hard."

"Then Mom's breathing *really* hard."

"Put some cotton in your ears," he said. "If your mom wakes up to find you gone, she'll punish *both* of us."

"But my stomach hurts. I have to go to the bathroom."

"Then *go*," Peter snapped. "You don't need me to help you."

When they reached the door, Tim suddenly stopped. "Peter . . ."

Peter anticipated a stall. A glass of water? A bedtime story? He wondered which tactic Tim would try. In the month they'd been together, Tim had tried every excuse imaginable. Peter didn't mind. He remembered doing the same thing to *his* father. And, just like his father, he'd fall for an excuse sometimes, while other times he wouldn't. Peter looked down at the boy and knew with a sad certainty that Tim would be the closest thing to a son he'd ever have. Normal family relationships, marriage, and children were not part of his future.

A sense of loss and regret crowded in on him. He vowed to spend more time with Tim in compensation. It wasn't too late, right? He could take Timothy out tomorrow and show him how to set the traps. It was a start.

"What do you want?" Peter asked.

Tim was hesitant. "When I was really little, Dad used to give me a hug before I went to sleep."

Peter knelt. "Is that it? You want a hug?"

"Only if you want to," Tim said.

Peter pulled the boy close for a hug. In that moment, he thought, *You can be the son I'll never have, and I'll be the father you lost. It's a game we'll play to keep from losing our minds.*

"And *then* he said a magic prayer to keep the monsters away," Tim enthused.

"Now you're pushing it."

"He really did!" Tim insisted.

Peter looked at him warily and wondered if Tim meant imaginary monsters or the ones that were real: the ones that were hunting them. Maybe there wasn't a difference. All the nightmares of his childhood had been fulfilled in the reality of his adulthood. The death and decay that he thought waited for him in the shadows of his bedroom closet now stood before him in the shadows of this church. Placing his hand ceremoniously on the boy's head, he cleared his throat and spoke in a mock drone. "Now I lay me down to sleep, I pray the Lord my soul to keep. And 'til I wake this next good day, please keep the monsters far away."

"Amen," Tim whispered, satisfied. "Goodnight, Peter."

"Goodnight."

Peter watched him drift through the doorway. He shook his head and returned to Sam's table to pour another cup of coffee. "Magic prayers," he said, chuckling.

He looked over at the stranger. Maybe he should say a few of his own.

CHAPTER 12

Bobby took his usual place at the edge of the alley and watched the deserted streets of Woodville for any sign of the police. Just opposite, a blue-and-green neon light announced the name of a beer through a large window. The low thump of a muted bass beat reverberated through the tin siding. A good dance number. A dance he was supposed to share with Heather. Depressed, he shoved his hands deep into his coat pockets and shot a glance down the alley. The night air was heavy with a promise of snow, but that didn't stop the two shadowy figures from taking their jackets off. It was a mere formality for the fight to come. No sense getting blood stains on the leather.

One of the figures muttered the worst kind of obscenities, the condensation of his beer-drenched breath rising like exhaust from an old pickup truck. He kicked a bottle that rattled along the pavement. A rat squealed and scurried down the edge of the wall to some hiding place behind stacks of garbage.

"Keep it down, Clay!" Bobby rasped.

"Yeah, keep it down," a man grumbled as he pushed at the sleeves on his flannel shirt. His tongue was thick with liquor. The man was named Jake and he had a body like an anvil.

Bobby worried about Clay. Clay was a lean, blond-haired kid with a chiseled face and wiry arms. He might outmaneuver Jake, but one solid hit from one of those fists would do Clay some serious damage. Bobby wanted to warn Clay to stop the fight. But he knew it was too late for that. He checked the street again for cops.

"Let's get on with it," Clay said.

Jake snorted as he lifted his fists. He took a step and stumbled as if the weight of his hands was too much to carry. Clay also held up his fists, wiggling them around like he wasn't sure how to use them.

Bobby watched the two circle each other. He knew how it would turn out. It always ended the same way. Clay was his best friend and it seemed important for him to witness the details—if only to tell Clay tomorrow what had happened after the liquor wore off and the bruises had to be explained.

Jake threw a punch and missed. He staggered forward and Clay sent out a hard right to Jake's jaw. It sounded like a weak slap. Jake staggered back and glared at Clay. He looked offended, swore, and threw his whole body at the scrawnier man.

From Bobby's vantage point, it was a confusing mass of wrestling, grunts, blows, upended boxes, breaking bottles, and curses amidst the clattering trash cans.

The noise would draw attention, Bobby knew. Somebody would call the police.

He tried to work up an explanation if they were caught. Nothing sensible came to mind. This fight would be hard to excuse. Everyone in town knew that Jake had threatened to turn off the utilities at Clay's father's farm. Clay's father hadn't paid the bill in two months. There simply wasn't enough money for it. That didn't stop Clay from wanting to beat the living daylights out of Jake. In this town, you were expected to look after your own, not the interests of a big utility company. Clay was going to beat the idea into Jake's head.

Bobby doubted the police would be sympathetic.

A light in a window blinked overhead and Bobby looked up. Someone peeked out to see what was going on. Bobby turned in time to see Clay throw a few wild fists at Jake's face, driving the larger man back until he fell over a crate. Jake hit the ground hard, pathetically sprawled out and unconscious.

"Get up!" Clay demanded and started kicking the prostrate figure. "Get up!"

A siren wailed in the distance. Bobby grabbed his friend's arm. "Let's go, Clay."

Clay kept kicking. "Get up, you no good—"

"He's down! We have to get out of here!" Bobby tugged at Clay's arm.

"Go ahead—try to turn off our power," Clay said as he delivered one last kick to Jake's head. He yielded to Bobby, walking backward as he grabbed his jacket from the top of a trash can lid. The two men ran out of the alley together. They had reached the end of the street and rounded a corner just as a police car raced past.

"Are you all right?" Bobby asked.

Clay rubbed his jaw. "I think he tried to headbutt me. I paid him back ten times over."

"Are you satisfied? Can we go home now?"

"Satisfied?" Clay asked, as if the idea was an impossibility. He pushed Bobby away and strode across the street to Hank's Place. Pushing open the door, he stepped into the dimly lit, smoke-filled bar. Bobby groaned and followed him.

CHAPTER 13

The dull morning light found Sam exactly as the night's darkness had observed him: sitting on his cot, flipping through the pages of some books he'd found stashed in the corner of a cabinet. The priest may have put them there to get rid of later, or maybe he didn't want the book-burning mob to find them. Sam doubted it was the latter. These books were novels, mostly. Thrillers about the second coming of Jesus. Sam recognized the titles. They were stories in which true believers miraculously disappeared, rescued by God from the suffering that would come before a terrible persecution began. They were solidly Protestant in their point of view, going so far as to make the pope an ally to the anti-Christ. But they were big sellers in their time. The priest may have read them just to find out what the fuss was about.

The irony was not lost on Sam. If there had been a miraculous evacuation of the faithful, he had certainly missed it. So had everyone else in the world. As far as he knew, there had been no sudden exodus, no catastrophes of the kind he knew some Christians believed. It was all wishful thinking on the part of the authors—an age-old desire to avoid suffering.

Sam knew better. The New Testament was filled with references to suffering. In fact, it seemed as if Jesus and the Apostles said more about suffering than a lot of those other subjects that Christians had grabbed onto for hope. Now that Sam was living in a time of persecution—maybe the so-called End Times—he saw firsthand the difference between fiction and reality. And he prayed, as Christians always had, for Jesus to come back and put things right.

Putting the novels aside, he held onto the single Catholic book he'd found so far: a Roman Missal from early in the twentieth century. How it had missed the bonfire was more than he could guess. He now turned the pages, finding himself enamored of, and puzzled by, the unfamiliar structure. His hope was that the Missal's prayers would help him. Maybe Ruth or Peter could explain the other parts.

He heard the soft jingling of a bell. Someone was summoning them all to breakfast. He stood and began to dress, suddenly remembering the small town where he used to visit his grandparents. On Sunday mornings, he would lie in their guest room and listen to the church bells announcing the start of services at the nearby Methodist church. It was a lifetime ago. He couldn't remember the last time he'd heard bells of any kind ringing for any reason. Nowadays he was aware of only sirens and alarms.

He wondered when the world decided it didn't need church anymore. What shift in the world's axis led the mass population to believe that mysteries of faith and their physical manifestations—like bells and steeples and statues and crosses—were no longer needed by humanity? And where was he when it happened?

He knew where he was: asleep in the arms of his lover, Academia. Now he may never be able to sleep again. Regret was like that, carrying with it a sharp memory of things done and left undone. *Mea culpa*.

Sam took care of necessities, then padded quietly down the hallway to the sanctuary. He passed the kitchen, where Ruth and Mary were setting the table for breakfast. He gave Ruth a quick nod and a gesture to suggest where he was going. She nodded back.

He assumed all would be well but couldn't escape a sense of foreboding that he might find Peter unconscious and the stranger gone. The cold, damp mustiness of the room reached him before he reached it, and then, with relief, he saw the stranger still buried under the blankets and Peter leaning back in a chair at the table.

"Good morning." Sam moved to the stranger and touched his forehead. The man was drenched in sweat. The fever was gone.

"I think it broke an hour or so ago," Peter said.

Sam checked the stranger's pulse.

Peter stood up. "Nothing happened last night. I don't think he moved at all."

"Did he say anything in his sleep?" Sam asked.

"No. In fact, he was so quiet that I kept thinking he died or something. I must have checked him a dozen times."

Sam looked down at their guest. Until this moment, he hadn't fully appreciated how much the man had stirred hope in his heart. While the stranger slept, hope was possible. The essence of any mystery was that you could project anything you wanted into it. This mysterious stranger could embody hope or despair. Sam remembered a poem he'd once studied in school:

Oh, man of mystery!
Be ye prophet or messenger of doom

Keep still thy lips
   and hold fast your sickle of destruction
For the wrath of God is found in death
   and not in life alone.
  Cast a cold eye on life, on death.
  Horseman, pass by!

The stranger might be a redeemer or an angel of death. Who was to say he wasn't one and the same?

"Get some sleep," he said to Peter.

Peter nodded but didn't leave. He looked around the church. "Looking at it now, it's hard to imagine anyone ever worshipping here. It's so cold and dark."

Sam let his eyes trail up to the modest arches supporting the ceiling and the gray chandeliers. Everything was cobwebbed and soot-covered. Any semblance of beauty and grace was long gone. "I doubt it was always so dark and cold."

"I've been to one or two Catholic churches that were."

"It's all you would have known in the first few centuries of Christianity. They hid and worshipped in the gloomy, cold caves and passages that made up the underbelly of Rome. The catacombs. There they were hunted and, if caught, tortured, and killed. Maybe time has gone full circle and—"

Peter yawned.

Sam smiled. "Go to bed. I'll keep an eye on our friend here."

Luke stepped through the doorway. "I've been praying all night," he announced. "God has been preparing me to heal this man. The spirit is moving within me."

Sam and Peter exchanged a knowing glance. "Go get the others, Luke," Sam said. "It's time for breakfast."

Luke frowned. "No. We must meet here in the sanctuary. We must study the Word and pray for the stranger." He turned to them and spoke with an unmistakable strain in his voice. "It is why I have come. I know this man." Sam saw tears well up in his eyes.

"How do you know him?" Sam asked. This was the first time Luke had said anything to indicate he remembered his life before the shock treatments.

"I don't know. Somewhere." Luke's face knotted up with concentration. "Before ... before ..."

Sam wondered how far Luke's memory would go—if he could go back to a time before the pain he'd obviously endured.

"What happened?" Luke implored. "What happened to me? Please, tell me. I don't remember."

Sam thought about the nature of mercy: when God allows us to forget our pain and when He allows us to remember it clearly. It wasn't the same for everyone. "Maybe I will tell you sometime, Luke. But first, we must join the others."

Luke's face cleared, like a child who'd been offered a candy bar to forget about his skinned knee. "Yes. And then I will call on the power of God to heal the stranger." He ambled away happily.

"It's heartbreaking," Peter said.

Sam shook his head. "It's better he doesn't remember."

Shortly after arriving, the fugitives had tried to gather for a time of prayer and Bible study. It was awkward and clumsy. They attempted to sing old hymns, but the verses were elusive and jumbled until the song eventually petered out to a comical standstill. Luke often rambled incoherently. Tim couldn't sit still. Beck was irritable.

All the same, Sam figured it was the closest thing to a proper church he would ever experience as an adult. Sad but true. He'd missed the opportunity to attend a real church by quite a few years.

He imagined that Mary and Ruth, who had attended churches throughout their lives, felt the greatest loss. How does one feel when stripped of something so vital but so easily taken for granted?

Now, huddled together in the kitchen, the Church of the Last Fugitives met in the name of the Father, Son, and Holy Ghost and shared in a communion of eggs, bacon, and bad coffee. Peter had gone to his room. Amy stationed herself at the doorway of the kitchen to watch the hall, just in case the stranger called out or emerged.

"How's the mystery man?" Beck asked.

"Better," Sam reported. "His fever is gone." He looked around at the gaunt, sleepless eyes that gazed back at him. This wasn't a church; it was a concentration camp.

"We need to talk about leaving," Beck said.

Sam put up a hand. "Not so fast."

"Fast?" Beck snorted. "If we don't get out of here now, the snow will make us stranded. *Without* food."

"What are you suggesting we do?" Ruth asked. "Pack up and leave? To where?"

"We don't have to be stupid about it. First, somebody should sneak down to the town and scout around. Let's find out what's going on in the real world. Maybe we'll learn what's become of our contact, or how to connect with someone who can help us."

"It's too dangerous," Amy said.

"No, I think it's an excellent idea." Sam rose to his feet. "And I want to thank Mr. Beck for volunteering to do it."

Beck spun in his chair to face Sam. "Now, wait a minute. I didn't say *I'd* do it. I thought we could take a vote and . . ." Trapped, he slumped in his chair and folded his arms.

"So much for old business," said Sam. "Any new business?"

No one spoke.

Sam clasped his hands behind his back and paced around the table. "We are *not* going to starve to death, in spite of what some of you think. I know we're down to some pretty skimpy meals and it may become uncomfortable—"

"To say the least," Beck said.

"Jesus promised that He would never leave us or forsake us," Ruth stated.

"Amen," Luke whispered.

"So, let's hang on as best as we can and don't let wild fears get in the way of our faith—or our clear thinking." That was as much as Sam could think to say.

"Can we pray together? *Please?*" Mary asked.

"If you want to." Sam knew that this had been difficult for them to do. Too often it became a depressing exercise of highlighting their current difficulties and bringing up present grievances. "What would you like to pray about?"

Mary cleared her throat nervously. "I've been having trouble sleeping lately. The strangest dreams keep waking me up." Her voice trailed off as she looked down at her knotted fingers. "I won't say any more than that."

Sam remembered his own dreams. "It's understandable. The fears we hide during our waking hours run rampant in our sleep."

"I will keep him in perfect peace whose mind is kept on Thee." Luke was quoting the Bible.

"I know, Luke," Mary said, "but it's the violence in my dreams that wakes me up. The running lost through the woods, the gunfire in the church . . ."

Mary stopped suddenly and looked stricken as Ruth and Amy turned to her, their eyes wide and mouths agape. Sam felt his heart throb in his ears.

"You're describing the same kinds of dreams I've been having," Ruth said.

They all looked at one another, aware that something strange was happening.

"We've all had the same dream?" Amy asked. "Is that possible?"

"There was a time I would have said that it wasn't." Sam shook his head. "Not now."

"I don't dream." Beck said.

They slipped into silence. Sam felt the pressure of saying something, but he had nothing to say. He didn't know what to make of the phenomenon. He'd have to think long and hard about it. And, even then, any guess would probably be wildly inaccurate. He pressed on. "What else should we pray for?"

"Our friend." Amy nodded toward the sanctuary.

"If he *is* our friend," Beck corrected her.

Amy continued, "And we should pray for Moses, Elijah, and the work of the Resistance."

"Yes, yes, we must pray," Luke announced, standing and quickly moving past Amy into the hallway. "I will pray for the stranger."

Amy looked at Sam. "Should I bring him back?"

"No." Sam felt resigned. "He can't do any harm."

"We'll see about that," Beck muttered.

Ruth suddenly giggled. All eyes fell on her. "I'm sorry. I was just remembering back at my home church when we prayed for things like guidance about the color of our carpet, or the upcoming potluck dinner, or Claudia Pilford's cat— with all the fervor of Moses standing before the Red Sea."

"We didn't know how quickly everything would change," Mary said.

"Is there anything else?" Sam asked.

Timothy spoke in a small voice. "Pray for Joshua. I can't find him again."

"Oh brother," Beck snorted.

Sam folded his hands. "All right. Let's pray."

CHAPTER 14

He was running. Running hard, aimlessly, though his fevered mind had forgotten why. He had to keep moving, keep climbing—that was as much as he knew. Something beckoned him like a siren's song that drew him up into the mountain. Exhaustion was near, however, and he fell. His mind screamed at him to get up, *get up*! His body refused.

He lay there in the damp leaves listening to the songs of the birds and the shallow sound of his own breathing. He thought back to when he lay in his bedroom listening to birds outside the window. That was another life, a real bed. Nothing was soft like that anymore.

He opened his eyes. He wasn't in the woods anymore. Dim lights flickered somewhere through a haze. *I see men as trees walking,* a blind man once said. Why had he thought of that? The lights, that was it. They twinkled in a strange, unsettling way. Candles? He couldn't tell. Everything was still too blurry.

He pressed his palms against his eyes. Had he gone blind? Why couldn't he see where he was? He'd been running in the woods and now ... now he felt clammy and damp.

A gentle hand touched him on the forehead. Normally he would have reacted, sprung into a defensive position to protect himself. But the touch of this hand wasn't threatening at all. It rested just above his brow, then on his eyes, and the blurriness fell away like scales. He blinked. Above him stood an old man with wild white hair and beard—a Sunday School picture of John the Baptist. He'd seen him somewhere before. Was this some kind of a vision?

The old man looked at him kindly. "Stand up."

"I . . . I can't seem to move. Who are you?"

The old man smiled wearily. "Why have you been running?"

"To escape. Just like everyone else."

"You are not everyone else," the old man said. "You were called to more important things."

"It was a mistake."

"Whose?"

"Mine. For saying yes."

"The Blessed Virgin said yes and saw far worse things than you. Now rise. You have work to do."

The old man was gone in a flash, along with any clarity of sight. Darkness covered him like thick earth, as if he'd been buried alive. He struggled against it, pushing hard, getting to his knees, and pushing, pushing. He felt the weight give way—enough to believe he could break through. He continued pushing until he was standing on very shaky legs, the weakness in his muscles and joints threatening to drop him to the ground again. The darkness turned to a dull gray light.

If it was a dream, then he had to wake up. If it wasn't a dream, then he had to open his eyes to see clearly where he was.

With all his might, he fought toward consciousness.

In the kitchen, the fugitives had their heads bowed in prayer. Amy had slipped further in to join them.

"He is risen!" Luke declared from outside in the hall.

"He is risen indeed," Ruth said, completing the old exchange.

Amy looked at Luke from the corner of her eye, then went back to prayer.

Sam started to pray about their food shortage and their hope for the contact to come very soon.

Suddenly Tim gasped.

Sam lifted his head to see what had startled Tim. Then Mary screamed, gesturing to the doorway. Everyone now spun in that direction. Sam turned around and saw Luke's expression of unbridled joy. Then, stepping like a shadow from behind Luke, the stranger appeared, wrapped carelessly in a torn blanket like Lazarus unbound.

CHAPTER 15

It took great restraint for the group to keep quiet while the stranger drank his coffee. All the while, they assaulted him with their eyes, scrutinizing his every move and gesture, searching for unspoken clues. Even Beck waited patiently. Sam was slightly amused to see them treat this awakened stranger like the visitation of an angel. Their fates were in his hands.

Hunched under the bulky blanket that still draped his shoulders, he looked small. His patchy beard, sunbaked skin, and matted hair made him look like a field worker. The coffee cup shook unsteadily as he raised it to his lips. Before drinking, he glanced up self-consciously at the seven pairs of eyes staring at him.

"How do you feel?" Ruth asked.

"Compared to what?"

Ruth chuckled. "Compared to how you felt before we found you in the woods."

"Compared to other days, I feel terrific," he replied. "We're in a church, right?"

"Yes," Sam said.

"Sam!" Beck snapped. "Don't tell him anything until we know more about him."

As much as Sam hated to agree with Beck about anything, he nodded and looked solemnly at the stranger. "Maybe you should answer a few questions first."

The stranger rubbed his forehead wearily. "If you promise to keep them easy."

"What's your name?" Beck asked.

"Smith," he answered. "James Smith."

"Sounds fake," Beck snorted. "Who were your parents: John and Pocahontas?"

"Mr. Beck!" Amy cried out.

"I'm actually the son of John and Patricia," Smith said. "And if you'll check your history, you'll find that John Smith and Pocahontas never married, let alone bore children. Next question?"

"What are you doing up here, Mr. Smith?" Amy asked.

"Would you believe me if I said I got lost while taking a long walk?"

"No," Amy replied.

"Taking a long walk from where—to where?" Beck asked.

Smith regarded Beck thoughtfully. "You don't have to be afraid of me. I'm a Christian."

There was a palpable feeling of relief around the room.

Beck didn't accept the news so readily. "What makes you so sure we're Christians? How do you know we won't turn you in?"

Smith gave them a confident look. "You are and you won't."

"Where's your identification?" Beck persisted.

"My—?"

"We looked through your knapsack and you don't have papers, cards, scanning codes ... nothing," Beck said.

Smith looked down at his coffee cup. What little color he had in his face drained away. "I'm on the run. I'd be a fool to carry an ID." He slumped a little more.

"We'll save the rest of our questions for later." Sam was trying to be diplomatic.

Smith lifted his hand. "It's all right. I can answer your questions. I don't want to return your kindness by being rude." He tried to smile. "It must have been a shock finding me in the woods."

"It certainly was," Beck grumbled. "Carrying you back was no picnic, either."

"Then I have you to thank."

"You do."

"And Peter," Amy interjected. "He's sleeping right now. He stayed up with you all night."

"Thanks to you both."

Sam hedged for a moment, then decided to ask the question they all needed answering. "Mr. Smith, are you our contact?"

Smith looked surprised by the question. He answered uneasily. "No, I'm not."

The relief of a moment before turned quickly to disappointment. Sam eyed him, unsure whether he believed the answer.

"How long have you been hiding up here?" Smith asked.

"Almost a month," Ruth replied.

Smith gave them a sympathetic look. "I'm sorry to give you bad news, but there'll be no contact for a while. The Resistance has been ... disrupted."

"Disrupted? What does that mean?" asked Mary.

"What happened?" Sam asked.

"Captain Slater," Smith answered, then realized that the name meant nothing to them. "He is breaking up the Resistance. He's obsessed with capturing Moses and Elijah. Everyone is laying low until a new strategy can be formed."

"How long will that take?" Mary pleaded. "Winter's coming. We'll never survive."

"Stay calm," Sam interjected. "We'll find a way to survive." He wanted to cut the conversation short and wait for the opportunity to talk to Smith alone. "Mr. Smith must be hungry. Let's get him some solid food."

Ruth was on her feet. "I'll take care of it."

"The rest of us can give the poor man some space." Sam shooed everyone but Ruth out of the kitchen.

As he shepherded Beck further down the hall, Beck reeled on him.

"I don't trust him. He's not telling the truth. We better keep an eye on him."

He then stormed off to his room.

Luke was nearby, standing against the wall and staring at his hands.

"You prayed for him, didn't you, Luke?" Sam asked.

"I did."

"Good work, Luke." Sam patted him on the arm.

Luke smiled.

"Did Luke *really* wake Mr. Smith up?" Timothy asked.

"Maybe," Sam replied.

"Wow." The boy wandered off with amazement beaming on his face.

Sam looked back at Luke again. The old man was still staring at his hands, but there was a knowing look in his eyes.

"He's not what he seems," Luke said.

Sam looked at him, puzzled, but the old man walked off without another word.

CHAPTER 16

Jake Janovitch sat in his easy chair and stared sullenly out his apartment window. The eye that wasn't swollen shut ached, though he was flying from painkillers. The afternoon moved in slow motion. He watched the bus depot below and saw a blue-shirted clerk put tags on luggage for the three waiting passengers, their collars turned up and their hats pulled down against the wind. The 2:45 bus was due.

The weather reports were calling for a heavy snowfall—a half a foot of accumulation, maybe a foot. Jake knew they were gearing up for any contingency at the utility company where he worked: employees on standby, checking and double-checking the grids, rerouting circuits to accommodate any sudden surge of power from furnaces and space heaters being turned on. It had been a mild autumn. But now the snow would fall, and everyone would overreact as if it had never snowed before. *Idiots.*

The 2:45 bus came around the corner. Its long blue and silver body was almost as tall as the bus depot, which was nothing more than a convenience store and gas station. The driver did a wide U-turn and jerked to a stop.

Jake sat up, wincing at the pain from his three broken ribs, and reached for his phone. The neck brace rattled. A sharp pain shot like lightning through his left shoulder. He groaned and then uttered the word "Work." The phone dialed his office. Brenda, their catch-all secretary, picked up.

"Put me through to Terry, will you?" he asked.

"Are you feeling all right?"

"A touch of the flu."

"That's not what I heard," she teased.

"Just get me Terry," he said.

After a few clicks and some "hold" music, Terry picked up. "Hiya, bud. How're you doing?" He was his usual cheerful self. Jake could hear the clink of his spoon tapping against a mug.

"Not bad," Jake mumbled. His jaw was very nearly broken, and it hurt to talk. His words were slurred. "I need a favor."

"Sure."

"The Hunts," Jake said. "They're two months behind. Time to disconnect them."

"After what happened last night?"

"Who said anything happened last night?"

"Everybody knows what happened. Natalie wasn't going to keep *that* quiet."

"What happened to patient privacy? Does she talk about everyone she treats at the ER?"

"The interesting ones."

Jake swore under his breath.

Terry chuckled. "Besides, Johnny was at the other end of the bar last night. He saw you two get into the argument and leave."

"Tell Johnny he didn't see anything." Jake made a mental note to have a little chat with Johnny as soon as he was able to have little chats again. "Now, cut their power?"

"Clay will come looking for you."

"They're *two months* behind," Jake reminded him.

"We'll enjoy your funeral." There was a loud clicking as Terry tapped at his computer keyboard. He hummed for a moment. "Here they are." More humming. "Not a chance."

"Why not?"

"They're on the old system. It has to be done at the house."

"Then do it."

"You think I'm going to drive all the way up there *now* with the snow coming?" Terry asked. "They still own guns, you know."

"It needs doing, so do it."

"No way, Jake. This is a score you'll have to settle yourself."

"Wait a minute, hold on." Jake's dull brain was on the edge of another idea. "Bring up the grid for the area."

"The grid? Okay." Terry tapped away at the keyboard again. "Got it. What do you want to know?"

"Who do they share with? Anybody else on the grid?"

"That's a large area. Let me see. I see the Hunts and . . . the Cantors Farm."

"Burnt down last year," Jake said.

"Right."

"Anything else?"

"A building. Code 4K. What's that?"

Jake struggled to remember. "Code 4K means . . . abandoned. Must be an old school or a church."

"I remember now. It used to be a Catholic church. We used to go past it on the way to Amber Lake." He paused. "Strange, but there's power running at that site."

"Hikers. Maybe drifters. So, is that it?"

"Uh huh. Why?"

"You can save yourself a trip to the Hunts' place and turn off the entire grid."

"Good point. Okay." Terry banged away at the computer for another minute. "Grid for Zone 12 is now *off.*" He punched the button.

"Thanks," Jake wondered if it was too soon to take more painkillers.

"Are you sure you want to make Clay mad again?" Terry continued. "He's an animal. Sounds like he tore you apart."

Jake looked at the clock on the wall. It was too soon. "What's Clay going to do when they send him to a reallocation camp?" Everyone used to call them "poor camps," but the government insisted that no one was poor anymore.

"You're really going to report him?" Terry asked.

"Hey, the law says we have to," Jake stated.

Terry grunted. "You can be a real nasty piece of work when you want to be."

Jake disconnected the call. He wanted to laugh but instead let out a howl of pain.

CHAPTER 17

Amy rinsed the last of her laundry in the cold, clear stream. A flannel shirt dripped heavily in her hand. The clouds had gathered in the last couple of hours, and she knew the snow was coming. She looked up at the woods and the mountains beyond. *Impenetrable*, she thought. How were they going to escape? What if they got snowed in? *Heavenly Father . . . what are we going to do?*

It was a half-hearted prayer, as prayers often are when the one praying already knows the answer. There was nothing that could be done.

A stray lock of hair fell into her face. She pushed it back and the gesture, so simple in and of itself, took on a vain significance. She wanted to look pretty again. Was it so wrong?

She thought of Mr. Smith and dropped the shirt into a broken laundry basket. She sighed yet again. A deep sigh, from the heart. This wasn't the life she'd had in mind for herself.

Closing her eyes, she touched her face. Her skin felt dry and rough. No longer the face of a young girl. Her hands were rugged and masculine. Her youth was gone, taken away from her by a cruel kidnapper who hadn't even bothered to leave a ransom note. Her parents had been taken away. Mental incompetents, she was told. It was just her, left to take care of her younger brother and sister. That's when the lines began to form on her forehead and around her eyes. Her mouth—always ready to smile—now pulled down at the corners. She couldn't do enough to satisfy the government regulations, no matter how hard she worked. Her sister was taken first; she died in the State-run children's home. Her brother became a model student and citizen, proving his loyalty to the Committee by betraying her faith to them.

How was a girl expected to keep her youth when the Committee stole it away, leaving nothing behind except the conviction that family ties, love, even the future were in its hands alone. Ultimately, it was the loneliness that caused her the most trouble. It greeted her everywhere she went—and lingered nearby no matter who she met or talked to. It honored no sacred spaces, invading her prayers and worship.

Now, crouching at the edge of a stony mountain creek, scrubbing someone's jeans, she felt like Cinderella without a fairy godmother. Hiking clothes instead of a peasant dress. Hopelessly plain. Would someone like Mr. Smith look twice at her? No, why should he? All she had to commend herself for was a knack for survival. In the end, she suspected that would fail her.

No, this wasn't the life she'd expected for herself. Hers was supposed to be a *normal* life: to grow up with normal experiences, to marry a normal man, have normal children. But the Committee was a fickle interloper. Normal was no longer acceptable. Everyone was told to be *exceptional*—be unshackled from the past, celebrate the new freedom of ideas, emerge like a butterfly from ancient cocoons. Be yourself in conformity with everyone else.

When the persecution against the faithful started, she determined to join the Resistance. Be heroic. Stand firm and die if she had to, just like a modern Joan of Arc. She would gather with Christians everywhere to become beacons of light, knights adorned in the whole armor of God. Moses and Elijah exemplified all that she aspired to be. Without violence, they attacked the Committee—disrupting infrastructures, breaking into indoctrination camps, hacking broadcasts and programs to speak the truth. Stories of actual miracles circulated. Believers were inspired to a gallant and courageous ideal. She wanted to be part of it, to play her part with a radiant dignity.

It was not to be. Her heroic faith was choked by a basic desire to survive. People died for the faith, she supposed, but not many. Most were thrown into camps until their minds were changed, or the drugs and shock treatments reduced them to drooling idiots. Where was the gallantry in that? It didn't really count as martyrdom—to drool rather than die for the cause. Where was the heroism in growing old before her time, helpless and undernourished, washing clothes in a mountain stream with little chance of ... of what?

She put her hands on her hips and choked back the gall of self-pity. It was pointless to feel sorry for herself. She knew it. So, why was she feeling it so acutely now? Was it because of Mr. Smith? Had his arrival unearthed something inside of her that she thought she had buried? What was it? Maybe it was the suddenness of a new kind of hope, something she hadn't realized she was missing until he arrived. Maybe it was a schoolgirl fantasy that he was the white knight she'd given up on, now come to rescue them all. Whatever it was had stirred up *everything* inside of her. With heightened hope came a deepening sense of disappointment. With a heightened faith came a deepened sense of doubt.

Impatiently, she threw the remaining clothes into the basket and snatched it up. She made her way back to the church.

She told herself—willed it—that by the time she reached the door to the church, she would no longer feel sorry for herself or indulge in vain romantics. She would look to God for answers, she pledged to herself. She would not look to a stranger to save her.

Sam and Peter looked at the fuse box. It was a collection of unlabeled switches, all in the *on* position.

Sam lightly touched the controls. "It doesn't look like anything's wrong."

"So why did the power go off?" Peter asked.

Sam pushed the largest switch to *off*, waited a few seconds, then turned it on again. He looked up at the light above them. It was dead.

"Well?" Ruth asked from the bottom of the stairs. "Did we blow a fuse?"

Sam didn't realize she had followed them down. "It doesn't look like it."

"Just when I was wondering if anything else would go wrong," Ruth said.

"So, *you're* to blame for this," Sam teased. "You shouldn't be wondering about bad things."

"What about the gas?" asked Peter.

"The stove is working if I use a match, but not the oven." Ruth looked anxious.

The three of them looked at the furnace.

"Gas," Sam said, as if answering their unspoken question.

"Then it'll work?" Ruth asked.

"Not without electricity." Sam drummed his fingers on the side of the unit. "We'll have to use the generator. Ben said it has some fuel left."

They made their way to the stairs.

Peter frowned. "Why would they turn off the electricity now? Do they know we're up here?"

Sam shook his head. "I doubt it. We'd be surrounded by now. It must be something else."

"Let's hope they don't turn off the gas," Ruth said. "There's an old woodstove in the corner of Beck's room. We may have to put that in the sanctuary for us all to use, if it comes to that."

"I'll start collecting wood when I check my traps," Peter offered.

Sam gave Peter an appreciative nod.

"This won't help morale," Ruth told them once they were on the main floor again.

"It may be just the thing to force us out of here." Sam rounded the doorway into the kitchen. "How's Smith?"

"Sleeping, last I checked," Ruth replied. She went to the stove, turned on a burner, and put a lit match to it. A flame popped up. "Thank God," she whispered.

Peter eyed the hallway. "Smith hasn't said anything else about the Resistance?"

"No," Ruth said.

Peter folded his arms. "I can't believe it's been destroyed."

"*Disrupted*," Sam corrected him.

"What's the difference? Both mean we're stuck up here longer." He pounded a fist against the tabletop. "I don't get it. I've heard so much about Moses and Elijah—the way they've evaded the police, escaped under impossible circumstances. How could God let the work of his prophets be *disrupted*?"

"Be careful with that 'prophet' talk," Ruth advised.

"Okay, forget Moses and Elijah for a minute," Peter conceded. "What's Smith *really* doing up here?"

Sam gave a half-shrug. "It's anybody's guess."

Ruth, too, checked the hallway and spoke quietly. "I've noticed that he's very clever about how he answers questions. Evasive without sounding like it."

"What's the rest of the gang think?" Peter asked.

Sam looked to Ruth for an answer. Like a true mother hen, she was the best gauge of everyone's feelings. "Well," she began slowly, "Luke is convinced he healed Smith and it's some kind of sign."

"Maybe it is," Sam suggested.

Ruth continued, "Beck said he doesn't trust Smith. Mary is disappointed that he isn't our contact. Tim thinks he has a new playmate. And Amy—" She stopped and gave Peter a coy look.

"Where is she now?" asked Peter.

"Down at the creek, doing laundry."

Peter scowled. "Smith's?"

Ruth nodded.

"What do you think, Ruth?" Sam asked.

"He seems nice enough, but he's quiet," she replied. "I never could trust quiet men."

"What about you, Sam?" Peter asked.

"I've never been accused of being a quiet man."

"What do you think about *Smith*?" Peter said.

Sam shoved his hands into his pockets and leaned against the table. "I want to believe he's a Christian. Why pretend? But he's holding back a lot of information. Why he was unconscious in the woods ..."

The thought faded away, followed by a dull silence.

A voice from the doorway startled them. It was Smith. "Has the jury reached a verdict?"

———————— ••• ———◆——— ••• ————————

Howard Beck steadied himself against a tree to try to get his breath back. Why was he so out of shape? It hadn't been that long since he was playing tennis at the club, had it? He yanked a handkerchief out of his coat pocket and dabbed at his forehead. *It's the altitude. Higher altitude, less oxygen.*

Squinting, he scanned the area for anything that might look familiar. But the trees all looked the same. Well, what did he expect in the woods? He had hoped for some kind of clue, something Smith had left behind. It shouldn't be that hard to find the spot again.

The forest was enshrouded in a dull grayness. He couldn't see anything that didn't look familiar from yesterday's outing. He turned slowly around and tried to guess how far he had walked from the church. A mile? Two miles? Carrying Smith yesterday, it felt like a hundred.

He started off again and had only gone a few feet when he banged his foot against a large tree root. He cursed it for being in the way. A blackbird responded with a loud squawk from above. Beck cursed the bird. The bird cursed him back. He grabbed a small branch and threw it at the creature. It flapped away to another tree.

He imagined the bird plucked, basted, and served with a plum sauce.

His stomach growled. *Blast them and their rations*, he thought. They can suffer and commend themselves for having faith in God, but he was a practical man. He wasn't about to starve to death—not in that church, not anywhere.

He stopped in his tracks again. He could be anywhere. This was a waste of time. Shoving his hands into his coat pockets, his fingertips brushed something hard and plastic. He dug deeper, past the old tissues and lozenge wrappers, and wrapped his hand around a familiar shape.

His cell phone.

He thought he'd left it behind. He was supposed to. It was a tracking device, he'd been told. Maybe it was, maybe it wasn't. He looked at the black screen. The phone was an older model, simpler and probably pre-dating the government's chip mandate. If he turned it on and got a signal, even for just a moment, he could look at the GPS and figure out where he was.

He pushed the small button on the side. The screen lit up. A logo of the manufacturer appeared and then his familiar screen settings: icons set against a picture of a pristine beach with stunning blue water in the background. The signal indicator was at its lowest level. He tapped the GPS app and a new screen appeared, mere pixels at first and then a circle slowly appeared like a radar beacon.

Is that where I am? he wondered as the circle showed a seemingly endless forest in all directions. Then the image focused, and he saw an area that might be a farm or ranch with a house. Thumbing at the screen, he followed a sliver of a road … maybe a driveway … to another road. Further along was a small town.

Another loud, sharp squawk from the blackbird made him jump. *What if it really is a tracking device?* He powered down the phone and shoved it back in his pocket.

They couldn't track him. Not that quickly. He shrugged it off, confident that the government was too incompetent to ever spot him in the middle of nowhere.

He was about to turn back for the church when his eye caught sight of a tree with a tear-shaped knot in the side.

He'd seen it yesterday, right before Peter found Mr. Smith. Now he could retrace his steps. Beck smiled. He knew what he had to do.

Smith pulled the blanket around his shoulders and gingerly stepped into the kitchen. "Well? Do you find the defendant guilty or not guilty?"

"We're still reviewing the evidence," Sam told him.

"May a witness take the stand?"

"Of course," Sam nodded.

Smith sat down at the table and looked up into the faces of Sam, Peter, and Ruth. He folded his hands in front of him and Sam thought he was about to pray. "You're suspicious. I don't blame you. I'm feeling a bit cautious myself."

"So, we've noticed," Ruth said.

Smith acknowledged the comment with a nod. "You don't have to be afraid of me. I'm harmless. And, as it is, I don't plan on staying."

"It's not your staying that we're worried about," Sam confessed. "It's your *leaving* that's worrying us." He watched Smith's face closely, looking for anything that might help him understand more about the stranger's intentions. Smith was expressionless.

"I travel best on my own," Smith stated.

"The evidence says otherwise," Ruth quipped.

"A fair point," Smith said. "But I had an accident. I was probably concussed."

"Where were you in an accident?" Sam asked.

Smith shook his head.

Sam frowned at him. "All right, then. Where will you go from here?"

"Into the mountains. I'll eventually make my way to the border."

Peter leaned on the table. "Are you going to another hiding place? Do you know of another stop in the underground?"

Smith lowered his head. "I told you. I'm not your contact."

"Then what are you doing here?" Peter snapped.

Sam put a hand on Peter's arm. "Calm down."

Peter stepped away, gesturing to the stranger. "But, Sam, this isn't right."

Sam grabbed a chair and sat down opposite Smith. "Mr. Smith, I'm at a loss here. I'm a college professor, not an expert in wilderness survival. You see our situation. Our food is running out. Peter hunts and fishes, but so far it's yielded very little. You know it'll get worse when the snow comes." Sam paused. Smith was watching him impassively. "I don't think God is going to drop manna from heaven or give us fuel for the generator. Somewhere there's a line between the kind of faith that waits and the kind of faith that acts. Right now, I'm not sure on which side of the line we should be."

"I understand," Smith said.

"We're desperate, Mr. Smith." Sam wanted to say more, then realized there was nothing more to say.

Smith kept his eyes fixed on Sam. "I can't help you."

"Then who can?" Sam asked. "The Resistance?"

"I don't know."

Sam fought a growing feeling of helplessness. "Is there a way to contact them? A contingency plan for a situation like this? Surely someone knows we're here. Someone will come."

Smith fidgeted. "I'm not sure about that."

"Then what are we supposed to do?"

Smith put his hands against the top of the table and pressed hard, as if it were in danger of flying away. "I don't know what to say."

"Then I have to ask you, or *beg*, whichever would be more effective ... please take us with you."

Smith sat upright, his eyes darting from one face to another, "All of you? We'd never make it."

"We have to try," Sam insisted.

"It's unreasonable for you to ask. It's more than I can do." Smith scrubbed his hands over his face. He sounded weary. "Give me time to think about it."

"Pray about it," Ruth said.

Smith didn't respond.

CHAPTER 18

The room was no more than six by six feet in any direction and pale green from top to bottom. The deep cracks in the cement looked like rivulets on a map to some foreign land. *Maybe Switzerland,* Ben thought. He was sitting in the center of the room, his wrists cuffed to a ring in the middle of a scarred metal table. His chair was also metal and uncomfortable, tilting a little to the right where the legs had buckled or were bent; it was surrounded by beaten and bent metal chairs. A mirror was fixed to the wall directly in front of him—a camera behind it, no doubt. The wall was covered with soundproofing pads.

With the knuckles of both forefingers, Ben lightly brushed each side of his thick walrus mustache. He had to bend his neck to do it. The length of the chains on the cuffs didn't allow him a lot of maneuverability. He then rested his large hands on the edge of the desk and tapped them lightly, working into the rhythm of a song he once loved.

He was trying to look unconcerned about his arrest, just in case they were watching him. Not too unconcerned, though, and not too little. Who in their right mind wouldn't be a little agitated when dragged by the police to the local station without a word of explanation, accusations, or charges? He needed to look innocent while, at the same time, appear as if he's concerned about being in the interrogation room.

He leaned back and tried to fold his arms. The chains wouldn't allow it. He rolled his eyes—a proper suggestion of annoyance for leaving him to sit there for an hour.

If he offered a prayer now, would he look as if he was praying? He never had reason to think about it before. What did he look like when he was praying? He would have to ask his wife when he got home.

He wondered why they wanted to talk to him. For that matter, he wondered *who* wanted to talk to him. He'd been so very careful—except for the discovery of the panels under the van's flooring. Bootlegging, they had said. Extra storage, he had said. They had to let him go.

The trick, Ben thought to himself, was to forget everything he knew. They couldn't trick him into admitting to anything that he put out of his mind. It was something he had learned while studying drama at college: *be* your character, believe who you are, believe what you know, shut off your mind to any other reality. He was a freelance delivery driver. That was all. He was a simple man with a simple life.

The latch on the door clicked. His eyes darted in that direction. He hoped the camera didn't catch his instinctive worry. The door opened and two men, engaged in a con-versation about what sounded like a horse race, walked in. They weren't local enforcers, not in those suits—a good make by a good city tailor. That made him uneasy. Why were federal agents here to talk to him?

The first man was slender and average in height. He had wavy red hair and an unpleasant hawk-like face. It was so bird-like, in fact, that Ben thought he'd had some kind of surgery done to cover a birth defect. Or maybe he'd been scarred in an accident.

The second man was tall and muscular with an open, friendly face—the kind of guy you could have over for dinner or go bowling with. His brown hair was styled short, giving him a just-graduated-from-college look. *A rookie*, Ben thought.

"Ben Greene, right?" the redhead asked. He sat across from the prisoner. The rookie remained standing.

"Yes, sir. That's me."

"Good. It's embarrassing when we bring in the wrong people." The redhead smiled, his thin lips cutting a gash across his face. "I'm Captain Robert Slater of—well, let's say a special division of a federal agency. This is my partner, Agent Williams."

"Hi." Ben was all friendliness.

Williams nodded and leaned against the wall with his arms folded.

"I'm sure you're wondering what's going on here," Captain Slater said.

"I sure am. I was in the middle of lunch when—"

Slater held up his hand. "I'm sorry for the inconvenience. We have just a few questions and, depending on your answers, you can get back to your lunch."

"Sure. What questions?"

"How long have you been transporting insurrectionists in the back of your van?"

Ben felt like he'd been slapped across the face. "What?"

"Maybe I didn't speak clearly enough," Slater said. "I asked you, how long—"

"I heard you, but I'm surprised. Transporting *insurrectionists*? I deliver a lot of *things*, but not rebels. Just ask the Maidstone Bakery Company and—"

"Please, Mr. Greene," Slater spoke softly, then glanced up at Williams. There was a communication in their look. "We know who you work for. We know almost everything about you. It's what we don't know that we want to clarify. Let's get to the facts. While you were sitting here trying to look calm and composed for our little camera behind the mirror, we were doing a forensic search of your van. We tested the bay underneath your fake floor and were amazed to find a variety of fingerprints, sweat, human hair, and fabric."

Ben held up his hands. "It's a *working* van. Lots of delivery guys are in and out of there." His mouth had gone dry. He wished he had a glass of water.

"Giving you the benefit of the doubt, we cross-checked some of the fingerprints. A few matched up with people you do business with. But, strangely enough, quite a few of them didn't. Those fingerprints belong to people who are on our watchlists because of their connections to insurrectionists. Some of these people have disappeared over the past few weeks." Slater leaned forward. "How do you explain that?"

Ben struggled to stay composed. "I won't try to explain it, since I don't know why those fingerprints would be there. *Except* that I occasionally loan my van to other drivers."

Slater looked at Williams again, "He's clever, isn't he?" To Ben again, he said, "You have the names of those other drivers."

"Of course." Ben's voice sounded more high-pitched than usual.

"The truth would be helpful. You Christians are big on the truth, aren't you? 'And you shall know the truth and the truth shall make you free.' That's what the Bible says, right? 'Thou shalt not lie.'"

To hear Scripture spoken so coldly by Slater made Ben's skin crawl. It was like perfume on a snake. Maybe he should cut his losses, try a different tactic. "Look, the problem is that I ... I've used my truck for some off-the-books work. Including a few ... um ... special clients."

Slater rubbed his chin and repeated mechanically, "Special clients."

"Clients who want to ship cigarettes and alcohol without paying the tariffs. A few illegal immigrants. I don't know what their religious beliefs are—or how they show up in your system ..."

Slater gasped from mock incredulity. "*You* do that? A good Christian man like you? I'm having a hard time believing it."

"You keep saying that I'm a Christian," Ben complained. "Why do you keep saying that? I'm just a guy trying to make ends meet."

"Do you see what he's doing?" Slater asked Williams.

"I see."

"What am I doing?" Ben asked.

Slater wagged a finger at him like an angry schoolteacher. "You hope that by admitting to some bootlegging that you'll sidetrack us from the more important questions. You're thinking that we won't ask you about your Christianity or the Resistance or how you transport your fellow believers. That's what you're doing, isn't it, Mr. Greene?"

"I'm trying to say that you're barking up the wrong tree," Ben said.

Slater gazed at him a moment. "Are you a strong man, Mr. Greene?"

"I beg your pardon?"

"It's one of the more fascinating things about Christianity: all the contradictions and conundrums. You know, strength concealed as weakness, weakness concealed as strength. It's maddening for those of us who like plain speaking." Slater stood up. "Are you a strong man?"

Ben tried to imagine what answer would be correct in this verbal chess game. "I suppose I'm fairly strong—physically, if that's what you're asking."

Slater shook his head. "Physical strength doesn't interest me as much as strength of will. Do you have strength of will?"

Ben gave him a blank expression. "I don't know what you're getting at."

"I'll give you an example." Slater circled the table. "If I told you that your wife was in one of the other interrogation rooms—"

Ben sat up, alarmed. "My wife?"

"Yes."

"She's not well," Ben explained. "Her health is fragile."

"Is it? Well, that will speed things up," Slater said. "You see, Agent Williams here is an expert at the art of physical persuasion. Don't let his boyish good looks fool you."

Ben shifted in his chair, his body tensing. "My wife has nothing to do with this."

"With what? The bootlegging or the transportation of Christians?"

"Anything," Ben said. "Leave her out of it."

"I'm dealing with a hypothetical situation, Mr. Greene. A little game of 'What if?' *What if* Agent Williams will get your wife to tell us what you won't."

Ben looked at Williams. Surely, he wasn't the type of man who tortured women in the line of duty. But the current regime regularly employed cruel and ruthless men. "She doesn't know anything about my work. She'd be hard-pressed to remember any of the companies I work for." Ben pleaded, "Please, leave her alone."

Slater shrugged. "*Hypothetically*, I might be lying to you. Hypothetically, it's possible that Williams has already interrogated your wife and she confessed everything: the way you've brought renegade Christians to your home, put them in the bottom of the van, transported them out of town to various points in the country, or in the mountains . . ."

He's bluffing, Ben thought. "You're trying to trick me into admitting something I haven't done."

"Haven't you?" Slater dug into his jacket pocket. "Under the circumstances, I don't think your wife would lie to us."

"You haven't talked to her," Ben said. His hands were clenching and unclenching.

Slater found whatever it was he was looking for in his jacket pocket. He placed on the table a small plastic bag. Inside was a gold chain with a small gold cross at the center. "Your wife's?"

Ben stared. It was a gift he'd given her for their first anniversary. She wore it under all her clothes. He was the only one who'd ever seen it. He began to grind his teeth, fighting back the words that wanted to come.

Slater dropped a second plastic bag. Inside was a handkerchief with a splash of red on the white fabric. "Sorry about the blood stains," Slater said.

Ben roared and lunged at Slater, pulling the chains and the table with him. Williams stepped forward, a taser in his hand. Ben was undeterred. Williams pulled the trigger. There was a crackling noise as Ben felt a blast of electricity shoot through his body, sending him sideways and down, the table tipping over him with a crash. He was dazed, but still conscious.

Slater knelt next to him. "Your wife isn't hurt, apart from the embarrassment we caused when searching her. However, I want you to understand the degree of force we'll use to get the information we want. Your wife *will* be hurt, Mr. Greene, if you don't cooperate." Slater stood up again. "The effects of the taser will wear off in a couple of minutes. I'll expect you to use that time to make a sensible decision."

Ben groaned. Even in the numbness, he felt foolish and weak. But this wasn't the kind of weakness that produced the strength of God—not the way the Bible talked about it. This weakness was very human. It was defeat. The answer to Slater's earlier question was *no, I am not a man of strong will. I thought I was, but I'm not. Pride made me think I could withstand whatever you threw at me. But . . . not my wife.* The realization gave Ben a profound feeling of loss. He wanted to weep for those he was about to betray.

CHAPTER 19

Clay stood in the kitchen of the farmhouse. He went to the coffeemaker. It was lukewarm. "Dad!" he called out, ready to complain. He listened. Silence. He knew every sound the house could make. It was the place of his birth and the place of his younger brother's birth and the place of the same brother's death ten years later from leukemia. It was the place where his mother spent the "best years of her life" until her suicide last year. It was the place where his father insisted they stay and work until they, in turn, returned to the dirt from which they'd all come.

Clay hated the place. It was an ongoing symbol of poverty and oppression. One way or another, he would escape from this mountain. And he'd long passed the point of worrying how his father would fend for himself alone. It didn't matter anymore. Let the man return to the dirt if that's what he had his heart set on. Then he realized that the refrigerator, an ancient model that normally buzzed loudly, was quiet. He opened the door. No light. He flipped a light switch nearby. Nothing. He flipped it up and down, just in case. Nothing happened. He glanced at the clock. It had stopped just a half hour ago.

He knew it wasn't a blown fuse. And he hoped that Jake had the good sense to leave town. Jake was a dead man otherwise.

He poured coffee into a mug, thinking it would be better than nothing. His mouth felt like he'd been sucking on used gym socks all night. His head throbbed.

I have to get out of here, he thought. There must be a plan, a scheme, to get off the mountain. He wasn't a particularly bright boy—he knew that—but he was pretty sure he had the minimal intelligence needed to escape. His lack of success until now didn't discourage him. Sure, a lot of schemes had come and gone over the past few years. Some faded from lack of follow-through, some from lack of spirit (back then he had his mother to think of), and some were blatant failures. It seemed unfair that determination alone wasn't enough. Circumstances kept working against him. He needed a lucky break. And money. He wouldn't survive long without money.

He gulped his coffee and spat it out into the sink. Maybe he should just have another drink from his stash in the bedroom. The "hair of the dog" and all that.

He looked out the window. A dull scene. The dull brown yard leading to the dull brown fence and the dull brown fields and barn beyond. His father stood at the fence, hunched over like the old man he was. A well-dressed stranger was there, though the clothes looked frumpy and dirty, as if the man had walked to the ranch. Clay craned his neck to check the driveway. No car.

What would a well-dressed stranger without a car be doing here? A breakdown on the road? Maybe it was the police. Jake might have reported him.

Clay's father nodded at the stranger, then gestured to him to wait. He turned and shuffled back to the house, pulling at his suspenders as he did.

The stranger leaned on the fence and looked cautiously around. He had a smug expression—the kind that well-dressed people often had. It was the kind of expression Clay wanted to punch off the man's face.

He heard his father's footsteps on the gravel just outside the door, then his two steps up, the screen-door wrenched open, and the inside door banged inward.

"What's up, Pop?" Clay asked.

His father shot him a disgusted look. "So, you're finally up." He went through to the pantry and started rummaging through the shelves.

"Who's the man?"

"Hand me that cardboard box over by the back door."

Clay obliged him. "What are you doing?"

"Not your concern." His father was putting cans and dry goods into the box.

"You're giving him our food?"

"A little. Not much."

"We don't *have* any to give away."

"I'll be the judge of that."

"Did you know the utilities are off?"

His father stopped to look directly at Clay. "I know it. What do you expect, after that stunt you pulled last night? What did you think Jake would do? Or didn't you think at all?"

"Jake?" Clay was all innocence. "What are you talking about?" *How did he find out about this stuff? Who did he talk to?*

"Never mind," his father said impatiently. He went back to stockpiling the food. "I'm sure you'll be happy when we wind up at the poor camp. It won't be long now."

You might go to the poor camp, but I never will, Clay thought. "If you're worried, why are you giving our hard-earned food away to some stranger?"

"Because, for the time being, he needs it worse than we do."

"Why doesn't he sell off that nice coat—or those fancy shoes—and buy his own food?"

"He can't."

"He's on the run, huh?"

"Just forget about it."

"Maybe we should call the police."

His father scowled. "Why? The phone won't be working anyway."

"What if he's one of those rebels?"

"Forget about it, Clay." He moved the box to the table and shuffled the contents around. "By the way, a lot of those 'rebels'—if that's what they are—are people who believe like your mother did. Do your three brain cells let you remember back that far?"

"I remember."

"I won't turn the man away empty-handed, if only for your mother's sake." His father grabbed the box and headed back across the chipped linoleum to the door. "See if the generator's working."

"You gave it away, *remember*?" Clay reminded him. "To that Catholic church up the hill."

The door slammed hard enough to rattle the windows. Clay watched his father through the torn curtains. The well-dressed man was visibly delighted with the food. Clay couldn't help but be delighted, too. There were rewards for the rebels. And, if his guess was right, the man had walked down from the Catholic church.

My lucky break, he thought. If it all worked out the way he thought it would, he could be off the mountain within the next couple of days. Maybe he'd take Bobby with him.

He spat again and pulled his coat off the hook next to the door. *Chores'll wait*, he thought. *I'm going hunting.*

CHAPTER 20

*You want to know what I think about death? I don't know. I've
been so busy trying to stay alive that I haven't really thought
about it. I just hope that when it comes for me it'll be quick.
I'm not very patient and when it's time to do something I want
to get it over with. I feel the same about death. I wouldn't
want it to drag out ... not like it did with my parents. No—
I want it done fast.*

—Peter, as quoted in
The Posthumous Papers of Samuel T. Johnson

"They were here all along," Williams whispered to Slater.
"Right under our noses."

Slater lifted the night vision binoculars to his eyes again.
They were standing under the arched brick doorway of a
closed shop not two blocks from Central. Apart from the
sounds of late-night traffic on the main road three blocks
away, all was silent. A rat, black and hunched, sniffed along
the step, looked up at the two men to see if they were of any
particular importance, then moved on without hurrying.

Williams squinted against the drizzling rain, thrown at
them in waves by the wind. The yellow glow of the streetlight
had a Dickensian look as it covered a section of driveway
leading to a large warehouse. "I expected our surveillance

cameras to see them," Williams complained. "They're *two blocks away* from our office!"

"I told you. They're roaches," Slater said. "Our surveillance cameras pick up *human beings* in this city. A pickpocket in Longmont Square and we've got him. A carjacking on 6th Street and we're there. But *roaches*—not a chance. That's why they can operate right under our noses. That's why they're probably operating right inside our building: using our phones, eating our lunches, filing our paperwork."

Williams' headset crackled softly. "Someone's coming," a voice reported. It was Wilson, their agent on the roof.

The two men retreated into the shadows of the doorway until Williams' back was pressed against the door.

Footsteps clicked on the pavement. Someone was coming down the alley, walking with a rhythm worthy of a metronome—perfectly paced and timed. "It's a policeman," Williams whispered just before the cop entered their view.

"Let's see if he notices us," Slater suggested.

The officer, dressed in standard-issue blue, strolled past without a glance at the two men. He couldn't have known that another dozen men were positioned all around the area.

"I want someone to grab him as soon as he's clear," Slater said into his headset. "Get his name and badge number."

"Any particular reason?" one of the agents asked.

"For not seeing us!" Slater snapped. "He was within five feet of two men hiding in a doorway and didn't notice."

Williams grunted. "I guess that explains how the roaches can operate two blocks from our office."

But the officer didn't follow the sidewalk to the next street. Instead, he turned down the driveway and continued to the large garage door. He glanced around quickly, then pushed a few buttons on a pad next to a smaller door. The door clicked and opened. The officer ducked in and closed the door behind him.

"He's working with them," Williams said. "Let's take them now."

Slater shook his head. "Not until they open the big door—which they will if Mr. Greene wasn't lying to us."

The mention of Ben Greene sent Williams back to the interrogation room and the memory of that big man with his walrus mustache weeping uncontrollably on the floor. It was hard to tell what affected him the most: what would happen to his wife, the thought of going to a Rehabilitation Center, or having betrayed his co-conspirators. It seemed to Williams like a waste of tears in either case since he was found hanged in his cell two hours later.

Slater asked, "What time is it?"

"Nine-thirty."

"The checkpoints will be changing their shifts now. If they're going, this is the time."

Slater's words seemed to serve as an "open sesame." The warehouse door lurched, then rose.

"Positions, everyone. When it's three-quarters up, move in," Slater whispered into his headset. "And remember: I want them alive."

The rising door revealed two delivery vans just inside, the engines running.

"Go," Slater said.

The driveway suddenly came alive with agents appearing from all directions, moving with speed and stealth, their guns poised. The reaction inside the garage was instantaneous. The van doors were thrown open as people leapt out to make a run for it—not only men, but women and children. There were more passengers than Williams expected.

"How many people can they fit in those vans?" Slater asked, surprised. He stepped out of the doorway and walked toward the scene.

The agents were efficient and quickly headed off the fugitives. A shot was fired, and a man went down hard on the floor.

"No!" Slater shouted into his headset, sprinting to the garage. "I said not to shoot!"

The uniformed policeman who'd walked past them earlier suddenly appeared from the back of the van, his hands held up. "Stop! Stop! Don't fire!"

Williams followed with his gun drawn. The garage smelled of exhaust and fuel, making Williams cough as soon as he crossed the threshold. The Christians, who were now assembled in the center of a circle of agents, were told to drop to their knees with their hands behind their heads. One of them, the man who had fallen when the shot was fired, lay whimpering off to the side.

"Is he all right?" Slater shouted.

The agent nearest to the whimperer reported that the man hadn't been shot but had fallen from the fright of the sound.

"Who fired?" Slater asked.

Reluctantly, a young agent—one of the new recruits—raised his hand. "I did, sir."

Slater marched over to him. "Why?"

"I thought I saw him draw a gun," the young agent stammered.

Slater reached down to the whimperer and grabbed his hands. He was clutching a small black Bible. Slater snatched the book away and threw it at the agent. "There's your gun," he snarled. "Thirty days' probation for disobeying orders."

The young agent's face fell. "Yes, sir."

"Empty the vans," Slater shouted to the agents. Several harnessed their guns and jumped into the storage areas. Knapsacks, bags, and boxes of food were systematically brought out. Slater watched silently. All in all, it looked like a refugee camp.

Williams scanned the group of Christians closely for any suspicious moves. He knew they were generally peaceful, but it took only one zealot to pull a knife to defend their cause. Circling them, he was struck by how ordinary they all looked—people in plain clothing who could have been out for a day of shopping. They were quite a contrast to the stark, black-dressed agents who surrounded them.

"Who's in charge of this exodus?" Slater asked.

No one responded. All eyes were fixed on the ground.

"Save yourselves a lot of pain and me a lot of trouble," Slater said impatiently.

"Who's the leader here?"

A martyred silence.

Slater pulled out his gun and carelessly waved it around a girl of five with big green eyes and a ponytail. "Do I have to ask again?"

"It's me," the man in the police uniform admitted.

"Yes, officer, of course," Slater said. "I should have figured that out for myself. Are you really a member of the force or just dressing up?"

"Dressing up."

"I can't wait to hear how you got the uniform. But right now—"

One of the agents came alongside Slater and leaned in, saying something Williams couldn't hear.

Slater's brows lifted. "Really."

Williams moved closer to his boss.

"Do you have the folder?" Slater asked Williams.

Williams nodded, reached into the inner pocket of his jacket and pulled out an electronic notepad. It was packed with information and profiles of suspected Christians. He handed it to Slater.

Slater thumbed at the screen. "Agent McKenna thinks our dress-up policeman looks familiar."

Williams glanced at the man in question. He had a narrow face with jet black hair and the stubble of a beard. Williams caught his eyes—a penetrating blue that looked as if they could see through anything.

"There." Agent McKenna pointed to the screen.

Slater looked at the screen, then down at the prisoner, and then to the screen again. "Good work, agent." Slater passed the notepad back to Williams and said to the uniformed man, "You're Brad Nichols."

Brad Nichols turned his gaze to Slater and held it there without speaking.

Slater was unaffected. "You don't have to say anything. But it is nice to meet you after all this time, *Moses*."

CHAPTER 21

The clouds never broke, so it seemed as if night had merely absorbed their gray light with its blackness, like pouring ink onto a ball of cotton. The forest took on the look of burnt matches. Ruth and Amy prepared a painfully modest meal of canned mixed vegetables and baked beans—the smallest portions possible.

The decision was made not to use the generator to run the furnace unless the temperature dropped well below freezing. The potbelly stove was brought in from Beck's room—under protest from Beck—and placed in the dining area. It gave the normally drab room a pleasant warmth.

Ruth served the food and jabbered about Peter's mother, telling stories of when they were young girls together. Peter laughed and threw in a few of his own memories. They laughed even more.

Amy was pleased to hear Peter laugh. She felt relieved, too, since she wasn't sure how Peter would behave after their talk the other night. She had rebuffed his feelings. A lot of young men wouldn't take it so well.

Ruth and Peter's conversation didn't seem to light anyone else's mood. They sat nearby, lost in their own thoughts, subdued by their own memories.

Amy expected Mr. Smith to be reserved. He sat staring at the woodstove, occasionally rubbing his clean-shaven face. The change made him all the more handsome. He could have been a movie star—one of the intense silent types that gave up no secrets willingly. His expression revealed nothing. Suddenly, he stood up, bid everyone goodnight, and slipped away to the sanctuary.

Sam was preoccupied with writing in his journal. The sound of the nib of his pen scratching against the paper weaved in and out of the hiss and crackle of the fire in the stove.

Luke sat closest to the orange glow of the stove, reading Sam's Bible. His lips moved and every now and then he would roll his eyes upward like a Shakespearean actor who'd just come across his favorite soliloquy from *Hamlet*.

Howard Beck, who normally had plenty to complain about, held his tongue, too. He didn't seem contented, just quiet. That made Amy suspicious, though she couldn't explain why. *He's up to something*, she thought.

Mary merely sat and listened with a cow-eyed look. And Tim, who normally put up a fight about bedtime, went off with his mother quietly.

Amy had watched them all, then said goodnight and walked to her room. She paused at the door and battled the conflicting emotions inside of her. Shrugging them off, she stepped inside. The room was already chilly. She'd have to sleep in her clothes. She put on a down vest and crossed her arms, hugging herself for more warmth.

Her room had once been an office that doubled up to store office supplies. She'd placed her cot between a desk and a worktable. She paced for a moment—only a handful of steps in any direction. Her eyes went up to a poster on the wall of a pair of hands clasped together in prayer. At the bottom was a Bible quote: "Pray without ceasing." Someone in the mob had taken a knife to the paper, a crosshatch of slashes. But the razor-thin cuts hardly marred the message.

Amy knelt next to her cot. *Oh, God . . .* No other words followed, so she prayed the Lord's Prayer. As soon as she finished, she stood up and paced again. She searched her memory for a psalm or an encouraging verse, something that would clear her mind so she could sleep. She sat on the edge of her cot, ran her fingers through her hair, then put her face in her hands.

Suddenly, she looked up as if remembering a forgotten duty. Should she check to make sure Mr. Smith was comfortable? Did he have everything he needed for the night?

Ruth had probably asked already. But what if she hadn't? It wouldn't hurt to make sure. She stood up and moved slowly to the door, hesitating with her hand on the doorknob.

She knew it was nonsense. She wanted to talk to him. Would that be so wrong?

In the hallway again, she made her way carefully back to the sanctuary. She paused before reaching the kitchen doorway. The heat from the stove radiated out to her. Peter said something that made Ruth laugh. She peeked around the corner at them. Both were at the sink with their backs to her. Ruth was washing the dishes, and Peter was drying. It could have been a normal family moment in a normal family kitchen.

Amy crept past, feeling foolish—even childish—for sneaking around. One of the two doors was open. She saw Smith standing near Sam's table. He was talking quietly with Luke. It, too, looked surprisingly normal. A real conversation with eye contact and normal tones of voices. She had never seen Luke do that with anyone.

Amy heard Smith say, "So you don't remember?"

Luke shook his head firmly. "My memory isn't what it once was. The Rehabilitation Center is a merciful blur now."

Smith nodded, then he saw Amy. "Is something wrong?"

Luke looked over at Amy and stood up. "Hello. Is it time for the night watch?"

"No. I ... uh ..." She spied a water pitcher on Sam's table and went to it as if it was her reason for being there. "I was checking to see if there is anything you needed. Fresh water? Ruth said you need to rehydrate. Drink a lot of liquids. I brought a couple of buckets up from the stream. I think it tastes better than the water through the tap."

"The pitcher is full," Smith told her. "I filled it up earlier. I can do that, you know. I don't need room service."

"God keep us safe this night." Luke held his arms up like a benediction as he walked out.

Smith watched him go, then turned to Amy. "Do you know anything about him?"

"Not much," Amy replied. "He was declared mentally insane because he was a preacher. They gave him shock treatments until he ... well, you see how he is. Though Sam says he's improving."

"I wouldn't be that optimistic."

They stood wordless for a moment and Amy realized she was still standing there with the pitcher in her hands. "You're right. It's full." She sat it back down on the table.

Another pause.

"Is it snowing yet?" she asked.

He looked at the boarded-up windows. "Hard to tell from here."

"When I was little, I loved it when it snowed. I always felt *alive*." She avoided his gaze and picked up the pitcher again, realized it was still full and put it down. "Mr. Smith, I'm glad you're here."

Smith cocked an eyebrow. "Are you?"

"You have given me—all of us—a new sense of hope." She blushed and wondered why she felt like she was back in high school.

"I don't know why," he said. "I didn't bring any hope with me. I forgot to pack it. That's always the way, isn't it? You take a long trip and always forget something important." He smiled, a dimple forming just to the right of his mouth.

She was caught off-guard. It was the first time she'd seen anything other than a stern expression from him—and it sounded like he'd even made a joke. Her heart spun as if she'd been given a very special and secret honor.

It gave her confidence to continue. "You're such a mystery, though. No one knows what to make of you. They're afraid to ask you any specific questions, and I've noticed the way you evade the ones they *do* ask."

"I've never thought of myself as mysterious." He kept his gaze on her. "Do *you* think I'm mysterious?"

She hoped that his prolonged look meant something. "There's a lot you're not telling us. We just can't figure out what it can be."

He kept his eyes on her and a shadow seemed to cross over them. Something had changed. "Sometimes it's better not to figure everything out. Dig too much and you'll find something you'll wish you didn't know."

"Cryptic," she said. "See? You're being mysterious again." She didn't want to lose the moment.

"I've told you everything you need to know."

A stiff silence returned, but she was so convinced that they were establishing some kind of bond that she pressed on.

"Peter is so excited about you being part of the Resistance. He wants to join." Why was she talking about Peter?

"There isn't anything to join." He turned away from her and knelt next to his knapsack. He began to sort through its contents as if he'd lost something.

She wondered if this was his way of telling her to leave. She didn't feel like she could. "They killed his parents, you know. Peter's, I mean."

"I'm sorry."

Amy felt a wave of embarrassment. "I know. It has become a cliché. We'd all sound like an obituary page if ... well, we've all lost loved ones. We've all heard the knock on the door in the middle of the night and the torture of not knowing what happened to whoever they've taken— whether they're dead or alive and suffering in some rotten cell or work camp." The words came in a torrent, along with the tears. She felt like a small boat in a gale and clung to the table for support.

Smith was on his feet. He took one step toward her, then stopped. "Amy, I don't know what to say ..."

If he had taken her in his arms to comfort her, she might not have felt so bad. But he had stopped, and she stood alone with her raw emotion. "I'm sorry. I'm being childish."

"There's nothing childish about any of this," he said.

She wiped her eyes with the back of her hand. "All I wanted to say was that Peter wants to join the fight. I guess what moves me to tears moves him to action."

"There's no fight," Smith stated. He returned to his knapsack and whatever it was he hoped to accomplish there. "We're—we *were* trying to help our brothers and sisters in Christ. That's all."

"But what about Moses and Elijah—the miracles they've performed? I heard about the time they struck an entire regiment *blind* while they—"

"You can't believe everything you hear."

"Then what can I believe?"

Smith shrugged. "When you find an answer, let me know."

This stung Amy. She wondered where the conversation had gone wrong. Bewildered by his cynicism, she asked, "I don't understand."

"I can't help you," he said, his body stiffening. He didn't look at her. "Are we through with this conversation or are you assigned to guard me for the night?"

She felt as if someone had injected ice-water into her veins. She stammered, "I didn't mean to ... I mean, I didn't come here to ... Obviously I made a mistake."

From his crouched position next to the knapsack, he turned his head to her. "Sometimes I think we all made a mistake."

She didn't know what he meant by his remark. She didn't stay to find out. She pushed herself from the table and strode out of the sanctuary.

———————————◆———————————

Sam was awake, lying on his makeshift bed and thinking about everything that was happening outside of his room.

He had seen Luke go into the sanctuary after Smith had said goodnight. That wasn't a big worry; he doubted that the conversation consisted of anything more than Luke's joy over having "healed" Smith. What was on his mind now was Amy. She'd been acting strange since Smith arrived. Was she overcome with hope? Was it a schoolgirl crush on a mysterious stranger everyone had hoped would rescue them? He hoped it was nothing like that. And yet, he knew she had slipped into the sanctuary to talk to him.

He lay with his arm tucked behind his head. A noise from the hallway jolted him. He realized then that he'd dozed off—and his arm had fallen asleep with him. Pins and needles worked their way up to his elbow as he gingerly slipped his legs off the sofa and crept to the door. He heard what sounded like a broom against cement, then the soft padding of footsteps toward the kitchen. Beck wouldn't be trying to sneak a midnight snack, would he? Maybe. But those weren't Beck's footsteps. They were unfamiliar.

He opened the door and was grateful the hinges were quiet. A dark figure had just slipped into the kitchen. Sam quickly followed and, fumbling in his pocket for a match, had just reached the doorway as the figure was about to open the back door.

"Who's there?" Sam asked.

The figure stopped. "It's me. Smith."

A packet of matches in hand, Sam lit one and held it up. Smith was standing by the door with his coat on and his knapsack slung over his shoulder. Sam moved to the lamp on the table and lit it. "Was it something we said?" he asked.

"It's better this way." Smith didn't move, his hand on the doorknob.

"Better for whom?" Sam asked. "Everyone will be disappointed. They thought—*I* thought you'd help us get out of here."

Smith frowned, the creases on his brow made more intense by the lamplight. "I can't help what they or you thought. You don't know anything about me or what I've been through."

"You can tell me now," Sam offered. "It might help me to explain to the others why you've abandoned us."

"Is that what I'm doing?"

"Yes."

"I'm not responsible for any of you," he stated. "If your people want a leader, why don't *you* lead them?"

"I wouldn't know where to take them."

"Pick a hole, any hole. The mountain is full of places to hide."

"You've seen us. We'd never survive."

"You won't survive with me." Smith gave him a harsh look. "I'm a sure way to die. Ask anyone who has trusted me. For the last three years—" He stopped himself mid-sentence, shook his head, then continued. "I'll give you this advice: Slater's a bloodhound. It's just a matter of time before he and his men will find this place. Get out before you're trapped by the snow."

"To where?"

"I left you a map on your table," Smith told him. "Hiking trails and contact points. It's the map your contact would have used. But it's risky. The trails could be watched. The contacts might be compromised. It's the best I can do."

"That's something, I guess." Sam replied, watching helplessly as Smith pulled at the door. "Why are you running, Mr. Smith?"

Smith turned to him. "We're all running."

"Not like you," Sam countered. "*We're* running from the police. You seem to be running from something else."

Smith tugged at the knapsack on his shoulders. "I'm just trying to escape."

"So was Jonah." His tone was caustic. "I just hope this mountain doesn't become the belly of the whale."

Smith gazed at him. Then he opened the door fully to a biting wind and seemed to launch himself into it. The door closed with a bang.

"He's gone?" Ruth asked from the hall.

"Yeah, he's gone."

"You said he would leave. How did you know?"

"Because it's what I would have done," Sam replied.

CHAPTER 22

I've been thinking a lot about death lately. I don't know why except that I've been thinking about my family. I know that death is the only way I'll get to see them again. I hope it's true. They all knew Jesus and loved Him very much. So, I picture that one day we'll have this great reunion in heaven where we'll sit down at a gigantic picnic table and eat potato salad and barbecue and hot dogs and … angel food cake, I guess. And since we'll be in heavenly bodies, we can eat all we want and not have to worry about calories.

—Amy, as quoted in
The Posthumous Papers of Samuel T. Johnson

Sam wasn't so new to Christianity that the ironies of Christian behavior—his own in particular—hadn't escaped him. After Smith left, he went back to his room and prowled anxiously. He read a few psalms in his mother's Bible. Then he turned to the Roman Missal and sought out prayers there. It was a vigil unlike anything he'd experienced before. He wondered why it took a crisis like this to drive him to his knees. Why did it take someone like Smith to show him how fragile his faith really was? He'd put an unreasonable amount of trust in Smith. He realized now that he was so hungry, so desperate for someone else to take on the burden of responsibility for the group that he was willing to entrust their lives to a stranger.

One thing he believed: Smith was right. They needed to move on *quickly*.

As dawn crept over the mountains, Sam pored over the map Smith had left. The map itself was dated from twenty years ago, but the red markings were new. "Stations" the red marks were called. The route was a combination of trails and back roads. He wondered how their contact had planned to transport them. By foot alone? That would have been impossible. It was hundreds of miles to the border. Maybe they planned to use a network involving cars and trucks, too?

Without knowing any of the answers, Sam could only guess that it would take them weeks to reach the border. How could they possibly survive? And once they arrived, what would they encounter: armed guards, a giant wall, a trap?

God knows, Sam told himself. *We must take it one step at a time, one station at a time.*

Assembled in the kitchen for their morning meeting, Sam told his fellow fugitives that Smith had left them. Once that shock had subsided, he told them about Smith's map and what he had advised them to do.

"Why should we listen to anything that man had to say?" Amy said scornfully. "He was unreliable and—"

"An ingrate," Beck snapped. "I *told* you we should have left him in the woods."

Ruth turned on him. "That's not helpful now, Mr. Beck."

Mary, ignoring the bickering, asked Sam what he thought they should do.

"We pack whatever provisions we can carry and make our way to the first station on the map. It's a day's walk."

Peter agreed enthusiastically. Amy conceded that it was their only option. Ruth agreed.

"The Lord will go before us into parts unknown," Luke declared. "And where He is taking us will require neither staff nor sandals."

"I take that as a yes," Sam said.

It was then that Sam realized Timothy wasn't with Mary. "Where's Tim?"

"He was sick all night."

"With what?"

"An upset stomach. He was vomiting—a lot. I don't know what brought it on. He's only been here with us." She wrung her hands. "Sam, I'm sorry. I don't think he can travel. Not today."

"What is it?" Ruth asked. "A flu bug?"

"I wish I knew. I've never seen him so ill." Mary turned to Sam. "When do you want to leave?"

"As soon as possible. We had a dusting of snow overnight. I'm pretty sure a storm is coming, maybe from the south. I hope to get ahead of it."

"Seems like I had that idea, too," Beck grumbled, then threw his hands in the air. "The whole plan is ridiculous. You want us to pack everything up and follow you into the woods—in the hope that Smith's map is any good?"

"You could stay behind, if you want," Peter offered.

Beck looked indignant. "You'd like that, wouldn't you? You'd *all* like that—to leave me behind to starve."

"As if you'd let yourself starve," Peter said.

Beck turned on him. "I suppose you must be feeling foolish now that your hero has walked out on us."

"*Children*," Sam interrupted, "we don't have time for this."

Beck stood up, knocking his chair over behind him. "*I* don't have time for this." He marched out, returning a few moments later, wearing his coat. He headed for the door.

"*Wait*, Howard," Sam said. "Where are you going?"

Beck ignored him and continued to the front door, slamming it behind him as he left.

Peter shook his head. "He's up to something. He's been taking long walks and ... I don't trust him."

"Go after him," Sam responded. "Apologize and bring him back."

"*Apologize?*"

Ruth put a hand on her nephew's arm. "Peter, *please*."

Peter stood up reluctantly, a chastised schoolboy being sent to the corner. He marched out.

Sam looked at the faces of the remaining fugitives, noting the look of anxiety on each one. "Let's start packing. We need to be ready as soon as everyone is ready to travel."

◆

Mary stepped quietly into her room. She had covered the single window with a heavy blanket and had to squint into the dim light. The shapeless bundle on the cot didn't stir.

My baby, she thought and held back a sob. She hadn't told Sam how sick Timothy really was. She was afraid. She knew they considered her a compulsive worrier, a fragile woman who might collapse into fits of tears at any moment. It's the way she'd been treated her entire life. As a child she was the frail and sickly one in her family. She had missed a lot of school, missed friends, missed everything a normal child experienced, usually from a cold, a flu, pneumonia, infections ... It set her apart, alienated her from the rest of the world. The ravages of adolescence were even worse.

"Tim? Sweetheart?" she moved to him, but the unmistakable smell of stale vomit held her back. She put her hand to her nose and went over to the wall. A bucket sat beneath the fractured blackboard. She took it to the door and sat it out in the hall. She'd have to give it a good scrub outside.

Turning to the room, her eye went to torn drawings hanging from a chipped corkboard. They were of Jesus on the Sea of Galilee, Jesus feeding the five thousand, Jesus teaching in the Temple, Jesus hugging a group of small children. These were the remnants of the Sunday School class once held in the room.

"Tim, it snowed last night. Did you know that?" She put on the sing-songy voice she often used with him when she was deeply worried. Sometimes she thought it had the same effect as singing "Mary Had a Little Lamb." The foul smell came at her again. She would have to change the sheets.

Tim groaned from somewhere under the blankets.

"How are you feeling?" She knelt next to him. At certain angles, he was the image of Robert, his father, back when they first met in high school. What a surprise Robert had turned out to be. She had given up on the idea of marrying, resigned herself to a life without companionship. When Robert first asked her out, she thought it was a cruel joke. He was the quarterback of the football team, after all. But her pride was not so strong—or weak—that she refused. She held onto the belief that the rumors about him being a Christian were true. A Christian wouldn't have asked her out as a joke.

That's what made Robert so exceptional. Before it was outlawed, Christianity had become the domain of people like her: misfits, the socially stunted, the ones with nowhere else to go for friendship. It was a refuge, a crutch. And people like Robert didn't need it because they had everything else.

The date turned out to be a social program at his church. He introduced her around as she smiled crookedly and tugged nervously at her stringy brown hair. That night every awkward movement, every misplaced comment, every spot and blemish seemed magnified a hundred times for her. She spilled her punch. She fell off her chair. At the end of the night, she ran to her front door tearful and humiliated, sure that the punchline to the joke was coming. He patiently followed her, not for a goodnight kiss, but to ask her out again. She couldn't find the words to reply and had nearly slammed the door in his face. Once inside the safety of her front hall, she stood in the half-light and cried for an hour.

More dates followed that weren't as awkward. Then came their prom. Then a summer missionary program together. As they continued into college, Mary slowly transformed from the proverbial ugly duckling into the beautiful swan. He cherished her. She worshipped him.

Robert asked her to marry him two years into college. He studied law while she dropped out to work, be a wife and, within a year, become a mother. The family seemed so complete, so perfect. He was the hardworking student, faithful husband, and dedicated father. She was the doting wife. He passed the bar with honors. She tried to give him a home of which he could be proud.

She remembered those days now like a dream that had never happened. Timothy was her only reminder of their reality, bringing with him a dull ache that sometimes made it hard for her to look at him. Sometimes the loss of happiness was too much for her to bear.

She got pregnant again a couple of years later but miscarried. That was the beginning of the nightmare, she reflected. It was a foreshadowing: the first crack in a perfect surface. Though she had recovered sufficiently, the world had become damaged in other, more fatal ways. The revolution came without a fight; then the persecution, which Robert battled with all his legal prowess; then the arrest—

Mary clenched her eyes shut. She'd drawn a mental line in the sand—and this was it. Across that line were the details and the pain of absolute desolation. Her reason to live had been taken from her. She was a beaten swan turned once again into an ugly duckling. Robert was gone and had left her with a God whom, without her husband, she didn't recognize.

That's why she seemed so frail. Rebuilding her life—her faith—took more out of her than she dared to think about. But she could be strong again, she believed. She had to be. For Timothy. How else could she have survived the horror of her husband's murder? When she was at the very brink of madness, she clung to her wits for her son's sake. He was her link to reality.

Sometimes, in the deepest part of her heart, she worried that she had replaced the god of Robert with the god of her son. Surely the real God understood. In the rebuilding of her faith, the God she hoped to know better *had* to understand. It was part of an unspoken deal.

Mary pushed back the stiff lock of hair on her son's forehead and felt for a fever. He was cool. It perplexed her, and she went through her mental checklists of his symptoms: no fever, stomach cramps in the night, vomiting but no diarrhea, lethargy.

"Guess what, darling? As soon as you feel better, we're going to take a long walk. Would you like to take a long walk and leave this place?"

"Are we leaving?" he asked weakly without opening his eyes.

In the dim light, she could see how pale he was. She lifted the blankets to tuck them under his chin. The smell assaulted her. "Tim?" She tossed the covers aside.

He opened his eyes lazily. "What's wrong?"

"You had an accident in your bed." She pulled him off the cot and tried to help him to stand up. His legs gave way. "Put your arms around my neck," she said, putting his arms on her shoulders. They slid off. "Please try, Timothy. Everyone's going to be angry with us if we don't get you better. They want to leave."

"Mom, can I bring Joshua with us?" he asked. His voice came in dry, rasping sounds. "I don't think he'll—" He suddenly coughed, then fell back, gasping for air.

Mary screamed.

Standing in the center of the sanctuary, Sam looked down at his solitary knapsack on the floor. So far, he was the only one who'd packed for their escape. Peter and Beck were still gone, and he wondered why it would take so long for them to return. Something was wrong, to be sure. He didn't have the inclination to guess what it was. One crisis was enough.

Ruth and Amy were helping Mary with poor Tim.

"What about you?" Sam had asked Luke in the hall.

"We bring nothing into the world, and we take nothing with us when we go," Luke announced. He strolled away, his hands clasped behind his back and an expression of complete serenity.

Sam mused grimly that circumstances seemed to be conspiring to keep them at the church. He heard footsteps in the hall and looked up hopefully. Ruth walked in with a dour expression.

"How is he?" Sam asked.

"Not well," Ruth replied softly. "Mary's almost hysterical. Amy's with them now. I can't figure it out. He's having trouble breathing and has no strength at all. His muscles are rigid and his stomach is distended. He can't swallow and he says his vision is blurry."

"A virus?"

"I don't know."

"Could it be rabies?" Sam asked. "He plays with that chipmunk ... I'll look around some of the places Tim likes to play. Maybe I'll find something that'll give us a clue."

Ruth rested her hand on Sam's arm. Her expression asked him the question her lips wouldn't form.

"If we have to take him to a doctor in town, then that's what we'll do. Pray that we don't." Sam wished he hadn't spoken the words out loud. He feared they might become prophetic.

Ruth sighed. "I'll go pack."

After a comprehensive search of the main floor of the church, Sam ventured out into the snow. It fell feather-like and eased his mind. It was too pretty to pose a substantial threat. He paced around the church grounds with his head down and eyes moving, like a man who'd lost a valuable heirloom. He skirted around the areas he'd seen Tim playing, hoping to find something that would give him a clue to Tim's illness.

The wind suddenly kicked up and sent a wet chill through Sam's frame. He made a hasty retreat into the church. Women's voices echoed somewhere down the hall. He searched the sanctuary and peeked into the various rooms. There weren't many places Tim could play without being seen. He spotted the door to the cellar and remembered that Tim had gone there at least once that he knew of. It was forbidden after that, but that might not have been enough to thwart the boy.

Lighting one of the lamps, Sam descended the stairs. The wooden steps groaned and creaked. Sam could understand how the clutter of boxes and shelves of worthless odds and ends might be fascinating to a boy like Tim. Sticks could become swords and boxes could turn into pirate treasure. For a moment, Sam envied Tim his youth, wishing for a renewed sense of carefree wonder and excitement about the world: a belief in miracles.

He lifted the lamp higher and continued on. Something skittered off to his right—maybe field mice, maybe even the chipmunk.

Over his head, he heard muffled voices through the ceiling. One was the high, shrill voice of Mary, speaking in a rapid flow of words that ran close to hysteria. Ruth and Amy were speaking in soothing tones.

Sam reached the bottom of the stairs and remembered his visit to the basement the night they had arrived. *So long ago*, he thought. But what a relief to have shelter and running water and electricity. Looking back, he felt blessed. Looking forward, he felt cursed. They had to leave but he didn't know what awaited them. They needed food but he didn't know where to get any. They needed help but he didn't know where to find it.

He felt a frustration that edged a deep anger. Why did he find himself in charge? Who put this responsibility on his shoulders?

He slumped down onto the bottom step and felt like St. Peter, who had dared to step out on the storm-tossed sea with Jesus but became frightened by the waves. There was nowhere to go but down.

"Lord, save me," he whispered.

He stood and made his way through the cellar—looking left and right at the various shelves and boxes. Something scurried just out of the corner of his eyes. He craned his neck to look. Maybe the chipmunk would guide him to the place Tim had played.

His gaze went to a stack of cardboard boxes. He was sure they were placed differently than he remembered. They now looked like they'd been squared off to form a kind of wall— maybe a kid's attempt to create a fort. Sam peered over the boxes. A blanket was there, with a few coloring books and crayons. The light of his lamp reflected off something shiny. It was a spoon. And then he saw a can next to it.

CHAPTER 23

Death? I don't think I know what that is.

—Timothy, as quoted in
The Posthumous Papers of Samuel T. Johnson

"What's going on in here?" Amy asked urgently as she rushed into the sanctuary. She had been in with Ruth and Mary tending to Timothy when she heard doors slam and Peter shouting. Fearful that Timothy might awaken, she ran to investigate.

Peter gave Beck a hard push toward Sam's table. Amy had never seen Peter so red-faced and highly strung.

"Peter, what's going on?" Amy asked.

"Where's Sam?" Peter snapped.

"I don't know—around somewhere—why?"

"Find him," Peter commanded, then turned on Beck. "How many times did you go there?"

Beck looked at his fingernails. "I don't have to answer your questions."

Peter moved toward Beck like a lion about to pounce. *"How many times?"*

Beck stepped back, then bumped into a chair and sat down. "A couple of times. I don't know. I didn't keep count."

"Peter, what's wrong with you?" Amy demanded. "What happened?"

183

Peter looked at her as if she were a stranger asking stupid questions at a road accident.

"I discovered our good friend Mr. Beck making a deal with a farmer a couple of miles from here," Peter told her.

Amy was dumbfounded. She spun to Beck. "Is that true?"

Beck looked at her impatiently. "We were running out of food. I had to take a chance. Getting caught has to be better than starving."

"After all we've been through—" Peter began, then stopped, speechless in his anger. In two quick steps he had Beck by the lapels and yanked him to his feet. "Do you have any idea what they'll do if they catch us? Do you? Torture, death!"

"Peter!" Amy cried. "Let go of him!"

Peter pushed Beck, who staggered like a drunken man and crashed against the chair. He grabbed the table to keep from falling.

"Does the farmer know where you came from?" Amy asked him.

"No," Beck gasped.

"You told him we're here, didn't you?" Peter asked.

Beck looked away.

Peter moved toward him again, his fists raised. "*Didn't you!*"

"Yes! It was the only way I could get more food."

"*More* food?" Amy asked.

"I told him how many of us there were so he'd give me more food to bring back."

Amy was puzzled. "But you haven't brought any food back here for us."

Amy looked at Peter, then glared at Beck. "You kept it for yourself? What kind of a man are you?"

"You risked *our* lives to fill *your* stomach," Peter said.

"You don't understand." Beck's voice took on a childish whine. "I don't want to be a martyr. I don't believe in all that hogwash about being privileged to suffer for my faith. I'm afraid of pain ... of death. I want to survive. I don't even know what I'm doing here."

"You're pathetic," Peter snarled. Then his eyes darted to the doorway. "Sam—"

Whatever Peter was about to say was cut short. Amy turned, startled by Sam's appearance. His face was marred with soot and dirt, giving him the look of a coal miner just coming from a shift. His eyes were swollen and red. In his hands he held an empty can and what looked to Amy like Tim's Swiss Army knife.

"Sam, what's wrong?" Amy asked.

Sam shook his head. "I don't know what we're going to do."

"Do?" Amy asked. "Do about what?"

Sam wasn't listening. "I've been surrounded by books all my life. Academics is what I know. I've tried to base all my decisions on good sense. I've tried my best. But everything we've been through goes beyond anything I know how to do. It has been difficult up until now. But *this*—" He held up the can. "This is beyond me."

"Sam, what are you talking about?" Peter asked, alarmed.

"I found this in the cellar." He sounded anguished. "The boy ate what was in this can—in a lot of cans. God knows how long he's been doing it. His symptoms ... I know what they are now ..."

They waited, a sense of doom moving across them like the shadow of a fast eclipse.

Sam looked at them helplessly. "He has botulism."

Chapter 24

"Mary ..." Ruth knocked softly on the door. She didn't hear an answer. She slowly opened the door. Enough light squeezed through the coverings on the room's single window that everything looked covered in gauze.

Mary knelt next to her son, keeping vigil.

Ruth whispered, "Mary."

"He looks so fragile," Mary said as she lightly touched his hair. "I keep waiting for him to open his eyes and say 'boo' like he sometimes does when he wants to scare me. He thinks scaring me is so funny. But you're not trying to scare me now, are you, Tim?" She caressed his face and sobbed. "He's breathing easier."

Ruth touched her shoulder. "Come out to the hall, Mary."

Mary shrugged her hand away. "I've tried and I've tried but I can't understand why God is putting us through this nightmare. He's my son, Ruth. He's all I have." She drew her hands together and knotted her fingers. "Hard as it is, I can accept God's will in the world, in our society, but not with my son. Not him."

Ruth waited. The words she wanted to say wouldn't form. Peter and Sam were going to carry Tim to the town doctor in the tiny hope that it would save the boy's life. There was nothing else for them to do. A killer had been let loose inside Tim's body and no one there could stop it.

Mary clutched Ruth's hand. "Pray with me, Ruth."

"Mary—"

"No, don't say anything. We must pray. God must be merciful. If He loves me, He'll make my son well again."

Ruth held her breath. "No, Mary, please don't use Tim as a test of God's love."

"He's using Tim to test *my* love, isn't He?"

Ruth was speechless. Now was not the time for this kind of discussion. "God sees and does things so much differently than we do."

"Let's pray, Ruth."

"We will pray, Mary, but there's something I have to tell you."

Mary looked at her with shadowed, suspicious eyes.

How much more can she take? Ruth wondered. *How much more can any of us take?* Ruth knelt next to her. "Mary, how would you like to take your son away from all of this? How would you like for him to escape now?"

"Why are you asking me a question like that?"

"If you could spare him from all the violence and suffering we might face ahead, wouldn't you?"

"Yes! Of course, I would! But why are you asking me that? What's wrong, Ruth? What's wrong with Tim? You're not telling me something."

"Sam and Peter are going to take Tim to a doctor."

"A doctor in the town? Is it that serious?"

"Yes."

"But they'll be caught—we all will. We can't take him to the town. The police will take him away from me!"

"You may lose him anyway, Mary."

"Why?"

Ruth hesitated, her determination draining. She spoke before it all but vanished. "He has botulism."

Mary's face was blank. "Botulism?"

"Tim opened some of the cans in the cellar. Green beans, beef stew ... He ate them. He must have been doing it for a while."

"What does that mean?"

"If we don't take him to a doctor right away, he'll—" Ruth stopped and rephrased her thought. "The Lord will take him home, Mary."

Mary's eyes widened, her face an expression of total horror. "No! God wouldn't take my baby away from me. He's all I have! You're wrong!" She put her arms over Tim. "God's not going to take him away from me!"

Sam and Peter slipped into the room and looked apologetically at the two women.

"Mary ...," Ruth said, signaling with her eyes her need for help. "We have to take him."

She held fast to her son. "No, I won't listen to you! I won't! You have no faith. If we pray, Timothy will get better. You'll see!"

It was an awful moment for Ruth, one she would never forget. She grabbed Mary's arms as Peter and Sam came forward. They struggled to pull Mary's hands from Tim's blankets.

"No!" she growled, fighting them. "He'll be all right. You'll see. We don't have to take him anywhere!" She put up a fight, lashing out wildly. Ruth locked her arms around Mary's arms and pulled her back.

"Mary, please," Ruth gasped. The effort knocked them both off balance and threw them both backward. Mary kicked out, catching the side of the cot with her foot and toppling it over. Tim spilled out onto the floor.

"Timothy!" Mary screamed when she realized what she'd done. She broke free from Ruth, scrambling on all fours to get to him. Sam and Peter dropped to their knees next to the boy to gather him up.

"Oh, God ...," Peter said.

Ruth saw Tim's face. His eyes were open and unseeing.

"Timothy!" Mary cried.

Sam dropped back on the floor, shuffling backward.

"Is he ...?" Ruth asked breathlessly.

Sam nodded and buried his face in his hands.

Mary wailed her son's name again and again as she pulled his lifeless body into her arms.

CHAPTER 25

Why in the world are you asking me about death? I'd rather not think about it. No, I don't want to think about it at all.

—Mary, as quoted in
The Posthumous Papers of Samuel T. Johnson

Mary wept over her son. Ruth and Amy gathered around her, praying, and struggling to find some semblance of comfort to offer her. It may have been sheer exhaustion that finally allowed her to let him go. She kissed him, then gave him up.

"Mary, I'm sorry." Sam's voice trembled as he lifted the boy and laid him on the cot. "We'll bury him now."

"Now?" she asked.

"Today's nearly gone, and the snow is falling heavily." Sam lifted a blanket and began to tuck it around the body.

"No! Don't put the blanket over his face!" Mary shouted. "He's afraid of the dark."

Peter stepped forward. "I'm going to take care of him, Mary. Will you give me the honor?"

Mary looked solemnly at Peter and moved her head in a barely perceptible nod. "You loved him, Peter. You understand."

"I do. I'll take care of him." Peter carefully wrapped the child in the blanket.

Sam watched him and wondered why it always seemed that the children were the first to suffer in times like these.

"I'll come with you," Sam offered.

"No, I want to do this alone," Peter said softly. "Maybe you should have some kind of service while I'm gone."

Sam agreed.

Peter carried Tim out of the room. Mary collapsed into Ruth's arms, wailing from her grief.

Peter carried Tim to the sanctuary where he put the body down long enough to get dressed for the cold afternoon. He was aware of Beck standing off to the side, watching silently.

The sky was a sheet of gray, with a sliver of crimson near the treetops to the west. There was an inch of snow on the ground. He walked to the graveyard and stopped at the edge of the headstones. He put the child down and sprinted off to grab a shovel by the lean-to shed next to the church wall. Digging would be hard, but he was determined to do it.

When he returned, Luke was leaning over Tim.

"What are you doing?" Peter asked. "Praying for healing? Will God bring him back to life? Is that what you're doing?"

"He is alive, but in a different place now." Luke put his hand on Peter's shoulder and looked deeply into his eyes. "You understand, don't you? We have been praying for help and God in His wisdom has answered that prayer for Tim."

The statement was so simple and so coherent that Peter nearly forgot that he was talking to a man who was supposed to be mentally deficient.

"Time is so very short," Luke said. "Short for life, short for love, and suddenly time is gone—but the end of time is not the end of us. Remember: it isn't the end."

Suddenly he turned his head as if something caught his eye. Peter waited, thinking he might say more. He didn't. He merely stared vacantly as if the meter had suddenly run out on whatever coin had given him this moment of lucidity.

Peter zipped up his coat, grabbed the shovel, and gazed down at the small body. He lay like an unkept promise. What was left for them? They could leave now, but could they ever really escape?

Peter patted the last shovelful of dirt onto the grave. *This is only an empty shell,* he reminded himself, *a hollow vessel.*

Maybe Luke was right. God had provided Tim with the best possible escape.

He stood up straight, every muscle in his body aching from working the hard, frozen earth. He was aware of being watched by the stone angels with chipped wings among the weather-beaten crosses and the moss-covered headstones. There were vases, too, now empty, as if ghosts had grabbed the flowers and run away with them.

"God, bless Tim and help us now." He paused, then said, "Hail Mary, full of grace, the Lord is with thee. Blessed are thou amongst women and blessed be the fruit of thy womb, Jesus. Holy Mary, Mother of God, pray for us sinners now and in the hour of our death. Amen."

Peter performed the Sign of the Cross and stepped back from the bald patch of earth. The snow lighted on him like heavy tufts of cotton—white tears from the eyes of God, falling quickly now. The wind rustled through the trees and somewhere there came a mournful howl. For a moment, he thought he heard the sounds of an engine, but dismissed it.

With a final glance down at the grave, he slowly turned and made his way back to the church. Sam would want to leave as soon as he they could. Peter was ready. The church now had the memory and smell of Tim's death. How were they expected to bear that? How was Mary supposed to endure it? They had to leave now for whatever waited ahead.

He blinked against the snow and looked ahead to the church. He stopped, stunned. His eyes must be playing tricks on him. Then he threw himself behind one of the granite monuments. His mind raced.

A dirt-covered Jeep was parked next to the door. Two men with rifles were climbing out.

CHAPTER 26

Williams was having a hard time concentrating, which wasn't normally a problem. His mind, usually a reliable machine, was now thrown off its calibrations. Moses—real name Brad Nichols—had proven to be a difficult interrogation. Reasonable persuasion did not affect him, which Williams expected. That was the normal first step. The second step of mind games, twisting the reality Moses had embraced, did not wear him down. The third step was old-fashioned pain applied through the latest technological methods. This was where Williams had the highest expectations. He was disappointed. The prisoner screamed as most men did but wouldn't yield any helpful information. When it got to be too much, Moses resorted to phrases from Scripture. "The Lord is my light and my salvation; whom shall I fear? The Lord is the strength of my life; of whom shall I be afraid?" They'd been at it for six hours and now Williams was losing his patience—the very thing he couldn't afford to do. To lose one's patience meant that one was becoming emotionally involved. Emotions were a no-go area for well-trained interrogators. It meant that control had been lost and might give the prisoner the upper hand.

They would normally move the prisoner to a cell and put him through intensive forms of deprivation: no sleep, no food, no silence—a bombardment of the worst kinds of noise. But they didn't have time for that.

"Do you think man is basically good or evil?" Moses asked Williams, his voice hoarse, his wan face bruised. He dripped sweat and blood. The room smelled of it: flesh and blood and all its in-betweens.

"I ask the questions here," Williams said as he washed his hands in the basin on the far wall of the interrogation room.

"Of course," Moses croaked. "You're not supposed to talk to me. Talking would make me human to you. If you remember that I'm a human, you wouldn't do this. Not without severing yourself from your own humanity."

"You're a talking roach," Williams replied, drying his hands and ambling over to a control panel. He casually touched a button on a pad. It sent a signal through the wires to an electrode they had drilled into the man's front tooth.

Moses cried out long and hard.

"Like I said, *I* will ask the questions," Williams reminded him.

Moses slumped. "The Lord is my fortress … my help … my rock …"

Williams rounded the heavy wooden chair and tugged at the straps holding Moses in place. "I want the details of your transportation system."

"For God so loved the world that He gave His only begotten Son—"

"We need names of your drivers, the kinds of trucks they drive."

"—that whosoever will believe in Him may not perish—"

"Pick-up and drop-off points, your contacts."

"—but have eternal life."

"John 3:16!" Slater cried out happily as he walked into the room. "Do I win a gold star?"

Moses groaned. A long sliver of bloody saliva slid down his chin. "You'll win more than a gold star if you take it to heart."

"I'd rather have the gold star," Slater said. He turned to Williams. "He's a tough one, isn't he? He wants to be a martyr."

Williams frowned. "He's in terrible physical shape for a man of thirty-nine. I'm afraid his body will give out before he will." They spoke as if the prisoner had left the room.

"The spirit is willing but the flesh is weak," Slater smirked.

"I don't get enough exercise." Moses' words clicked somewhere inside his throat. "Would asking for a sip of water be inappropriate?"

"Ask away," Slater offered.

"May I have a sip of water, please?"

"No!" Williams snapped.

"Oh, now, don't be like that," said Slater. He went to the basin, grabbed a small glass on the side, and filled it up. He returned to the prisoner and held the glass a few inches from Moses' mouth. Moses leaned forward, straining at the straps. "Tell us about your partner in crime."

Moses looked at the water, moving his chapped lips. A tear slid from the corner of his eye.

Slater moved the glass a little closer to the prisoner. "Tell me about Elijah."

"He's a mystery," Moses said.

"How so?"

The prisoner turned away from the water. "If you don't have him, then I can't tell you where he is. He simply disappeared."

"You don't expect me to believe that," Slater scoffed.

"It's true. We thought you had him locked up somewhere."

"We did. But you helped him to escape."

Moses coughed. "From the Rehabilitation Center? We didn't know he was there until after he escaped. Then ... we didn't know where he went. He didn't rendezvous with us at the appointed place."

"Oh? And what appointed place was that?" Williams asked.

"God is my refuge and strength."

"Tiresome, isn't it?" Slater asked Williams.

Williams nodded.

Slater crouched in front of Moses. "If what you say is true, then what do you think happened to him?"

"He is just like his namesake. He felt alone against the corruptions of the Ahabs and Jezebels. A kind of melancholy, I guess. But God will raise him up for mighty deeds. His work has not been completed."

"You're assuming he's still alive," Slater said.

"He is. I can feel it." Moses gazed at Slater through half-lidded eyes. Williams recognized the look. His body was shutting down.

"Where is he?"

"In the belly of the whale."

"What?"

Moses lifted his head. "Do you believe in dreams and visions?"

Slater smiled. "I dream of a day when our world will be rid of roaches like you."

"Jacob wrestled the angel and overcame him, as we all wrestle the forces of light and darkness. All things work together for the good of those who love God and are called according to His purpose ..." His voice faded as he closed his eyes.

"What's he saying?" Williams asked as if Moses had spoken a foreign language.

"Gibberish," Slater said. "Are we losing him?"

"I think so."

"Bring him back!" Slater stood up and threw the water in Moses' face. The prisoner didn't react.

Williams moved to the door. "I'll get the doctor."

"Wait. He's coming around."

Moses slowly opened his eyes. In a thick mumble of words, he said, "Captain ... you lost this battle ... before you began."

"I'll be the judge of that," said Slater.

"You'll be the judge of nothing," Moses whispered. "For the Lord Jesus Christ sits upon the throne. You will be judged. Accept His mercy before it's too late."

"As a non-existent entity, He has little power to offer judgment or mercy. So, let's go back to Elijah, shall we?"

"God did not send His Son to condemn the world, but to save it through Him," the prisoner declared with labored breaths. "Those who believe in Him are not condemned; but those who do not believe are condemned already. You are a condemned man, Captain. You are dead—and you don't even know it."

"This is getting us nowhere," Slater said to Williams. "I think we're being too easy on him."

Williams watched his boss slide around the table to the control panel. "I've already given him the permitted maximum."

"Permitted?" Slater asked as he perused the buttons.

"Leave it to me."

"Leave *what* to you?" Slater snarled. "You've had him for hours and you haven't gained anything!"

"Patience, sir. Go out in the hall for a minute."

"*You* go out in the hall if you want. We don't have time for this kind of coddling. Whatever they taught you at college isn't doing the job."

Williams knew now that tackling his boss and dragging him out was the only thing he could do. And he wasn't about to do that. Slater was a cat who toyed with his prey for only so long before he went for the kill.

Moses' head dropped. "Captain Slater, your soul is required of thee. I knew your father, you know. I remember his visits when I was a boy—"

"Be quiet!"

"He was a man of faith, a soldier of righteousness—"

"That's enough!"

Williams stepped toward his boss. "He's goading you. Don't listen."

"Your father was an inspiration to me. My work with the Resistance is a direct result of—"

"Shuttup!" Slater roared and dropped his fingers onto the control panel pad.

Williams leapt at him. "No!"

It was too late. Slater slammed the levers forward.

Moses howled as his body jerked and twitched like a spasmodic puppet as the strategically placed electrodes did their jobs. Only the straps kept him in the chair, but the violence of the blast of energy jolted the chair up and over onto its side. Williams heard the distinctive death-rattle in the prisoner's throat.

"Get the doctor," Slater shouted. He sat down in a nearby chair, as if the effort of pushing the sliders had been laborious.

Williams glared at his commander.

"Get the doctor and then we'll start again," Slater said. "He won't forget that kind of pain. When he comes to, he'll want to tell us everything he knows."

"Comes to?" Williams asked, incredulous. He marched over to the chair, knelt, and snatched up Moses' wrist to check for a pulse.

Suddenly the door pushed open, and a man named Nesbit, an interrogation monitor, ran in. "What happened in here? What did you do? His vital signs are gone."

Williams dropped the pulseless wrist. "Where's Dr. Kennedy?"

"He went to get coffee," Nesbit sped for the door again. "I'll find him."

"Is he dead?" Slater asked.

"As good as dead." Williams began life-saving procedures on the prisoner. It was a half-hearted effort. He knew there was no bringing Moses back.

"I didn't expect him to be so weak," Slater complained.

"He had a heart condition," Williams said. "If you'd read the file, you would have known that."

Slater grunted and walked out.

CHAPTER 27

It is the nature of grace to be present when you don't think it is. Only after a crisis or a catastrophe do you suddenly realize that grace had been there all along, giving strength at the point when there was no strength left. Sam had come to that conclusion months ago, in a time of relative safety, and now hoped to God he was right.

Sam looked at the group of refugees, gathered among their knapsacks in the sanctuary. They looked like a scene from a zombie movie. Life had been pulled out of them as if it had been wrapped up and taken away with the body of Tim. They were going through the motions now. If it wasn't true for them, it was true for him. Any leadership he asserted now was a sham. He was truly and fully helpless. Whatever happened now had to come from God.

A wind rattled through the church, groaning high in the rafters. Sam imagined that he'd heard a car drive up.

"Has anyone seen Beck?" Ruth asked.

"Not since Peter dragged him back from that farmer's," Amy replied.

"He's probably pouting in his room," Ruth suggested. "I'll get him."

Sam watched her leave and wondered how Beck would act now that their worst suspicions about him were confirmed. When Peter had explained, Sam thought it was unimaginable that Beck could do such a thing. But then he realized that it *wasn't* unimaginable. It was, in fact, predictable. *What Beck did, any of us could have done*, Sam thought.

Sam wanted to throw Beck out of the group, but Beck cut loose was a worse danger than Beck staying with them. Kept nearby, they could watch him.

Ruth returned a moment later with a grim expression. "His things are gone. I think he left without us."

"You're kidding." Sam shook his head in disbelief.

"He was humiliated by what happened," Amy observed. "He probably thought we'd throw him out anyway."

Ruth frowned. "Something was never quite right about him being with us."

"We'll have to forget about him." Sam stood up. "Let's find Peter and get out of here."

Ruth said, "It's still snowing, you know."

"Is it snowing?" Mary asked quietly. "The ground will be cold."

Sam walked over to Mary and knelt next to her. "Mary, I want you to know how sorry I am about Timothy. We would all like to stop and grieve with you, but we can't now. It's urgent that we leave."

Mary looked at Sam sadly, then nodded.

"Does it make sense to leave now?" Amy asked. "Maybe we should wait until morning."

"Who will separate us from the love of Christ?" Luke asked, quoting Scripture. "Will tribulation or persecution or famine? It is written, for thy sake, we are put to death all day long. We are considered as sheep led to the slaughter."

"Luke, please," Amy entreated him.

Luke continued, "But in everything we overwhelmingly conquer through Him who loves us. I am convinced that death nor life nor things present nor things to come nor powers nor height nor depth or any created thing can be able to separate us from the love of God which is in Jesus Christ."

"Everything in my being says we should leave now. We can reach the next station in just a few hours." Sam strode to the front doors. "I'll get Peter and we'll go."

As he reached for the doors, they were abruptly pulled away from his grasp. A blast of cold air and stark light hit him in the face. He made out the silhouette of a man—and a rifle pointed at him. Amy cried out and Sam turned to see a second man standing in an exit at the far end of the sanctuary.

"Freeze! Nobody move!" The second man held a pistol at arm's length in standard police fashion.

The one with the rifle scowled. "Bobby, will you stop it? We're not playing cops and robbers." He gestured at Sam to move inside. "Back off."

The one called Bobby ambled over to the group. He beamed happily. "It looks like we got a whole flock!" He looked like he'd just won the lottery.

"Looks that way," the one with the rifle said. He gestured to the knapsacks and bundles on the floor. "Caught them on moving day, too."

"Guess we got here in the nick of time," Bobby smirked.

Frozen by the shock and confusion, no one moved. Sam noticed that the two men weren't dressed as police. They wore large colorful hunting coats, thick wool caps, jeans, and heavy boots. He guessed they were in their early twenties and could have been students in one of his classes. The one with the rifle was tall and lean with a hard, angular face.

The other—Bobby—had gentler features and amused eyes. There was something comical about the two of them. They were kids with toys. *Dangerous* toys.

The one with the rifle eyed the small gathering. "Funny, I don't see our friend here. Where is he?"

Sam looked at him quizzically. "Who are you talking about?"

"The hoity-toity one with the silver hair. He came to my daddy's farm looking for food. I saw him from the window."

A sickening realization visibly worked its way through the group.

"Beck is gone," Sam said.

"Too bad," the rifleman said. "Less reward that way."

"Reward?" Sam asked. "For what?"

"Capturing Christians," the rifleman replied.

Sam cautiously moved forward. "Look, maybe we can discuss this ..."

The kid lifted his rifle. "You can talk to Clarisse here. She's good at shooting her mouth off."

Sam retreated. "I never argue with a loaded woman."

"Smart man." He turned to his partner. "Bobby, check for any stragglers. Then get the cops on the radio and tell them what we found."

"Snow's getting deep fast, Clay. The police probably won't make the drive."

"Then we'll have to take them down in the Jeep. Just get going."

Bobby pocketed his pistol long enough to give his cap a good pull over his ears, then he stepped out the way he'd come in.

Sam and Ruth exchanged a knowing look. Peter was out there somewhere. Did he see their visitors? Was he concocting a plan to help them? Sam hoped not. Peter was reckless enough to do something foolishly heroic and get them all killed.

Clay turned the rifle on Sam again. "Why don't you sit down with the rest of them? You look like you're thinking something stupid."

"That's my normal look," Sam said, sitting on the chair next to his table.

"What are you going to do with us?" Amy asked.

Clay's expression told Sam that it was the first time he'd noticed Amy—and he was impressed by what he saw. His tone changed noticeably. "Well, sweetie, I'm going to take you to the police and get a big fat reward for you. See, Bobby and me have been trying to get off this mountain and you folks are going to make it possible."

Ruth suddenly stood. "Listen to me, young man. Do you have any idea what'll happen if you turn us in? They'll probably kill us. Is that what you want?"

Clay shrugged. "What they do with you is their business. All I know is that people like you are wanted by the government, and they're willing to pay a lot of money for you."

"You don't care that they'll murder us?" Ruth asked.

"Just sit down, lady," Clay said. "This ain't no press conference and I ain't answerin' no more questions. All of you can just shut up."

Ruth sat down and stared crossly at the young man. Sam knew that her withering look would have no effect on the boy.

The front doors exploded open again. Everyone leapt to their feet. Clay swung his rifle around in case someone used the opportunity to attack. Peter staggered into the sanctuary, followed quickly by Bobby.

Falling on all fours, Peter was coughing. A trickle of blood slipped from his lip.

"What's going on?" Clay asked Bobby.

Bobby was breathless. "This one … he busted the radio, Clay!"

"What?" Clay shouted. "Let's pile them into the Jeep."

"Can't," Bobby said. "He flattened our tires, too. All four of them, just like pancakes."

With this announcement, Peter looked up at Sam with a wry smile.

With a stream of obscenities, Clay closed in on Peter with a few short steps. "You'll pay for that!"

Peter was on his feet quickly, ready for whatever Clay might do.

Clay lifted his rifle.

Bobby jumped between them. "Don't, Clay. You promised."

Clay tried to push past his friend. "Police don't care what kind of shape they're in when they arrive."

"*I* do." Bobby held Clay back. "You promised."

Clay spun away angrily and kicked at nothing. His face was flushed, his veins bulging out of his neck. He turned and pointed at Peter. "I oughta kill you, boy!"

"As if you could," Peter smirked.

Clay started for him again. "It'd be no problem."

Bobby pushed Clay toward the door. "Go out and cool down, okay? See if the other guy is around. Go on."

Clay hesitated long enough to scowl at the wide eyes staring back at him. Then he pushed Bobby aside and stormed off.

Peter sat down next to Ruth and rubbed his lip and jaw. A bruise was already starting to form.

"Now you folks need to listen to me," Bobby began as soon as he was sure Clay had gone. "Clay's got a fiery temper and when it kicks in, he stops thinking. Just do what he says and you won't get hurt. Understand?"

Sam said, "Bobby, you seem like an intelligent sort of person ... You don't want to do this, do you? I mean, we're human beings just like you. You can't turn us in for money. We're *people*."

There was a second—a fraction in time—when Bobby's eyes betrayed an inner conflict. Sam knew it well: it was a remnant of humanity in a very inhuman circumstance.

"Come on, Bobby ...," entreated Sam.

Bobby shuffled his feet nervously, then looked at Sam with a hardened expression. "It's the only way off this mountain."

Sam had no response.

"This place is a dump!" Clay announced from the hallway as he walked back in. He used the barrel of his rifle to poke at the bundles on the floor. "Where's your food?"

Everyone looked at each other awkwardly, as if drawing mental straws to decide who would break the bad news. Sam cleared his throat. "You've come to the wrong place for food."

"No food? How can that be? Your pal got lots of food from my daddy."

Sam spread his arms. "It never got here."

Clay kicked one of the bundles. "You hear that, Bobby?"

"What are we going to do?" Bobby asked.

"How am I supposed to know? It's snowing like crazy out there." Clay pointed the rifle at Peter like an accusing finger. "This is all *your* fault."

"And I feel *really* bad about it," said Peter.

"Don't rile me, boy. I'd just as soon kill you as look at you for trapping us like this."

Peter held his gaze. "Don't like the feeling, do you?"

"*Peter*," Sam snapped.

Peter kept his eyes fixed on Clay, but spoke to Sam. "They're willing to see us die for money; I don't mind seeing them suffer a little."

Clay moved toward Peter. Their faces were only inches apart. They were two animals locked in a primal contest of wills.

Sam stood up. "Let's calm down before something happens that we'll all regret." Sam looked to Bobby, hoping he would do something, say something. Bobby watched with an expression of fear.

Ruth grabbed Peter's arm. "Please stop," she urged him. "This isn't a tussle in the locker room at high school. For our sakes . . ."

Peter broke his gaze from Clay and turned to her. "You're right. I'm sorry."

"That's right; be a mama's boy and listen to what she says," Clay goaded him.

"I'm not his mother," Ruth said.

"Then what are you?"

"His aunt."

Clay turned to Sam. "You his uncle?"

"No," Sam replied. "Just a friend."

"And who are you?" Clay asked Luke.

"A humble servant," came the answer.

Clay pointed at Mary. "*You* must be his mother. You've got the look of a mother."

Mary shook her head.

"Will you please *shuttup*?" Amy shouted at Clay. "Hold us prisoner if you want, but don't talk us to death."

Clay looked at Amy, then crouched down next to her. "You know, for a group of Christians, you're a feisty bunch. Most people would be quivering in their boots at a couple of guys like us with guns. But not you. The fact is, I like feisty . . . in women."

"Cut it out, Clay," Bobby said.

Clay ignored him. "You're a pretty thing. I'll bet we could make good use of our time together, y'know, while we're stuck here."

Amy watched him with a bitter coldness. The rest of the group visibly tensed. Sam rested his hand on the back of his chair, ready to use it as a weapon against Clay if he had to. He'd read about turning the other cheek but wasn't sure how it applied to this situation.

Undaunted, Clay reached out and stroked her hair. "You'd like me a lot, I'll bet. Be sweet and maybe I won't take you in."

Amy spoke through clenched teeth. "Don't touch me."

"I could be the best thing that ever happened to you."

"Stop it," Peter growled.

"What's your name?" Clay asked, his smile cruel, his strokes harder.

Amy swiped her arm at him. "Leave me alone."

Peter stood up. "Keep your hands off her."

"Stay back!" Bobby held up his pistol. His hands were shaking.

"I think we're getting a little overheated," Sam said.

"Oh, yeah," Clay cooed to Amy. "Let's get a little overheated."

Peter took a step toward Clay, but Clay was upright again, his rifle trained on Peter. "Not another move, boy. You can't do anything, you understand? You're my prisoner and you can't do *nothing* about it."

"Yeah, you're tough with a woman," Peter said.

"Some like it tough," Clay said with a cruel smile. He suddenly bent down to Amy, grabbed her jaw and kissed her hard on the mouth. She tried to pull away, but his grip was firm. Suddenly he cried out and staggered back, his hand to his mouth. "You bit me!"

He clenched his fists and started for her. Peter leapt at him. Clay anticipated the move and skillfully sidestepped him, swinging the butt of the gun around. It slammed hard on the side of Peter's head, dropping him to his knees.

Ruth cried out, "Peter!"

As one, the group surged forward.

Bobby stepped in their way, waving his gun back and forth. "Don't take another step! I mean it!"

Mary let out a loud sob.

Clay leveled the rifle at Peter. "Just the way it should be, boy. On your knees."

Peter sprung at him again, wrapping his arms around Clay's legs and driving him backward to the wall.

Clay used both hands to bring the rifle butt down onto Peter's back. Peter still held tight. Another blow with the rifle butt, and then another. Peter let go and rolled from the assault. Clay followed, kicking wildly at Peter's back and ribs.

Ruth was screaming now. She threw herself forward, but Sam caught her by the arms and pulled her back.

"That's enough, Clay!" Bobby yelled.

"I'm sick of him!" Clay shouted. He grabbed the back of Peter's jacket and, with one hand, dragged him to the door. Peter struggled to get his footing but stumbled and fell again.

Bobby circled around the group, cutting them off from Clay and Peter. "Stay back!"

Red-faced, his nostrils flaring like a charging bull, Clay threw Peter at the doors. Peter landed on all fours.

Clay snarled, "I'll show you what happens when you break my radio and flatten my tires. And then I'll have your girlfriend and you won't do a thing about it."

Clay kicked at Peter again, driving him against the doorjamb. More kicks. More screams.

Amy broke free from the group and rushed at Clay. She made it close enough for Clay to swing his arm around and knock her back.

The distraction allowed Peter to launch himself at Clay with both fists.

Clay reeled back, the rifle jerking upward, level with Peter's chest. The gun went off with a deadly roar.

PART III

THE PATH

CHAPTER 28

The place was called Woodville. It was the quintessential Rocky Mountain town with a row of innocuous cabin-looking shops selling everything from dry goods, to feed and fertilizer, to rank imitations of the latest fashions. A large building of corrugated metal, a holdover from some older time, had been converted to a bar imaginatively called Hank's 2. Beck needed only to look across the street at another bar set in a log-cabin frame to find the original Hank's. A blue-and-green neon light displayed the name of a beer through smoky brown glass—the same beer advertised in the window across the street. It was a cheap government-sanctioned brand. He pondered both buildings, as if they offered him any different choices. The street was empty except for the whipping snow and a pickup truck waiting patiently at the single intersection for a light that refused to change.

Beck limped in the direction of Hank's Place. His feet were cold and ached from the long trek down the mountain. The snow had blown around his ankles and over the tops of his boots. His hands, though gloved, felt numb. His shoulders ached from carrying the knapsack he'd shoved his few belongings into. He knew he had to keep a low profile, but the wall of snow and the weariness from the walk made him reckless, as if no one could make him suffer any more than he'd already suffered. He had a sense of safety born out of the anonymity of the town; no one would care about him here. It was time to duck out of the snow and indulge in something that would warm his belly. A whiskey would be nice ... better yet a brandy. He pushed open the solid wooden door that said "C'mon In" in chipped letters. He blinked at the darkness, needing a moment to adjust his eyes. The place smelled of beer, sweat, and cigarette smoke. The combination made Beck feel slightly euphoric. It was a hint of civilization and normality. He felt like a prisoner who'd been released from solitary confinement.

The interior of the bar was true to the cabin motif established outside. Large wooden beams crisscrossed overhead, and the walls were rough and poster-packed with ads for beer and whiskey featuring scantily clad women in provocative poses. Logs also comprised the foundation of the large rectangular bar in the center of the room. Small round tables and uncomfortable-looking chairs dotted what was left of the floor space. The bartender, a burly bald man in a white shirt, presumably the Hank of legend, leaned against the counter reading a newspaper. He looked like a heavenly messenger standing amidst the sparkling glasses and multi-colored bottles within arm's reach around him. A few stools down, an old man sat hunched over a drink. Beck gasped, his heart jumping. The man looked exactly like Luke. Beck collected himself and shrugged it off. Of course, anyone with wild white hair and beard would remind him of Luke.

Neither of the men looked up at him. Somewhere a jukebox played an old song, the thumping bass being the only thing Beck could hear clearly. He sauntered up to the bar and slid onto a stool. Dropping his knapsack on the floor next to his feet, he folded both hands in front of him like a man in prayer. In a perverse way, he felt like praying, thanking God for deliverance from that church and the mountain, thanking Him for bars and stale cigarettes and bad music and liquor. Mostly the liquor. It was exactly what he needed to break from the past.

He wondered why he hadn't run away before. Why hadn't he escaped and come to the town sooner? He knew the answer to the question, but purposefully avoided it. There was no point in dealing with realities now. He was momentarily free and knew he had to enjoy it while he could. Now was the time to consider his options for the future.

The bartender suddenly looked up and eyed him suspiciously. "What can I get you?"

"Brandy," Beck said.

"You have money?"

"Of course, I do."

"Let's see it," the bartender insisted.

Beck frowned at the man, yanked off his gloves, jerked open his coat, and dug into his pocket for his wallet. Finding it, he produced a gold credit card. It was enough to satisfy the bartender's concerns.

"It says they executed him," the old man on the other stool said. Beck realized they were talking about the newspaper. The headline gloated that one of the leaders of the Christian insurrectionists had been caught.

"Good," the bartender grunted. "Those types need to be put down."

The old man continued, "I wonder why they didn't show it on television—the execution, I mean. Nothing better than an execution, except maybe wrestling."

"You've seen an execution on television?" the bartender asked.

"On the internet." The old man seemed pleased. "There are websites, you know."

The bartender put the glass of brandy in front of Beck and grabbed his card. "You want a running tab?"

Beck nodded, then rested the brim of the glass next to his lips, savoring the heady smell, building anticipation of the nearly forgotten taste. He closed his eyes and took the first sip. The warmth filled his mouth, then worked its way down his chest. It was liquid peace.

The old man tapped the newspaper page. "They executed him quickly for security reasons. Says he ran a significant risk. The other insurrectionists might have resorted to terrorism to free him."

Beck stifled a laugh, but it caught the ears of both men.

"Something funny?" the bartender asked.

Beck held up a hand. "No, no. It's that line about terrorism. What kind of terrorism would they resort to: wave a cross at a building, call down fire from heaven?"

"It's happened," the old man scowled.

"That's right," the bartender agreed. "You remember the fire two years ago. Where was it?"

"The Committee Building," the old man said.

"That's right. They blamed Moses and Elijah for that."

"Burnt the thing to the ground without any kind of those whatchacallits."

"Incendiary devices," the bartender added.

"That's right. Nobody ever figured out how they did it."

"They didn't do it by praying, that's for sure." Beck took another drink. This was just like the old days at The Inn, the place around the corner from his office. Endless talk about the latest business, the latest gossip. The fire at the

Committee Building was a set-up to elicit public hatred against the Christians. Making them look like they were fanatics with supernatural powers gave everyone the desire to kill them. It triggered another violent purge.

"What are you, some kind of expert?" the bartender asked.

"I used to work three blocks from the building," Beck said smugly. These local yokels would be impressed by that piece of information. Here was a big-city boy in their midst.

The bartender's bald head slid into creases between his eyes. "What are you doing here then?"

"Oh, I'm just passing through," he replied and took another sip of his brandy. It was doing wonders for him already. The snow, the church, the events up there were blurring quickly.

They looked at him with undisguised disbelief. They no more believed that he was a big-city businessman than they believed he was the Queen of England.

He glanced down at the worn sleeves of his coat and suspected that his face looked awful. When did he last shave? Did it matter? Beck shrugged. Let them think what they wanted so long as they brought him another drink. He pushed the empty glass toward the bartender. "Please."

"*After* I've checked your card," the bartender said and slipped over to the credit card machine. He tapped the card against the screen. The purchase was approved.

"Satisfied?" Beck asked.

The bartender brought him another drink.

This is the way to go, Beck thought. A single night in oblivion would make all the difference for him. Then he could ignore the feelings that nibbled at the edge of his conscience like rats on the other side of a wall. Those rats had to be fought. They had to be exterminated, drowned with lots of drinks. They carried with them the diseases of guilt and remorse: two things Beck had been fighting for years.

"Do you have rooms in this town?" he asked.

"What kind of rooms?"

"A place to sleep if I decide to ..." *drink too much*, was the finish of that sentence, but he left it alone.

"I've got rooms upstairs," the bartender offered. "You can stay in one for a fee. You can even have someone to go with it if you want."

Beck chuckled. "That depends on how drunk I get."

***

Central's Data Security Department hummed with life, twenty-four hours a day, seven days a week. The men and women who worked there wore glasses and light blue lab coats that matched perfectly with the light blue cubicles. From there, they monitored and distributed the information that streamed in from all parts of the world. Bank transactions, credit reports, purchases, tax returns, confidential memos, police reports, internet search histories, social networks ... they had it all. If you wanted to know what so-and-so paid on his November electric bill three years ago, they could call it up with just a few keystrokes. Need to know when the mayor last had the oil checked on his car? It was there. Data Security knew it all. They were to be honored and feared.

At least that's how Drew saw his job. Who needed political power or position when he had information? The keeper of the secrets would win in the end—and he had the secrets right there at his fingertips.

Laura, his assistant, popped up over the wall of her cubicle. It was like a desert rat peeking up from its hole. "A 971 just came in."

"So?" Drew asked. He was sitting with his feet up on his desk, twirling a pencil in his fingers. "Give it to Alex."

"I thought you'd be interested in this one." She looked proud of herself.

"Why?"

"It's not your usual bad check or late-on-alimony payments. Take a look."

He sighed and leaned forward to his keyboard. With a rapid-fire sound, he keyed in the report. It told him that an unidentified credit card had been used at 7:48 p.m. at Hank's Place in the town of Woodville. The system always flagged cards that didn't seem to have a registered owner, suggesting that the user wanted to be off the grid, probably for black marketing or money laundering purposes.

From that point, Drew could have followed the tracks in any direction: a complete history of Hank's Place, its owners, its yearly grosses, how much food and beverage it had purchased in the past day. Nothing was withheld.

"Do we have any other flags from that area?" he asked.

"Way ahead of you," she said. "A few days ago, the tracking system got a *ping* from Howard Thomas Beck's cell phone."

"In Woodville?"

"Near to it."

"Why is this important? Is Beck a person of interest?"

Laura moved around the cubicle wall and leaned in close. He could smell her perfume and the starch she had used that morning on her blouse. She reached past him and did some rapid-fire keyboarding herself.

The screen highlighted that Beck had been wanted for questioning regarding the First National Investment Company bankruptcy. Specifically, there had been allegations of embezzlement, misuse of funds, fraud, etc., etc.

"This was interesting in itself," Laura said, "but this is even better: Beck disappeared from our monitoring a month ago."

"That *is* interesting," Drew admitted. "So, he disappeared in the city and reappeared in the mountains. Not just any mountains, but a particularly out-of-reach area of mountains."

Laura tapped the screen to find another set of data: checkpoint logs. "He went there, but he's not showing up at any of the checkpoints along the way."

"I guess he sprouted wings and flew."

"He's on the run," Laura said.

"Except that he turned on his cell phone." Drew smirked at the stupidity of the man. "And what about that unregistered card?"

"It's the kind of card an embezzler like Beck would use." Laura pulled back, half-sitting on the cubicle's counter. "Coincidence?"

Drew eyed her. "Woodville—set in that whole section of mountain range—has been identified as a popular new route being used to get to the border. We better notify the boys upstairs."

Laura nodded and slipped out to make the call.

Drew returned to the main screen about Beck and began a more detailed review of the man. Within an hour, he knew more than he ever wanted to know about Beck's history. He then clicked over to a collection of surveillance photographs. This was the fun part for Drew. Here he might find some sordid pictures of his man in compromising positions. The government wasn't beyond blackmail. Neither was Drew. He often downloaded them and took them home for his personal collection.

For the most part, though, the assemblage of high-resolution color photos was boring—taken while Beck was being investigated for his shady business dealings. There was Beck sitting in a restaurant talking to an investor ... Beck meeting in a hotel lobby with the CEO of a big corporation ... Beck shaking hands with a local politician ... Beck trying to be discreet in sunglasses while negotiating with some other unsuspecting clown in a parking lot. The faces and names of all of Beck's contacts popped up for further cross-referencing if Drew felt so inclined. He didn't. He scrolled to the last photo they had of Beck: the man standing in a crowded thoroughfare talking to another man with a bushy mustache. The program identified the man's name, flashing like a warning sign: Ben Greene.

The system should have flagged this weeks ago, Drew thought, annoyed. *No wonder the Chinese are so far ahead of us.*

Laura returned with a cup of coffee for him. "Well, detective? Have you found anything interesting?"

"Maybe," he said and viewed the report about Mr. Greene. Suspected of being an insurrectionist of the Christian persuasion, Greene had recently been arrested and was later found hanging in his cell after an extensive interrogation by the head of Special Forces, Captain Robert Slater. Drew had had dealings with Slater before. He was hardcore.

"What's this?" Laura asked, leaning forward again so that her face was near his. She was such a tease. "Why would an embezzler like Beck have secret meetings with a Christian like Greene?"

"Maybe he thought the Christians were a way to escape," Drew suggested. "You know how saving people is like crack cocaine to them."

"I've never had crack cocaine," she said.

"Let's try it sometime," Drew suggested. "Meanwhile, let's get this report directly to Captain Slater." He glanced at the time on his screen. It was nearly nine o'clock.

As the night went on, Beck learned that Hank's Place was where the town's most sour-faced drinkers gathered. Hank's 2, on the other hand, was a dance hall for younger and more energetic drinkers. Tonight, however, there wouldn't be too many customers in either.

"It's a blizzard out there," one local announced as he came in. "Nobody'll be going anywhere for a while."

Beck's hope that the drinking would keep his mind focused on his options was misguided. He kept slipping from what he needed to do to what he'd already done. His conscience wouldn't be kept at bay. He soon found himself wallowing in self-pity: a back-door to the conscience. He fought the feelings with as much effect as a single man wielding a pencil against an invading army.

Why shouldn't I feel sorry for myself? he wondered. He wasn't like the rest of them at the church. Suffering was an ugly and cruel thing, to be avoided at all costs. It was insane to embrace suffering for some bizarre attempt at redemption or a mythical crown. Let the saints and the martyrs suffer. He was neither.

He thought of the boy. No doubt the martyrs at the church thought Tim's death was in some way his fault. If he had taken food back to share, then Tim wouldn't have eaten from the cans in the basement. That's what they would say. But how could they be so sure? He didn't know much about botulism, but he knew enough to argue that it couldn't have come on so fast. The boy must have been eating from the cans for days before then. So, it wasn't his fault. They had no right to think that it was. Since when was he responsible to them—to anybody other than himself?

The thumping of the jukebox's bass pounded in his ears, and he wished it would stop. "Can you turn that thing down?" he slurred at the bartender.

"Turn *what* down?" baldy asked.

"The jukebox."

"It isn't on, you moron," he said. The two other men at the bar laughed; the old man's was a high cackle.

Beck slumped over his drink and followed the scars in the counter with his finger. It was like a relief map. Where would the road take him now? Where could he go? He was a man without a community. He couldn't go back to the city. They'd catch him quick if he did. Where did he belong? *Nowhere*, he pouted. He was disenfranchised, a true alien in his own country. Regret welled in him like a backed-up sewer. He had weighed his options carefully and made his choices. But now he knew they weren't the right ones. Maybe he should have made a deal with the lawyers and trusted his luck. If everything had hit just right, he would have done some community service for a while. But what if things didn't hit exactly just right? He couldn't bear the thought of prison. Not even for a couple of years. He had to escape. But how? That was the question he had asked.

Not even the drink could dull the memory of that night when he stumbled into the alley and saw the tiny group slip into the doorway. He thought it was an illegal bar, the kind with potent drinks, not the watered-down stuff they served in joints like Hank's or even The Inn. He followed them in and was amazed to find himself in a secret gathering of Christians. It was a worship service played out with softly glowing candles, a whispered liturgy, and tearful prayers. Why they didn't suspect him, nor raise an alarm at his presence, he didn't know. They welcomed him, in fact, and when he heard them speak of the Resistance, his mind formed a plan for escape. He had enough Christianity in his background to say the right words, to fake the prayers. All he had to do was convince them long enough to get away.

His conscience had pricked him then. He had been used to fighting in a wolf's lair where sticking it to your neighbor, lying to get ahead, deceiving your closest friend to line your pocket was standard fare. Doing it to a flock of sheep was a different matter. He wasn't so cut off from his conscience that he didn't feel guilty. For a while. But a conscience ignored is a conscience controlled. It had no sway over him. He mastered any feelings of guilt, considered his options, and embarked on a deal with his god. With a wink and a handshake, he and his god plotted together. They were made in each other's image after all. Beck was certain that he could succeed in his plan.

His lawyers stalled the legal system long enough for him to wire what was left of his money into untouchable accounts and secure his place on the next transport out. It was so easy. Yes, he disliked the squalor of their meeting place, the indignity of hiding in a stinking truck with people who gave every appearance of being Christians because they had nothing else to do with their lives, but it served his purpose. They would get him across the border.

The jukebox continued to thump in his head as he finished his drink. He hit the glass hard against the counter and wiped his mouth. Leaning heavily on his propped-up fist, he fiddled with the glass with his free hand. Drink spilled out. The glass was filled up again. Hadn't he just finished it? He didn't question the blessing, but simply took another sip. The taste went sour in his mouth. His enjoyment of it was gone. The bartender was probably giving him the bad stuff.

That was the problem with life, wasn't it? No matter what he did, he wound up with the bad stuff. He had married a beautiful woman—Louise—who'd turned into a wrinkled, sickly hag. He had made shrewd business investments that brought him accusations of embezzlement. He had made a deal with his god and his god had gone back on his word. He was supposed to make it across the border, not get stranded at the church. He was supposed to travel with reasonable comfort, not wind up hungry and cold.

Well, what else was he supposed to do except explore his options? Going to the farmer for food made good sense. Sam and Peter and the rest were being ridiculous in their belief that it would all work out, that God would take care of them. He didn't, did He? He'd double-crossed Beck and He would double-cross them eventually. After all, what kind of God would let the boy die like that? Even Beck wouldn't have been so heartless.

He looked with unfixed eyes across the counter and saw the old man, still there. He was the spitting image of Luke now. A chill shot up and down his spine. It *was* Luke. "How did you get here?" Beck demanded to know.

"What?"

"How did you get down from the church? Did you follow me?"

"I don't know what you're talking about."

Beck was aware that the people around the bar had turned to look at him. He wondered how it had gotten so crowded when the weather was so bad. There were only a couple of them there a minute ago. He turned his gaze to see who his new drinking companions were. A woman whose face was in a half-shadow peered at him. It was his dead wife, Louise. She smiled in that crooked way he once found so odd. Next to her sat Tim, his face white, his eyes recessed in dark circles. Next to Tim was Peter in a blood-soaked shirt. There was Sam holding a pen made of a skeleton's finger. Ruth, Mary, Amy, adorned in linked dandelions. Even Ben the van driver was there, wearing a necktie made of hemp. They were all clearly dead and looked at him with expressions of accusation.

"What do you want?" he shouted.

The bartender leaned next to him, his teeth green and his breath smelling of old earth. He looked again and it was Sam. "We had a deal," he slurred.

"Your deal was with the wrong god," said Sam. "Your god is just like you: a liar and a thief."

Beck wanted to leave. He tried to stand but his legs were not cooperating.

Louise said sweetly: "You are your god, my love. You can't pretend like you didn't know it." He was not aware that she had moved from her stool, but was sitting next to him, her decaying face next to his. "Daddy always said you were a confused man. You confused strength with weakness, courage with cowardice. Every time you said you were being practical, I knew you were trying to take the easy way out. But I loved you for it. I really did. I thought your weakness was a virtue."

"No," Beck blurted out. "You loved me for my strength. You thought I was clever."

"Oh, Beck," she said sadly.

"Do you have any idea how many people you hurt with your cowardice?" Peter asked.

"You're a walking curse," said Amy. "Everything you touch is cursed."

"You bear the mark of Cain," the rest of them said like a Greek chorus.

"You're a condemned man, Beck," the bartender added pleasantly.

"I was being practical," Beck moped. "It's not my fault how it worked out."

Tim pointed at him. "It's your fault. It's all your fault."

"It's all your fault," the entire bar chanted over and over again.

He opened his eyes without realizing they had been closed. A cracked ceiling was the first thing he saw. He traced it over and down to the peeling wallpaper that looked like someone pulled the corners away to see what was underneath. Light streamed through the threadbare floral pattern on the loosely hung curtains. The place smelled of moldy linens. He was lying on a bed.

Where was he?

He swung his legs off the sinking mattress. He was still fully dressed. Sitting up, he battled a wave of nausea. How did he get here? On shaky legs, he crossed to the window and peeked out. The glass was framed with the fingerprints of frost, intensifying the brightness of the snow on the street below and the roof directly across—the tin roof of Hank's 2. Had he drunk so much that they had to carry him up and put him to bed? He supposed so. The last thing he remembered was encountering an entourage of ghouls at the bar. What an awful dream. The feelings it conjured hung on him like the taste of brandy and vomit. He'd been sick in more ways than one.

Collapsing on the bed again, he tried to ward off his feelings of guilt. What was the point of feeling guilty about anything now? It wasn't practical. But the feelings remained. *You're such a selfish coward.*

He wondered why his conscience now sounded like Louise.

"Let me die so I don't have to hear you complain about taking care of me," she had said the night before she died. "I'm tired of feeling like an inconvenience."

What kind of a man would make his dying wife feel that way?

A selfish coward.

He spun on the mattress and vomited in a nearby trash can.

Someone pounded on the door.

"What do you want?" he called out miserably.

The pounding continued. His annoyance turned to dread as he realized that whoever was pounding on the door was now body-slamming it. "Take it easy! Just give me a second to open the door!"

It was too late. The door wrenched from the lock, splintered the jamb, and flew open. Two men marched into the room with guns drawn.

"Howard Beck?" asked a man with bright red hair.

"What do you want?"

The red-haired man glanced at his partner, a tall, brown-haired, and congenial-looking fellow. A hint of a smile. He holstered his gun. "I'm so glad to meet you."

CHAPTER 29

Smith poked at the roaring fire, then sat back, nestling into a thick-cushioned wingback chair. He surveyed the small cabin. It glowed red and orange from the fire. The single window shone white with the glow of the high snow drift just outside. On one wall, nearest the makeshift kitchen, the shelves were thoroughly stocked with boxes of dry goods—cereal, rice, flour, powder, anything that wouldn't spoil—and canned fruits, vegetables, soups, jams, milk, biscuits. It was like an old-fashioned grocery store. On another wall, there were entertainments: books, recordings of music and films. The third wall was covered in framed prints by the Masters. The fourth held the large oak door and window. Whoever in the Resistance had chosen this cabin and stocked it had certainly done an excellent job. If Smith was allowed to choose his heaven, this would be it. He had everything he needed and no responsibility. There wasn't a soul to be found for miles. Alone with himself, he relished the chance to think clearly.

The cabin was one of only four structures in a deserted mining camp—apart from the tin huts that littered the mountainside. There was a large square building that had once been a hotel or a brothel; he wasn't sure which. A small wooden shack served as the general store. Next to that was the post and telegraph office. Then, away from the rest as though it had been shunned, was this cabin. Smith had arrived there from the church, pushing himself hard along the trail, passing other stations along the way.

He would stay there awhile. There was no reason to rush for the border when the accommodations here were so good.

The steam from his cup of coffee curled up and around his nose. The aroma rich and soothing. He picked up the book he'd taken from the shelf. A collection of poems. He turned to one by someone named J. C. von Zedlitz.

Uncertain Light

Without wood or path, man scales the rocks as a wanderer:
rushing streams, surging rivers, windswept woods,
nothing halts his stride!
Though darkly massing clouds billow over his head;
rolling thunder, streaming rain, a starless night, nothing halts his
*   stride!*
At last!— at last!—a distant light glimmers!
Is it a will o' the wisp, is it a star?
Ha! how friendly is its gleam; how it entices and beckons me!
The wanderer hastens swiftly through the night, drawn towards
*   the light.*
Is it fire or the light of dawn?
Is it love, is it death?

Closing the book, Smith felt a stab of sadness. He remembered, far back in his life, that he once thought he had a poet's heart and was capable of writing words like this. There had been a time when the world seemed colorful and alive, his eyes filled with visions of beauty and a longing to find the words to describe them. It was so long ago—long before the world turned into heavy black shadows, thick grays, and empty white pages. His poet's heart had been stolen and replaced with a machine that did little more than pump blood. It was a functional organ that allowed him to do his work—no, *God's work.*

Why did it seem like those who responded to God's call often found themselves lost in a colorless world? Was it the realization that beauty was an illusion, the top of the rock that merely disguised the earth, worms, and decay underneath? God's call got your hands dirty, it put you face-to-face with the ugliness of the world, its lack of peace, its futile attempts to find happiness.

But where did that leave the one who had answered the call? How was he expected to cope with visions of brutality day after day?

Smith couldn't. It was unfair of God to expect him to. He saw that clearly now. The human capacity to adjust to the worst possible conditions was unfathomable. For years he had been in survival mode. Now he wanted to live. In this cabin, he could feel the pull of life—in a full stomach, a warm fire, books of poetry. Perhaps he could immerse himself further in it once he got across the border and could work with his hands once again. Maybe his poet's heart would break through the machine.

He turned the page of the book, and his eye caught another poem by the same poet.

Assurance

You must look aloft, oppressed and weary heart,
Then your deepest pain will soon turn to delight;
You must look aloft, oppressed and weary heart,

Then you can grasp on to hope,
no matter how high the floods may reach,
how could you be abandoned when love remains in you?

He thought of the church he'd left behind, how it had stood like a large tombstone on the mountainside. He'd had an image—call it a vision—of the people he'd left behind. He saw the boy encased in dirt and the others walking like the living dead. He looked down at the book of poetry and suddenly flung it away as if it had condemned him.

Standing up, he scowled at the fire and then paced angrily around the small room. The snow still fell outside, carried by a wind that whistled down the chimney of the potbelly stove in the corner. He didn't want peace; his expectations weren't that high. But he might at least be allowed to enjoy some quiet.

How could he silence the voice that spoke deep within? It wasn't even his voice. It was Sam's.

The mountain was the belly of the whale. That's what the voice said repeatedly, like the distant S.O.S. from a crippled ship.

God, if you have something to say to me, say it directly, Smith thought. *Let's stop playing around.*

The fire spat and sparked at him indignantly, as if scorning his request.

His was an act of pride, he recognized. Making demands of God betrayed his attitude for what it was. Giving up was never an act of humility. It was useless to pretend otherwise. The source of his despair was pure selfishness. He'd had enough and wanted out. There was nothing noble or sacrificial about that. Where was the mortification in abandoning those strangers back at the church? Where was faith to be found in this cozy little cabin?

His eye went to the wall next to the bookcase to rest on a painting of the Virgin Mary. She was radiant in blue and white, her arms outstretched. She had said yes to the angel, come what may. She would store secrets in her heart, including greater pain than Smith could ever know.

Comfort is the enemy of faith. It was his father who used to say that. *Our faith is never so neutralized as when it is withdrawn from the hard edge of life.*

But why did it have to be this way?

It was an unanswerable question. That was the trick he'd taught himself over the past few weeks: keep the questions so abstract that they couldn't be answered. A vague idea went a long way in helping to avoid hard answers, because hard answers went hand-in-hand with taking action, and taking action created responsibilities, and responsibilities were the things he wanted most to avoid.

So, there was the truth. Even if God spoke to him directly, he wouldn't want to hear what God had to say. The questions would be too direct. The answers would be too hard.

He returned to the wingback chair and slumped into it. His whole line of thinking was spoiling the place. It was like trying to enjoy a meal with starving children watching from the windows.

Again, he saw an image of Tim encased in the earth.

Look aloft, oppressed and weary heart.

He rubbed his hands over his face.

How can you be abandoned when love remains in you?

Love remains. But what did he love? Was it something he was willing to die for?

He loved God's call and thought he was never afraid to die for it, though, in truth, he never believed he would have to. The call had made him feel secure, invincible. How could one be on a mission for God and not feel safe?

Was it coincidence, then, that he decided to run away just when his work was becoming more difficult—less secure, less invincible? There had been so many setbacks. The risks increased daily. Betrayal was in the eyes of every newcomer.

Was it dying that he feared, or the responsibility of living?

And what was it he loved? Did he love God's call more than he loved God?

The wanderer hastens ... drawn towards the light.

Is it fire, is it the light of dawn? Is it love, is it death?

He reached for the Bible on the bookshelf. *Where can I go from Your Spirit? Where can I flee from Your Presence? If I ascend to heaven, You are there. If I make my bed with the dead, You are there. If I take the wings of the morning and settle in the deepest parts of the sea, even there Your hand shall lead me and Your right hand will hold me fast.*

"God," Smith cried out, "why don't You just let me go? I'm not worth holding on to. I'm useless to You now, don't You see that? *I am driven away from Your sight. How can I ever look upon Your holy face again?*"

The wind was picking up. A branch banged urgently against the window. The entire cabin shook as if it might be ripped from its foundations and thrown aside. Suddenly the door blew open, the snow swirling in like searching spirits. Smith leapt from the chair and slammed the door shut. His heart raced as he fell back against the wall and slumped to the floor. The branch clawed at the window until the glass cracked and shattered, allowing the branch to poke inside. It pointed and shook at him.

He was afraid now: afraid that he had become addicted to his despair, that his heart could no longer be moved by the truth, by guilt, or by love. Worse than losing the passion of faith, he was afraid he'd lost his faith completely. And he wept with tears that felt hot and thick, as thick as blood.

CHAPTER 30

When I was a young girl, I used to love playing in my grandfather's house. It was a world unto itself with so many knickknacks ... oh, those knickknacks. Personal trinkets and mementos ... each one with a different story about his life. It was a treasure chest of memories, an escape to a different place and time. And he had a big featherbed in his bedroom that we kids jumped on like a trampoline. We loved that bed.

As he got older, he would say "Rutherford"—which is what he used to call me because I think he wanted me to be a boy— "Rutherford, one day I'm going to die but don't you be afraid or sad because death is just a doorway. Just like the doorway that leads into this house."

He died peacefully in his sleep in his bedroom, in that big featherbed. But they wouldn't let me in to see him. And after he was buried, they locked the door to his bedroom, and I never went in again.

That's what death seems like to me. A locked door. But one day I'll get through and it'll be just like jumping on that featherbed again.

—Ruth, as quoted in
The Posthumous Papers of Samuel T. Johnson

Sam grabbed the bucket of melted snow and, under the scowling eye of Clay, passed it around for everyone to drink. They had all huddled to sleep around the stove in the kitchen. He pondered them all sadly and wondered how they had endured the past couple of days together, trapped by the snow, choked in a vacuum of anger, hunger, and despair.

The small group's unified will had been broken. Each person's faith stood alone—quiet. They had been cast adrift on a life raft and now looked at each other through the dark, sleepless eyes of people who suspected they wouldn't be rescued.

Peter was dead. He'd been killed instantly by the blast from Clay's rifle. His corpse was wrapped in tarps in the cellar; the snow was too deep and the ground too frozen to bury him. Ruth wept at first, then seemed to call on an inner peace that astonished Sam. Amy and Mary were inconsolable. Luke was praying, his lips moving silently.

Though Clay was obviously shaken by what he'd done, he would not yield his dream of claiming a reward from the police.

Bobby seemed bewildered by what had happened. Sam noticed that the young man now looked at Clay with a watchful expression, as if he might be Clay's next victim.

Meanwhile, the snow piled up in windswept drifts around the church, sealing them in. If the group had felt mildly claustrophobic before, it bordered on a kind of insanity now. Their captors escorted them to the toilet, berated them for the lack of food, and occasionally knocked them around when Clay had had too much to drink from a supply of whiskey he'd kept in the back of his Jeep. Once he had tried to grope Amy but was too drunk to do anything more than fumble with her top, then pass out. There was a moment during the incident when Sam was sure that Bobby would shoot Clay. Sam still had Tim's Swiss Army knife and would have used it if Clay persisted.

The two captors took shifts to watch their prisoners and to sleep, but the result was that no one rested.

Clay took a drink from the water Sam handed him. As he did so, Luke broke the silence. "Jesus said to drink from the well that ends all thirst."

"Shuttup!" Clay screamed, adding a string of expletives. "Three days. Three *lousy* days. I'm sick of this. When it isn't snowing, the wind is blowing. And when the wind isn't blowing, it's too dark to travel. I never thought I'd see the day when my stomach would feel like this."

"There are some cans of food in the basement you can have," Amy said quietly.

"*Amy*," Ruth rebuked her.

Amy glanced at her, then Mary. "I'm sorry."

This is life as it really is, Sam wanted to say out loud. He gazed at the emaciated group and considered that maybe his life had been constructed on a false premise: life was meant to be peaceful and safe. Isn't that what he'd worked toward for years in his career with that mistress of his, Academia? That was his mistake. Peace and safety were illusions in this world. *This* was real life: this huddled group, this church. Here was a microcosm of the living world. Here was the struggle to know faith, to keep hold of it amidst suffering, to see death face-to-face and know what it is to live. God cannot meet man in comfort because man won't answer Him there. God must meet man at that place where everything has been stripped away, where life is raw and sweaty, where the sinews are stretched and the blood runs a deep red. God does not rest on cushions but on a cross. Life is found only there—His grace, too—and then maybe peace will follow.

"Mind if I go get my journal from the sanctuary?" Sam asked, wanting to write down his thoughts.

"Yes, I mind," Clay replied.

Bobby, who'd gone off to the bathroom, returned with a strangely animated look on his face. "Clay, it's stopped snowing. It looks like the sky's clearing. It'll be hard, but I think we can make it back to your farm!"

Clay leapt to his feet and dashed to the back door, rubbing at the small window. The drift obscured any possible view.

"The front door," Bobby said. "Go look."

Clay sprinted away.

Everyone looked at Bobby expectantly. "Are we really going with you?" Amy asked.

Bobby shrugged. "I guess."

"Can we take care of Peter's body before we leave?" asked Ruth.

Bobby pursed his lips. It was the first time anyone had mentioned Peter for quite a while. He looked as if he was weighing his options. "I don't see why not. If Clay makes a fuss, well, I'll ..." He looked away from them, as if he was suddenly ashamed. He spoke gently: "I'm sorry about what Clay did. He's never done anything like that before. I know it's hard for you to believe, but it's true."

Sam glanced uncomfortably at Ruth. Her expression was sadly compassionate, and he wondered if it was another kind of grace at work in her life that allowed her to forgive something so brutal. He imagined that Bobby had been an accessory to Clay's violence for years—and had done nothing to stop it.

Bobby continued, speaking directly to Ruth, "I know you were his kin and I'm really sorry. If I thought there was something I could do—"

"You can do something," Ruth said. "You can let us go."

Clay was back before Bobby could respond. His dour face was oddly alight with a newfound cheer. "Let's get them together, Bobby. We'll walk them to my place, then make our way to the town from there. Looks like we'll get our reward after all."

Bobby eyed Clay. For a fleeting moment, Sam hoped the boy would insist on letting them all go free. But he didn't say a word. Such an act of intervention would have to come from a place of strength that Bobby didn't have at present.

Slowly, like mourners at a funeral march, they made their way from the kitchen to the sanctuary. They picked through their belongings and prepared for the long walk to Clay's farm.

Sam was just about to walk over to the table to retrieve his journal when a new voice echoed through the sanctuary. "Going somewhere?" it asked.

Everyone jumped from the surprise. Clay swung his rifle around. Bobby clawed at his belt and eventually pulled out the pistol. But the voice had echoed from no single place— and no one could pinpoint where it had come from.

One of the doors creaked open and they turned to look, but no one was there. "It's not a good day for a walk," said the voice—and its owner stepped out of a shadowed area behind a space that once held an organ.

It was Smith.

His eyes were fixed on Clay and the rifle. "Put your toy away before you do any more damage."

Clay stiffened, still shocked by this new arrival. "Who are you?"

"The name's Smith. Sorry we don't have time to chat, but we have to leave before it starts snowing again." He turned to the rest of the group as if Clay and Bobby weren't there. "Get your things together."

Sam glanced warily at the two gunmen. "We're ready to go."

But no one moved. Clay and Bobby looked at the stranger, dumbfounded.

"We don't have time to waste," Smith said. "Sam, tell everyone to get their coats on!"

Sam looked from Smith to Clay and back again. "I would, but I'm afraid Clarisse will start shooting her mouth off again."

Smith sounded exasperated. "Let's go!"

With watchful eyes on Clay, they each began to put on their coats.

Their action snapped Clay out of his stupor. He stepped closer to Smith, his gun raised. "Now hold on just a minute. I don't mean to interrupt your big heroic entrance, but these folks are coming with me. As a matter of fact, you're coming with me, too."

Smith smiled indulgently. "Clay, you and Bobby need to go home. Your daddy is worried about you."

"What can you know about my daddy? I don't know you from a hole in the ground!" He raised the rifle, gripping it firmly. "Now move on over and join the rest of those folks. We're going back to my farm, getting the truck, and taking a ride down to the town. Got it?"

"But if we wait much longer, some of the people from the town are going to meet us here. I'd like to avoid that, if at all possible." Smith spoke in a voice so calm that Sam found it unnerving.

"You think you're tough, don't you?" Clay sneered.

"Clay—"

"Stop calling me that!" Clay screamed at him. "I don't know you!"

"Maybe we should wait outside until you decide what you want to do," Sam suggested.

Clay jerked the rifle at them. "Nobody move. I swear I'll start shooting. You know what happened to that other smart-mouth."

"Peter," Smith said.

"Yeah—and you're next." Clay held the rifle steady.

"Give me the rifle." Smith held out his hand like a father to a disobedient son. "Come on."

Smith's eyes seemed to burn into Clay, who stood immobilized, as if transfixed by them. Then he spoke in a low growl. "Buddy, you've got five seconds to get over with the rest of them. That's all I'm giving you." He put the rifle at eye-level and placed its butt against his shoulder. It was pointed at Smith's face. "One ..."

Smith moved toward Clay, his hand still outstretched. Sam reached into his pocket and found the Swiss Army knife. He'd stood by helplessly when Peter got shot. This time he would throw himself at Clay or Bobby.

"Get back, mister, he's not bluffing," Bobby pleaded.

"Two ..."

Mary began to weep, sliding down to her knees. "No, please not again ..."

The air didn't move, as if the entire church was holding its breath.

"Three ..."

"Clay, stop. I can't handle this," Bobby cried out. "It's not worth it."

"Four ..."

Sam readied himself to leap at Clay. But Bobby stepped around so Clay could see him. His pistol was held high and pointed at Clay's head. "Stop *now*! I swear to God I will shoot you, man. Put the gun down and let's get out of here."

Clay glanced at Bobby. "Don't be stupid."

"I mean it," he said, the pistol trembling, sweat beading on his face. "I'll shoot you before I let you kill anybody else. Understand? I'm done with this!"

The three-way standoff held silently. Every muscle in Sam's body had tensed.

"Are you gonna move or what?" Clay shouted at Smith, but his tone had lost its strength.

Smith shook his head. "It's finished, Clay. Listen to Bobby. Get out of here."

Bobby cocked the pistol. "Let's go."

Clay lowered his rifle. "I'll never forgive you for this," he muttered. Without another word he spun on his heels and marched out of the church, kicking the doors open wide as he went.

Bobby exhaled loudly. He dropped his arms as if his muscles had given out. His show of courage had seemingly exhausted his ability to speak. He simply nodded to them and ran after his friend. "Clay!" he called out—and then he was gone.

Sam leaned against the table, the adrenaline still surging through his body, his head throbbing. It didn't seem possible that they'd reached the end of it.

Amy buried her head in Ruth's shoulder. Mary put her face in her hands.

Luke, who had been watching the scene with an unconcerned look, mumbled something inaudibly.

Smith spoke next. "Do you have what you need? We need to hurry."

They moved sluggishly at first, then more quickly. Once again, this man, this stranger, had appeared and instilled hope in them. This time it looked as if he might really lead them to the promised land.

"This is going to be a difficult journey. I hope you're up for it."

"Anything to get out of here," Amy assured him.

Sam zipped up his coat. He couldn't believe they were finally going to leave. He grabbed his knapsack and checked one more time to make sure he had everything.

Smith was at his elbow. "I saw Peter's body in the basement. We don't have time to take care of it. I'm sorry. Where's Beck?"

"Gone."

"And Timothy?"

"He died. Food poisoning."

Smith nodded.

"I have a lot of questions for you," Sam said.

"I'm sure you do. But don't expect any sensible answers."

Coats were pulled on, knapsacks positioned on shoulders, final necessities taken care of, and then they were ready to leave.

Sam surveyed the sanctuary one last time. He wondered if other fugitives and hostages developed a twisted affection for their places of captivity as he had for the church. It was as if it had been all he ever knew. His time at the college, his apartment, all the elements of his previous life had been washed away by the baptism of suffering he'd experienced here. For a moment, he felt like Lazarus, walking out of the tomb to a new life.

"Let us pray for guidance and strength!" Luke called out as if speaking to more than just their group. Sam looked at him. What did his eyes see in his madness or his faith? Was the sanctuary filled with a congregation that only Luke could see? Phantoms? Ghosts? The communion of the saints?

As Luke raised his hands, the rest of them dutifully bowed their heads. "Father, we thank You for Your love and the peace You offer us through Jesus Christ, Your Son . . ."

There was a sound, barely discernible to Sam's ear, but insistent like a buzzing insect. It was low and mechanical.

"We thank You for the means of escape that You have provided through Your servant," Luke continued.

Sam peeked up and saw that Smith was already looking around, tilting his head, trying to get a fix on the sound. One by one, Amy, Ruth, and Mary also lifted their heads. Luke was the only one who seemed oblivious to what was happening. "Be with us on the journey ..."

"It's too late," Sam said, knowing it was true. Somehow it had always been true.

The sound was unmistakable now, growing ever louder. The church shook and rattled. One of the smaller windows shattered. The snow blew and billowed outside. A different sound faded in, too—a buzzing like someone had started a chainsaw somewhere. It wasn't a single chainsaw but rather several that drew closer and then surrounded the church.

No one moved, though Sam was certain that every fiber in their beings screamed for them to run. They seemed mesmerized by the cacophony of sound that had penetrated the quiet.

There were shouts and banging noises in the hall, then the sanctuary doors were thrown wide, and a stark shadow appeared, framed in the doorway. It was spectral and otherworldly as the outside light shone furiously around it. Other shadows appeared and the group shielded their eyes to see who or what it was.

The shadow stepped in and became a man: tall, lean, redheaded, with cat-like eyes and a thin, sharp mouth. "I am Captain Robert Slater with Special Forces. By the authority of the Committee, you are all under arrest."

CHAPTER 31

Law enforcers dressed in black tactical uniforms burst through every possible doorway, weapons raised and ready. Instinctively, the group huddled together and were quickly surrounded. Slater clasped his hands behind his back, his chin held high, and circled them, looking to Sam like a Nazi official from a World War II movie. *A cliché*, he thought.

"This is a fine catch," he proclaimed.

Sam noticed that Smith had positioned himself in the center of the group, his head bowed and his face turned away from Slater.

"What's this all about?" Sam asked, attempting a confident tone. He had tried the same thing with Clay and Bobby. It hadn't worked then either.

Slater gave him a curious look, as if he was an animal that had suddenly spoken. "All will be explained," he said, smiling.

Another man appeared in the doorway—he was in plain clothes, taller than Slater and had a pleasant face and dark, curly hair.

"Ah, Agent Williams! I'm so glad you could join us," Slater said. "Bring our friend in. No sense keeping him away from the rest of his family."

Williams nodded and signaled to someone out of sight in the hallway. There was a scuffle and Howard Beck was thrust into view like a child who wasn't quite ready for his part in the school play. Sam was shocked. The man had the stricken look of someone who had been in a dungeon: dark circles under his eyes and an expression fixed with pain. They had tortured him, Sam guessed, hoping that such torture was the only reason Beck had led them to the church.

Beck stood with his hands held in front of him as if he'd been handcuffed so long that he didn't know what else to do with them. Williams nudged him to walk on. He shuffled slowly, his head hung low, his eyes avoiding contact with anyone else's.

Slater gave Beck a patronizing pat on the shoulder. "Thank you for all your help. We couldn't have done it without you."

"I didn't—" Beck started to say but gave up and fell silent.

"I should have known," Amy said softly.

Slater stood still, eyeing each of his captives. His cool gaze gave Sam the creeps. His expression held the smug satisfaction of a successful hunter inspecting his prey, taking in every detail. He looked ready to put a few more notches in a belt already full of dead men's dreams.

Slater's eyes rested on Luke. "Why do you look familiar to me?"

Luke stared back at him without a hint of recognition.

Slater looked puzzled, as if he didn't know how to interpret Luke's dull-eyed look.

Ruth broke the silence. "Will you please tell us why you're here? What have we done wrong?"

"Insurrection," said Slater. "I know you'll deny it and we'll waste a lot of time getting to the truth, but I'm sure we'll—" He stopped mid-sentence. His eyes lit up, his slash of a mouth turning into a grin. "I'm speechless. It isn't possible. I couldn't be so lucky." He pushed past Sam and Amy to face Smith. "Finally."

Smith looked at him with indifference.

"I really didn't expect to find you here." Slater spoke as if welcoming an old friend. He turned to Beck. "You lied to us, Mr. Beck."

"I didn't!" Beck cried out, wincing as if he might be struck. "He wasn't here when I left. I swear."

All eyes went to Smith, and Sam felt the significance of the moment.

Slater gestured to his assistant. "Signal the helicopters. Get some reliable off-road vehicles up here. The snowmobiles will be useless. Until then, I'll do everything here. We can't take any chances."

Williams nodded and marched out, lifting a communication device as he went.

There was no mistaking the sudden shift of activity that Smith had caused.

"What are you going to do?" Ruth asked.

"Administer justice," Slater replied.

"Justice? Here?" Sam asked. "Surely you're taking us back for a trial."

Slater shook his head. "The trial will take place here."

"But you can't!" Ruth insisted.

"I can and I will," Slater responded curtly, pointing at Smith. "I won't lose this man again."

"Why?" Ruth asked. "Who is he?"

Slater looked genuinely stunned. "You don't know?" He flashed a taunting smile at Smith. "You didn't do any magic tricks to impress these people? You didn't pull a few prophecies out of a hat? No miracles?"

Smith simply looked at him.

"Oh, I get it. You're acting just like Jesus did before Pilate." Slater seemed delighted and paused for dramatic effect. Then he gestured grandly to Smith, bowing slightly. "Meet Elijah."

Everyone turned to Smith with dumbfounded looks. Except Sam. He had already guessed Smith's identity the night Smith had left. Who but Elijah or Moses could have been so weighted down, buckling under the responsibility for lives other than their own?

The importance of this moment wasn't lost to him now and reinforced his growing belief that, in this play, he and his fellow fugitives were little more than supporting characters in a greater drama. It was a battle between titans. Mere mortals like Sam wouldn't decide its outcome one way or another.

Smith kept his eyes on Slater, holding a passive expression.

"We captured Moses, you know," Slater told Smith. "He said he didn't know what had become of you. I didn't believe him, but now—well, I guess he was telling the truth. It's a shame because he died for it."

Smith tensed but didn't respond.

A hard smile spread like a shadow over Slater's face. "What happened, Elijah? Maybe you thought you'd take a little vacation from it all? Or maybe the cowardice that is inherent in your faith overwhelmed you and you ran away—like the rest of your sheep."

Smith remained silent.

Slater rubbed his hands together like a connoisseur about to set upon a lavish meal. "Let's get this over with. There are too many of you roaches for me to remain idle. So, here's the deal, plain and simple: renounce your faith and I'll let you go."

Smith rounded on him. "You're a liar."

Slater ignored him. "Keep your faith and lose your lives."

"You call that a deal?" Amy asked.

"It's the best you're going to get." Slater smiled again, smugly. "I harbor no illusions. I know you Christians love this. From the beginning you have thrived on being persecuted, whether real or imagined. You enjoy running and hiding and having your secret meetings. You crave the opportunity to suffer for your Master. Oh, the honor of it all. Nothing unifies you people more than to be attacked and pursued."

His statements were met with silence.

He continued, "If my superiors would listen to me, there'd be no persecution. I'd let you have whatever you want so you'd get fat, lazy, and complacent. You'd fight among yourselves and devour your own beliefs. You're your own worst enemies when you aren't hunted. But my superiors won't listen."

"Sorry to be such an inconvenience," Sam said.

"I'm giving you a choice. It's up to you. I'll leave you to give it some thought." Slater signaled for the tactical team to withdraw. He then nodded to another plain-clothes agent. "Watch them."

The agent saluted and positioned himself near the door. Slater walked out, his long coat floating behind him like the robes of the Grim Reaper.

The fugitives stood like mourners at a funeral, an invisible casket before them. Smith broke from the center of the group, moving off to the side.

Beck was on his heels, pointing an accusing finger. "So, you're the infamous Elijah. It was you they were after, not us."

Beck had the look and tone of his former self. Apparently, no amount of torture could change him.

Smith nodded. "It appears so."

"They interrogated me for three days. I couldn't figure out what they wanted." Beck turned to the group, spreading his hands in appeal. "I held out as long as I could. I thought you'd be gone by now."

Sam knew that no one believed Beck's words. The unspoken suspicion was that he had told Slater everything he knew at the first sign of pain.

"We tried to leave, but couldn't seem to get past the door," Sam explained. "Timothy and Peter are the only ones who made it out."

Beck frowned. "Where did Peter go?"

"He's in the basement," Ruth said.

Beck's eyes grew wide, seeking an explanation.

"The son of the farmer shot him." Amy nearly spat the words at him. "The farmer who gave *you* food. His son followed you. You led him here."

Beck's hand caught the edge of an upturned pew. It looked as though he might collapse. He slid slowly to the floor.

It was the first hint of humanity Sam had seen exhibited by the man.

Sam turned to Smith. "Why did you come back?"

"I was never a good survivalist," Smith offered.

"What aren't you telling us?" Ruth asked.

"The less you know, the better."

Amy moved around to face him. "You're all Peter talked about. You and Moses. He believed in you completely. I don't know if it's a blessing or a curse that he didn't know the truth about you."

"Amy—" Sam stepped toward her.

"It's all right, Sam," Smith said. He looked at Amy with an unruffled expression. "I'm sorry for not living up to Peter's expectations. I'm sorry that I didn't bring manna from heaven or call lightning down to scatter our enemies. I never claimed to be more than I am. I didn't ask anyone to put their faith and trust in me. Maybe you should have reserved those for God."

Amy held his gaze for a moment, then turned away. "Maybe we should have. I'm sorry. I'm sorry for all of us."

"Is your name really Smith?" Sam asked.

"James Michael Smith," he replied. "We chose biblical names for our work in the Resistance."

"What happened to you?" Ruth asked.

Smith drifted to Sam's table, leaning against it. He stumbled for the words to continue. "I couldn't go on with the work." He glanced at Sam. "You were right. I was running away from more than I thought."

"You cannot run from God," Luke declared. "Where can you go that He won't find you?"

"What will Slater do to us?" Amy asked. "He wouldn't dare execute us."

"Don't count on that." Smith scanned their faces. "He considers himself an exterminator. We're nothing more than vermin to him."

Beck looked up. "But it's *you* he wants. Maybe we can make a deal ..."

"What kind of a deal do you have in mind, Beck?" Sam asked, affronted.

"Haven't you done enough damage with your deals?" Amy snapped.

"How is this my fault?" Beck whined. "*He's* responsible for putting us in this situation. The police wouldn't be here if they weren't looking for him. They don't really care about us." He pointed at Smith. "You should talk to them. Make some sort of arrangement."

"Stop it, Beck." Sam felt his face going red. "He wouldn't be here now if he hadn't come back to help us."

"And we wouldn't still be here if you hadn't begged for food at the farmhouse," Amy added.

Beck slumped back, his eyes filled with panic. "But I don't want to make this choice. I don't want to die."

Ruth glowered at him. "None of us wants to die. But, in heaven's name if we have to die, then let's do it with dignity. Stop whining."

"Do not grieve as those who have no hope," Luke told them. "Our victory is in Jesus Christ. A seed must fall to the earth before it is risen. We will die, yet we shall live again."

Beck put his hands over his ears. "No, I don't want to hear about that. I want to live and stay alive. There must be a way to make a deal!"

Slater and Williams marched in from the hallway. Slater gave them an affirming look. "I'm impressed. This is the perfect hideout."

"Obviously not *perfect*," Sam countered.

A tip of the head from the captain. "Point taken. But it's remarkable, nonetheless. You seem to have everything you need here."

"Except food," Ruth said. "And the power was a problem."

"I'll see if I can fix that for the next group that comes through," Slater quipped. "Williams, can we find them something to eat? Sandwiches, drinks? Military rations? There's no reason to prolong their discomfort."

Williams gestured to the agent by the door, who took the suggestion and left to make it a command.

"Each of you will be going to your separate rooms now," Slater declared. "I believe you'll be able to think more clearly about this matter of life and death."

The tactical team marched in and corralled them out of the sanctuary like cows to a slaughterhouse.

Slater told the guards, "And don't let them talk to each other through the walls. I don't want any of their ridiculous camaraderie going on."

Back in his room, Sam looked at the mess made by the soldiers. They had rifled through the desk and cabinets while the group was talking in the sanctuary. He sat down in the pastor's chair and, for the first time in weeks, saw the blood stains on the desk. He didn't want to be here anymore. He didn't want to be anywhere else either. Whatever acts of violence had been committed in this place before seemed almost holy. It could be cleansed only by a washing with blood, like so many other things that God must redeem.

Sam knelt to pray. He had once asked God for the miracle of an escape. Now he asked for a different kind of miracle, a different kind of grace.

I'm going to die, he thought. In knowing that, he also knew a sense of peace. It knelt next to him like a friend he hadn't seen in years.

CHAPTER 32

"Now it's just the two of us," Slater said.

Smith gave him a look of indifference. "I'm thrilled."

Slater pulled a pistol from his shoulder holster and gestured to a chair. "Bring that here."

Smith obliged him, putting the chair in a clear space. He nodded to the pistol. "Do you really think you need that?"

"The mind of a desperate man often produces foolish actions," Slater said.

"I'm not desperate."

"You should be." Slater wagged the pistol at the chair. "Sit down, please."

Smith sat. He knew that this was all part of Slater's game.

Slater began a slow circle around him. "Jesus Christ is not returning in the nick of time to get you out of this."

"How can you be so sure?"

Slater laughed and continued his stroll around the chair.

"The group is hoping that, since you have me, you'll let them go," Smith explained. "I think they're being naïve."

"I think you're right." Slater was smirking. "I have a better plan. You see, I've had a lot of time to think about this while chasing you all over the country. You are Elijah—mover of mountains, man of miracles, leader of the *exodus*—"

"Moses led the exodus, not Elijah," Smith reminded him.

Slater ignored the correction. "You and Moses were and are an inspiration to Christians all over the country. Moses even more so now that he's dead. You Christians love your martyrs."

"What's your point?"

"It would do me little good to kill you, since your death would merely fuel the fires of Christian faith rather than put them out." He raised a finger, pleased with where his thoughts were going. "Instead, I want you to openly and publicly renounce your faith."

"Forget it."

"Hear me out," Slater said in a voice of calm reasonability. "Consider your situation. You're a second-rate rebel caught on this desolate mountain. Why were you here? I know. You got tired of all the heartache and the death, the constant drain of having so many lives depending upon your decisions. You gave up, thinking that one human being could only do so much and maybe, just maybe, your God would give you a break."

Smith wanted to argue with Slater but knew better. It all rang true.

Slater leaned close, his voice a hissed whisper. "God's giving you a break *now*, my friend. Why are you fighting? Why are you putting your people in harm's way? Renounce your faith so your people can live peacefully, *safely*. The State can be forgiving. I'm authorized to offer them clemency if they'll stop fighting us. Frankly, between the two of us, I don't even care if you mean it. It's the show we want. You won't get better terms than that."

Smith waited. The longer he let Slater talk, the more he'd learn.

Slater growled, "Don't you see what I'm offering you? This is an opportunity to end the running and hiding for you and all your people. Isn't it worth a minor sacrifice on your part to do it? The courtesy of a reply is customary at this point."

Smith shook his head. "I'm not interested."

The slivers of Slater's lips stretched across his face. "You're a stubborn man. But I know your stubbornness. It reeks of self-righteousness. The odor of a man who thinks he is forgiven. You ran from God but, somehow, some way, you decided to come back. What changed your mind? This church? The people you abandoned here? You came back and that makes you feel strong." He chuckled. "I'm not surprised. It's all too predictable."

"Give up," Smith said. "These old school games don't work."

"Yeah, I know." Slater offered a fake sigh. "We're at an impasse. You'll give up your life for your cause. I get it."

Smith watched him. There was another card Slater was about to play.

"Are you willing to give up someone else's life?" Slater asked.

Smith looked up at him, struggling to subdue a feeling of alarm. "What are you saying?"

"I'm adjusting the rules to our little game, Elijah. You agree to do what I say, or I'll kill the others. One by one. It's your choice."

Smith felt like he'd been sucker-punched. "You can't do that. The law doesn't allow for ..." his voice trailed off. The law had no place here.

"Williams!"

Williams stepped in from the hallway. "Sir?"

"Bring in one of the women."

Chapter 33

Ruth sat motionless on her small cot, her hands folded neatly on her lap, her mind turning her life over and over like an old heirloom. She inspected it, cherished it, regretted the various nicks and scratches. She'd had a full life—she believed that for sure. Her experiences covered everything she thought she would have wanted from it.

She was born and raised with the good sense and godly faith a country girl needed to survive. When her father died, she managed the farm and turned it into a profitable enterprise. Profitable enough that when it was sold, she was able to give her mother a comfortable existence for the remainder of her life, short as it was. No one in her family seemed to have the ability to live past the age of fifty. Her father had a stroke at forty-eight, her mother died at the age of fifty—two days short of her fifty-first birthday. The death certificate said it was from "unknown causes." Ruth was now forty-nine.

She had had two children. First was a small boy, whom she had named for her husband Andrew. The boy died of pneumonia at the age of three. She was pregnant with her daughter when Andrew Sr. was crushed under a tractor. Her daughter, Sarah, must have sensed in the womb that her father was gone, for she declined the invitation to life and died at birth from complications.

Ruth grieved a year for each, living in the endless dusk of self-pity and black shrouds of resentment. She was alone: isolated in the firm belief that no one could understand her feelings or pain. Friends and neighbors did their best—God bless them—but their words were only so many trite phrases and meaningless clichés. After all, she was only twenty-seven years old and who could know what it was like to be so young and to have lost so much? That sort of tragedy was supposed to be reserved for older and more mature people, who were equipped to handle it.

Yet, without realizing until much later, those years were for her a cocoon out of which she would emerge as an older, more mature person. There she had found God. Not the God of her youth—a thunderous being of Sunday School miracles and Genie-in-the-lamp prayers—but a real and living God of respect and love, compassion and chastisement, power, and fear. He came to her in the darkness on a wintry night when she had been contemplating suicide. She had been asking herself, "Why should I live?" and He said as clearly and audibly as someone standing next to her, "Because I live." He tore the mourning rags from her windows and let the light in. And she grasped life with a quiet determination and a new joy.

A cradle Catholic, she went to confession and then Mass and rediscovered the presence of Christ in the sacraments. She attended Mass every day from then on.

Peter was a young child—her sister's son—and he became like her own. She watched him grow as a boy. When the persecution began, she watched him become a man. He was the fulfillment of a promise God hadn't actually made, but she believed in: a covenant for her life.

She had held him so close, that one last time before they wrapped him up in the tarp and carried him to the cellar. She had hoped that his spirit would move through hers and touch it ever so briefly before making its way home. She was sure that it had.

Someone knocked gently on the door and then opened it. The agent called Williams stepped in. He looked at her as if he was about to invite her to a meal.

Ruth smiled at him.

"Look at her!" Slater exclaimed as Williams led Ruth in. "What a fine figure of a woman."

"Mr. Smith?" Ruth asked quietly, puzzled.

Slater strode away to the hall. "I'll leave you alone for a moment to think about your future."

Williams followed his boss. After they'd gone, Smith leapt to his feet and moved quickly, in one direction then another. "There has to be a way out of here."

"Mr. Smith, I've made up my mind," Ruth said. "I'm not renouncing my faith."

Smith stopped, turning to her. "It's not your choice anymore. If *I* don't reject Christ, he'll kill you."

Ruth was surprised. The lines on her face seemed to deepen. She spoke quietly. "You won't, will you?"

"I don't know." He checked the windows. "If we could wrench one of these boards away—"

"And then what? I'll run away?" Ruth asked. "To where?"

"The forest."

"They'll shoot me first. I'll be an easy target." She moved to him. "This insanity has to end somewhere, and this is as good a place as any."

Smith looked at her, not sure he wanted to believe her. "I appreciate your courage, but—"

"I mean what I say," she said, stern and stubborn. "You cannot compromise your faith on my behalf."

Smith grabbed his coat and took it to her. "I can create a distraction. Use the back exit by the choir rooms. Go straight for the cover of the graveyard." He took her arm and began to pull her across the sanctuary.

"Naughty children," Slater called from the doorway, his hands on his hips. He *tsked* loudly. "I'm disappointed, Mr. Smith. Now we'll have to handcuff you." He drew his pistol and aimed it at Smith.

Williams took the cue and guided Smith back to the chair.

Smith was fuming. "Kill me if you want but leave them out of it."

"Still trying to escape from the responsibility of making decisions. I would have thought you'd learned by now," Slater sneered. "You're no good to me dead. But these others are ... well, they're expendable." He feigned an apologetic look to Ruth. "Nothing personal, of course."

"It never is when people like you kill people like me," Ruth said.

"What's your decision, Mr. Smith?"

Smith stared coldly at Slater.

Ruth put a hand on Smith's shoulder. "Keep the faith, Elijah."

Williams had just produced a pair of handcuffs to secure the prisoner when Smith threw himself at Slater. They fell to the ground and struggled there until Williams, more powerful than Smith imagined, wrapped an arm around his neck and pulled him off.

"Stop!" Ruth cried out.

Slater joined Williams in wrestling Smith back to the chair, clasping the handcuffs securely around his wrists.

"Desperate thoughts and foolish actions," Slater puffed. His tongue searched out a break in his lip where a tiny thread of blood fell. "I take that as your answer."

Williams took Ruth by the arm and led her through the doors. A moment later, the main doors opened, allowing a blinding snow-induced light to spill into the relative darkness of the sanctuary. Smith strained at the handcuffs, his wrists cut by the hard edges.

The doors banged shut and the light was gone. Then came a single gunshot.

Smith slumped in the chair.

Slater asked, "Is your faith *really* worth the lives of all these people?"

The doors opened again, and Williams returned. He stamped his feet. Smith thought he saw a pink hue to the snow hitting the floor.

"Next," Slater said. Williams went back to the hallway.

Smith looked at Slater and spat. "How could you have the flesh and blood of a human being and be so inhuman?"

Slater was unaffected. "The decision is yours. You can stop this any time you want."

Smith now lowered his head and prayed. What did God expect him to do? It was never part of his understanding that he'd have to sacrifice the lives of other people to preserve his own faith.

Williams returned with Mary.

Smith saw her and groaned. "Oh, Mary ..."

She blinked as if unaccustomed to the light. "You don't have to lock us in our rooms, Captain. We won't try to escape." She looked at Smith, her brow creasing. "What have they done to you?"

"Your life is entirely in Elijah's hands. Talk to him about it." Slater bowed to her cordially and, with Williams, went to the hallway again.

Mary moved quickly to Smith, circling behind him. "What can I do? How have they bound you?"

"Handcuffs. Forget about it."

She stepped back from him. "What's going on here? Did I hear a gunshot?"

"Yes."

"Why? What were they shooting at? Did someone try to escape?"

"They killed Ruth."

She staggered back, as if hit. "They killed her? Because she refused?"

"Because *I* refused."

Mary put her hands to her mouth, but they couldn't stop the mournful whimper that slipped through.

Smith searched her face. Her red, tear-battered eyes looked back at him. "Mary ...," he began.

"Don't say anything, Mr. Smith." She rose to her full height, her head back.

"You don't understand," he said. But her eyes told him that she did.

"Losing Timothy was like death for me," she whispered. "I was afraid then. I'm afraid now, too, but it's different somehow."

"I'm sorry."

"Why? I have a husband and son that I hope to see."

She looked stronger and more determined than Smith thought possible. He had a sense that he was seeing her true self: a person who'd been buried by past circumstances and was only now coming alive.

"Well?" Slater asked upon his return. He looked eagerly at Smith and then Mary. When neither responded, he said, "So be it."

"Come with me." Williams guided Mary to the doors.

She didn't look back but faced directly ahead.

Slater watched them go and spoke with feigned remorse. "The shame is that no one will ever know what happened here. It will never be written or recorded. There's no book in which to place it. You, them—all will be forgotten like the decaying bodies in that graveyard outside. How does the saying go? Ashes to ashes—"

The shot rang out.

"—dust to dust."

Smith was hit with a wave of nausea.

"What's the point, Elijah? You Christians say you value life and yet here we are. You're casting life aside ... for nothing."

Williams did not stop in the sanctuary this time but continued down the hallway like a malevolent spirit.

"You could make the difference," the captain said. "You can make what happens here meaningful. This church could become a shrine to the diplomat who made peace between two opposing factions."

Smith jerked his arms angrily, the handcuffs scraping against the metal backing of the chair. "What is it about Christians that makes you do this? Is it because we have something you don't? Is that what eats at your insides? We have something you can't touch or take away from us. No matter how hard you try, you can't smother it or stop it. You may think you know human nature, but you don't know anything about the Spirit. And it's driving you crazy because you never will."

Slater leaned into Smith's face, his nostrils flared, his hot breath filling the air between them. "I know a lot more than you think."

"Why? Because of your father?"

Slater slapped Smith hard across the face.

Smith felt the burning sting, but pressed on. "You want to stamp out the Resistance because *your father* created it."

"Williams!" Slater called out, reeling back. "Bring me *two* this time!"

Smith clenched his teeth.

"You can't sit here and let these people die. You won't do it! No faith—not even yours—can bear the responsibility of killing them. Stop it *now*, Elijah! It's within your power to do it!"

CHAPTER 34

Alone with Howard Beck and Luke, Smith tried to think. Two men might have a chance to change the playing field of Slater's little game. If Beck jumped Slater, and Luke could get the better of Williams ...

No, it was absurd to think about.

"I want to know what's going on," Beck demanded. "I thought I heard gun shots."

Smith couldn't think clearly. *It's all my fault.* What if he hadn't run away? What if he hadn't come back? What if he gave up and went along with Slater's demands now, with the hope of escaping later? What if ...?

"Are you listening to me?" Beck snapped. "Captain Slater was ready to make a deal of some sort. So, what's the problem? Do what he wants!"

"You don't understand."

"What's to understand?" Beck asked. "You put us into this situation; you can get us out."

It sounded so easy, Smith thought. Why not? A simple nod from him and Slater would stop this massacre.

The words of Jesus came to him: *If you deny Me before men, I will deny you before My Father in heaven.*

Smith felt like he'd taken the cold grip of the devil's handshake. *So, what if I gain the world, but lose my soul?*

Smith looked at Luke and was startled by the serenity on his face. Was he really so oblivious to what was happening around him?

Luke caught Smith's gaze and smiled. This was not the dull, abstract expression he characteristically wore. He looked vibrant and alive.

A fist tightened around Smith's heart.

"There was darkness in the belly of the whale," Luke said. "There was darkness in the tomb, too. But it only lasted three days. Today is your day to rise."

Smith felt hot tears gather in the corners of his eyes. "Forgive me."

"What are you talking about?" Beck asked. "Forgive you for what? Be practical, Smith. If you go along with whatever he wants, then we're free to go, right? 'He who fights and runs away, lives to fight another day.'"

Smith spoke calmly. "If I deny Christ, then he'll let you go. Otherwise ..."

Beck looked at him, impatient. "Otherwise, *what*?"

"Those gunshots you heard ... he killed Ruth, then Mary." Smith felt the fist squeeze hard around his heart.

The blood drained from Beck's face. "What? No!" His eyes darted back and forth, reflecting a deep panic. "What are you going to do? You're not going to let him kill me, are you?"

Slater and Williams were now in the doorway.

Beck rushed over to them. "Captain Slater, you can't be serious about this. It's not fair to put my life in his hands. It should be my decision. We had a deal. You said no one would get hurt if I cooperated."

Slater brushed past Beck with an expression of disgust. "Smith?"

Smith looked away.

"Get them out of here," Slater commanded. Williams took Beck's arm to lead him out. Luke followed peacefully, obediently, the lamb to the slaughter.

"No, please!" Beck begged as Williams pulled at him. "Just tell me what you want! Smith, please help me! This isn't fair! I'm not ready to die!"

Williams continued dragging him out. Even after they were out of sight, Smith could hear Beck screaming.

"Don't do this!" he cried. "This is insane! You can't! Oh, God, forgive—"

The gunshot cut him off. Then came the second.

Smith's head dropped, the tears sliding down his cheeks.

On his knees in the wet snow, Howard Beck slowly lifted his head. Williams held his gun to the sky like he'd just signaled the start of a race.

"We said that *you* wouldn't get hurt if you cooperated," Williams explained. "Here are your coats, knapsacks, and some additional provisions. Now take your nutcase friend and run—into the mountains."

Beck stood up on trembling legs, the cold air jabbing at his skin like millions of pins. Luke was already standing, his expression unchanged from what it had been before.

"Both of us?" Beck asked, his brain still not grasping what was happening. He looked helplessly at Williams. Having been sure of his death, he now felt an odd disappointment that he was still alive. Relief, he hoped, would come later.

Williams jabbed a thumb at Luke. "He's useless to us. Take him and go."

"But—to where?"

"*Run!*" Williams shouted, then turned to go back into the church.

Beck quickly grabbed the knapsacks and thrust one into Luke's arms. "Let's go, Luke," he said and tugged at Luke's sleeve.

"We're leaving?" Luke asked.

"Yes." As they began to walk, Beck thought he saw something out of the corner of his eye. He didn't dare turn to look. He was sure it was two bodies.

They pushed through the pathless snow around the church, weaving through an assembly of soldiers and snowmobiles, until they found the path that took them into the mountains.

CHAPTER 35

The question I keep hearing—the one that keeps going through my own mind—is "Why is this happening to me? I'm a Christian—why are these bad things happening to me?" But I keep coming back to another question. "Why not?" Considering the ongoing corruption of the world, I have to wonder why terrible things don't happen to us all the time.

—from *The Posthumous Papers of Samuel T. Johnson*

Using Tim's Swiss Army knife, Sam made a crack between the boards covering his window. He could see beyond the patrolling guards to the blanket of snow, the majestic pines, and the high hills that rolled like ripples to the great wave that was a mountain. Deep patches of blue appeared like lakes in the sky. He hadn't noticed the beauty of the area before. It spoke to him like a gentle tap on the shoulder and a whisper from God.

Yet it hadn't been beauty that got through to Sam's heart. Not before he'd become a Christian, and not since. It had been through pain—the pain of a cross, the pain of separation, the pain of their experience in the church, the pain now of imminent death. Pain preceded a resurrected life. Sam didn't understand why, but that's the way it was. If God's own Son had to abide by that rule, then why should there be exceptions?

Two figures moved through the trees, but Sam couldn't make out who they were. Certainly not officers. They weren't dressed right. Before he could ponder their significance, the door opened behind him. He turned to see Williams standing there.

"I don't suppose you've come to play cards," Sam said.

A threadlike smile formed at the corners of Williams' lips. Sam followed him out of the room and down the hallway. As they approached the sanctuary, he could hear Slater saying, "Put an end to this heartbreak. Why endure it?"

They rounded the corner of the doorway. Sam saw Slater kneeling next to Smith.

Williams cleared his throat. "Sir."

The captain turned, saw Sam and, as if well-rehearsed, crossed the room to him like he was about to greet an old friend. He put a hand on Sam's shoulder and leaned in, speaking conspiratorially. "He's being stubborn. Reason with him." He tipped his head to Williams, and they slipped into the hallway.

Smith was a picture of suffering. His arms were stretched behind him, cuffed together behind the chair, which seemed to be the only thing that kept his hunched body from falling forward.

"I heard the shots," Sam said softly. "It's strange. I always thought that when it was time for me to die that I'd have something significant and profound to say. I don't."

Smith didn't respond.

"Right now, I feel a very quiet peace." Sam realized that it was the kind of thing he'd prayed for but never thought he'd experience.

Smith didn't respond. His head dropped again. His shoulders shook slightly. Only then did Sam realize he was crying.

"Mr. Smith . . ."

Smith slowly looked up, his body trembling as if the weight of his head was too great to hold. His eyes were bloodshot and swollen, tear stains crisscrossed like trails down his dirty cheeks.

"It was important that you came back here," Sam told him. "I've been thinking about it. I believe it was intended this way. Everything that has happened over the past few weeks has pointed to this moment."

"Why?"

"Why not?" Sam asked, shrugging. "We can all run like Jonah, but we must face our Golgothas like Jesus. The battle may seem lost, but we've won the war. So, in a way, it's incidental how it all plays out. Maybe that's what the early Christians understood about martyrdom."

Smith took a deep breath and closed his eyes.

"Besides, who said there can't be a happy ending in death?" Sam spun to the door and shouted, "Slater!"

Slater and Williams strode in from the hallway.

"Let's get this over with." Sam walked toward them.

"He's going to let you die?" Slater asked.

"I'm not giving him a choice," Sam explained.

Slater looked disappointed. He motioned to Williams.

"Guard your faith well, Elijah," Sam said, stepping ahead of Williams to the hall. He clasped his hands in front of him to keep them from shaking. He didn't want his reaction to the cold to be mistaken for fear. He was afraid, yes, but there was no reason to show it to Williams or the guards nearby. His knees trembled. He clenched his teeth.

"Would you like to remain standing or be on your knees?" Williams asked.

"My knees," Sam replied and knelt in the snow. It was wet and quickly soaked into his jeans.

Not far away, he saw the small pockmarks in the snow where other knees had been placed and a spray of red dots on the soft white skin like bad acne. "Aim well," he said to Williams.

A click from the gun was the last thing he heard.

Chapter 36

Smith tried to pray but Slater's voice kept cutting in.

"One more, Elijah," Slater was saying. "One more life here and many more elsewhere that you can save if you choose."

Smith was drained now. No matter how many ways he tried to console himself, guilt dug its talons deep into his soul. It seemed to tear through his most vulnerable places.

This is for me, he thought. *They're dying for me.*

He was beyond any other regrets: the *what ifs* of what he should or shouldn't have done. He had five deaths on his conscience and no time left to atone for it.

Lord Jesus, have mercy on me, a sinner.

He prayed that purgatory might hold him accountable.

But the sight of Amy in the doorway fractured his will. She was like everyone's first love to him; the kind of girl men hoped to marry and have children with. She was too young to be taken out of the world. Maybe if she survived, her youth and energy would somehow save what was left. She was a tiny ember of innocence that might start a new fire.

"She's such a sweet thing," Slater announced, like a slave auctioneer. "It would be terrible to lose her. But ... you haven't made up your mind, have you?"

Smith refused to look at Slater or Amy. If he saw her eyes, he would weaken.

Slater said to Williams, "How about it? Do you think our young soldiers outside would enjoy this young girl? Take her. Let's find out."

Smith's head snapped up as Williams grabbed Amy. "No!" she cried out. She struggled against his grip, but with no effect.

"They can do whatever they want with her," Slater shouted.

Amy fought every inch of the way as Williams dragged her to the door.

"She's a fighter." Slater smiled. "They'll like that."

The image of what those men would do to Amy filled Smith's mind. A bullet through the brain, other types of torture—he might have had the strength to withstand. But this was the desecration of hope, the total violation of innocence. He was too weak to keep silent.

"All right." It sounded like a growl.

"Wait!" Slater called out to Williams, then turned to Smith. "What did you say?"

"Let her go," Smith said. Whatever he believed, it wasn't worth this.

"You agree to our deal?"

Smith nodded so slightly that Slater didn't seem to catch it.

"*You agree?*"

Smith was about to say yes when Amy suddenly broke free from Williams. She stumbled and fell, dropping in front of Smith. "No! Any agreement with this man would be making a covenant with the devil. Whatever he says he'll do is a lie. You know that better than I do. Please ..."

Smith whispered, "You don't understand—"

Amy locked his eyes onto hers. "They can't hurt me inside ... not where it really matters. I'd rather lose my body than for you to lose your soul."

Williams yanked her to her feet.

"I don't care what they do to me," she cried out.

But the tears came to her eyes in spite of her resolve. In them Smith felt his own heart crack open and bleed. The blood slid down within him like lava. *This is for me,* he kept thinking in a hollow, prayerless void. The words bounced and reverberated like the cry of a small boy lost in a deep cave: *this is for me.*

Another voice entered into his darkness, not a distant echo but a very present sound that resonated in his ear. "This is not for you," the Voice said. "This is for *Me.*"

Slater strode to Smith. "I want your word."

Smith's and Amy's eyes were locked. She forced a smile through her stream of tears.

"I'm waiting!" Slater thundered, his voice betraying a crack in his composure.

"No." Smith lowered his head again.

"What?"

With more strength, Smith said, "*No.* I won't do it. No deal."

Slater's rage was sudden and explosive. "Get her out of here! Put her with the rest!" he roared.

Williams dragged Amy away, kicking open the doors and disappearing down the hall as his boss screamed after him.

"I want the bodies hung from the trees! Do you hear me? I want this place to be a curse to anyone who'll ever think of hiding here again!" Slater lunged at Smith, pounding him with hard fists. Then the captain grabbed the back of the chair and, with surprising strength, pulled him, chair and all, to the open doors. Down the hall they went, with Smith pulled backward, still stunned by the blows. They reached the doors to the church itself and Slater kicked them open.

With a loud grunt, Smith was thrown into the snow. He landed partly on his knees, the chair doubling him over so that he went face-first into the cold slush. Slater's hands were on the chair again, pulling him back to a sitting position. He felt the sting of ice shards in his face.

"You're a fool!" Slater shrieked. "I want you to see what you've done! Watch!"

Smith tried to turn away, but Slater grabbed his head, holding his face forward. He caught a glimpse of Amy standing in the snow, her back to him. Williams was pointing a pistol at her head.

"I want you to see how her blood looks on the beautiful white snow!"

Smith clenched his eyes closed just as the shot went off. The snow deadened the sound outside, but it echoed like a bark down the church hall. When he opened his eyes again, Amy was a lifeless heap in the snow. Her spirit had departed to another place.

Smith wept.

"You are to blame," Slater gasped. He leaned heavily on the chair; his breathing labored. He was expended now, the outburst subsiding.

"Bring him back in," Slater said to someone.

Smith and the chair were dragged back to the sanctuary.

What could Slater do to him now? He'd run out of bargaining chips. There was nothing left that could hurt him, which is as it should be when it comes to matters of faith. He now had no pride to cling to, no despair to wallow in. Smith looked into the eyes of faith and saw its simplicity.

God, how loving You must be to put Yourself into the fragile hearts of men.

"Well, murderer?" Slater snarled. "What do you have to say about your faith now?"

Smith's voice shook as he replied, "Jesus loves me, this I know, for the Bible tells me so. Little ones to Him belong. We are weak, but He is strong."

He lowered his head and could hear the chaos outside. Williams barked out orders to the men. Smith imagined their grim expressions as they took the bodies of those who'd been shot and carried them to the single oak tree that watched over the graveyard. Their ankles would be tied and then they'd be strung up like turkeys in a butcher's shop. *There is no dignity*, Smith thought. *Not in these bodies, not in this life—only in eternity.*

He heard the loud click of a semi-automatic being cocked behind him. It was Slater's, he had no doubt. The man had run out of moves to play; there was nothing left for him to do. Smith was no good as a pawn now.

"I forgive," he said through swollen lips, the taste of dirt and snow in his mouth.

If Slater replied, Smith never heard it.

Chapter 37

Slater staggered to the small table and leaned on it for support. He dropped the pistol on the tabletop, then rubbed his hands over his face. Losing control made him feel nauseous. It was a sign of weakness. He would get an earful from Williams about it.

His eye caught a stack of papers near the edge of the desk. *The Posthumous Papers of Samuel T. Johnson* the top page said in a neat cursive. He snatched them up to give to Williams as evidence, but the last page slipped out and fell on the floor. He picked it up and glanced at the words, suddenly curious about the final entry—whatever it might be.

It had been written the day before by Sam.

"Oh death, where is your victory? Death, where is your sting? Thanks be to God, who gives us victory over death through Jesus Christ. For we do not wish you to be misled, brothers and sisters, about those who have died, so that you won't grieve as those who have no hope. For if we believe that Christ died and rose again, even so, those who died in Jesus will be brought by God. For this we say by the Word of the Lord that the Lord Himself will descend from heaven with a shout, with the voice of the archangel and the trumpet of God, and the dead in Christ shall rise first. Then we who are alive and remain shall be caught up together with them in the clouds to meet the Lord in the air. And so we will always be with the Lord. And He will wipe away all tears and there will be no more death—or sorrow—or crying—or pain. Therefore comfort one another with these words."

Williams came alongside him. "It's finished."

"Burn it," he commanded and pushed the papers to Williams. "Start the fire with this." He stormed out of the church, shouting over his shoulder, "Burn it all."

EPILOGUE

Beck and Luke stood on a ledge overlooking the valley. In the distance, Woodville sat nestled like a toy town in a Christmas display. Closer, just below them, they could see the last of the authorities leave the church. Smoke billowed from the sanctuary, then tiny tongues of flame appeared in the sanctuary wing. The fire spread and grew larger until the entire church was engulfed. It went up quickly like the kindling it was.

Luke said simply, "God have mercy."

Beck sobbed, his breath rising in misty puffs. His eyes were already red from weeping, and they now burned from the irritation of his constantly rubbing them. Or maybe it was the smoke wafting his way.

He had made a final deal and had been betrayed in the most final way. He'd been released, not shot. The betrayer had been betrayed.

He wished with all his heart that Williams had killed him, if only to save him the trouble of doing the job later. It wasn't mercy that let him live. It was a curse, like the mark of Cain.

He turned away from the scene below and looked to the path ahead. It cut through the trees for a dozen yards, then forked. Which path should they take?

The thought came to him that he could take the path of Judas or the path of Simon Peter. One betrayed Jesus and hung himself; the other betrayed Jesus and found forgiveness.

Forgiveness seemed like an impossibility now. He had done too much, more than God Himself could accept. Killing himself was the better option. Throw himself off one of the many ledges they'll encounter. Be done with it. He glanced at the drop from this ledge and wondered if it would truly kill him. Cursed as he was, he might well survive it and be crippled for the rest of his life.

He was a coward, but he wasn't that much of a coward.

Luke sighed. He was facing Beck, his eyes brimming with tears.

Beck had to wonder, *Did the old man really understand what was happening?*

Beck peered over the ledge. If he killed himself, what would become of Luke? Maybe he was rationalizing, but he couldn't leave Luke alone in the wilderness, could he?

"What will become of you?" Beck asked.

"The Lord is our strength and provision," Luke said.

Beck shook his head. He had betrayed the others by wanting to stay alive; could he betray Luke now by wanting to kill himself? Perhaps Luke was meant to be his penance, his means of redemption.

No, he thought and slumped against a tree. No. He was trying to negotiate another deal with God and that was something he couldn't afford to do. Not again. At least Judas and Peter carried their betrayals to their full consequence— no deals. Beck had to do the same now. He had to make up his mind. Which path should he take?

He looked one last time at the burning church and then gestured to Luke. "Come on."

They strolled to the fork in the path and stopped.

Beck was stumped. "I don't know which way to go."

"I have something that will help." Luke reached into his pocket.

A collection of Bible verses, Beck thought.

Luke handed him a large square of folded paper.

Beck reluctantly opened it. He gasped. It was a map of trails with handwritten marks. *Stations.* "Where did you get this?" he asked, astonished.

"The priest gave it to me before the soldiers came."

"What priest?"

"Father Smith."

"*Father* Smith?" Certain that Luke was confused again, Beck corrected him. "Smith wasn't a priest."

"He was. He told me so."

"No."

"Then why did he give me this?" Luke reached into another pocket and pulled out a rosary. "This was given to him at his ordination. Blessed by the pope. He said so."

Beck looked at the rosary. The beads were wooden and worn from use. He looked at the map and chose a direction.

They took the path that would lead them further up.